FROM CZECHOSLOVAKIA WITH LOVE

KEITH EDMONDSON

First published 2016
by Rowanvale Books Ltd
Imperial House
Trade Street Lane
Cardiff
CF10 5DT
www.rowanvalebooks.com

A CIP catalogue record for this book is available from the British Library.
ISBN: 978-1-910607-23-7

I dedicate this book to the memory of Barry Hanson, a lifelong friend, who was always true to his Bradford roots.

CONTENTS

Praise for The 6ε Steppes

'The depth of political and historical research is superb, both nationally and locally... This is an imaginative and (despite the violence) warmly told tale. James is an honest gent, but with just the right amount of Yorkshire thrift and nous... An enjoyable, exciting, sometimes funny and often nostalgic tale, this is an up and down, and sometimes surprising, book in more ways than one.'

— Dr Phil Greaves

'The puns made me laugh but did not detract from the tension and excitement as the story twisted and turned to its conclusion. The plot is clever and the detailed writing took me back to 1963 and the Cold War. I thoroughly enjoyed this book and I would recommend it to anyone.'

— Andrew Pullen

'I read this novel in about four days. It is great, fast-paced and fun — I couldn't put it down!'

— Peter Ingham

'I thoroughly enjoyed this book.'

— Lynne Lewis

ACKNOWLEDGEMENTS

Grateful thanks are given to the following people for their encouragement, information and valuable comments during the writing of this novel.

David Allen, Phil Greaves, Keith Hannay, Barry Hanson, Peter Ingham, Mike Lee, Mike Palin, Penny Palin, Ian Piercy, Ray Pullen and Colin Starkey.

A special thanks goes to Julie Partis who took on the daunting task of proof reading the manuscript.

CHAPTER 1
CZECH MATE!

The aircraft banked sharply to the right and began its descent into Prague International airport just as the British European Airways stewardess announced, 'We have just started our descent, please fasten your seat belts, extinguish your cigarettes and remain seated until we have landed and the engines are switched off.'

I was jolted out of my torpor and started mentally running through the main points of my mission. As a newly-fledged agent, this was my first mission and, on paper, it was straightforward. I just had to meet up with a Czech scientist, who was coming to Britain anyway in a few months' time, and report back on why he'd suddenly requested an urgent meeting with us before he left. I was booked on the next flight back to the UK at about lunchtime the following day; a doddle really, and a good excuse to pick up some duty free. I was the logical choice for the trip as I had the perfect cover story. I had been trained up as a wool scientist, at the Wool Institute in Ilkley, to carry out technical service visits to countries interested in introducing new wool processes. The Czech scientist was due to be on a year's secondment to the Institute, too! The aircraft started to lower its flaps which resulted in increased sensitivity to a stiff crosswind, almost upending the comely stewardess in the aisle as she checked that all seatbelts were fastened. She dropped very neatly into my lap, which fortunately was conveniently placed.

'So sorry, sir,' she said, blushing. I dismissed it with a gesture indicating there was no problem; in truth, it perked me up no end!

Just over five years had passed since, as a temporary MI5 agent, I had been transferred to MI6, after being instrumental in foiling an assassination attempt on President Kennedy's life during his visit to the UK in 1963. The euphoria had been short-lived, as the President had been killed later on that year in Dallas. Nevertheless, the experience had opened up an alternative career which I never would have guessed at.

The aircraft made a good landing and we taxied to the disembarkation point.

'Goodbye, have a good stay, sir,' said the stewardess with a coy smile as I passed her on the way out.

After entering the airport building and walking for some distance along several corridors, I joined the queue for passport control. Finally, it was my turn and I handed over my passport to a figure partially hidden in a kiosk. On closer inspection, it turned out to be a small lady in uniform with a severe expression on her face, as first she scrutinised my face and then compared it with the photo in my passport. I watched her as she appeared to be examining every page in minute detail for a good three or four minutes. It amused me that, from a certain angle, she was the spitting image of Rosa Klebb, of From Russia with Love fame. I was tempted to remark that James Bond couldn't make it this time, but previous experience had taught me that passport officers, in any country, have their sense of humour extracted during training!

'Your purpose in this country, Mr Brittain?' she said huskily, suddenly coming to life.

'Business,' I said.

'What sort of business? Where are you going?' she barked loudly. I was sure it was Rosa Klebb, perhaps she was doing some moonlighting?

'Textile service business, I'm here for a meeting in Prague,' I responded, biting the tip of my tongue sharply to avoid adding 'Rosa'!

'OK, I let you in,' she said, ending the conversation as she stamped my passport with a flourish.

I picked up my small suitcase from the baggage reclaim area and presented it to the customs officer, who indicated that he wanted it opened. He was momentarily interested in the glossy, technical, promotional literature I had packed on top of a change of clothes and then I was quickly waved through.

I walked through a door into the Arrivals hall and looked at a queue of people standing behind a metal barrier, some holding cards with names on them, others just with eager faces, searching each new arrival, hoping to meet up with a loved one. My name was not on any of the cards, so I filed my way further into the hall and inspected the fewer people standing there. Nobody appeared to be waiting for me; the instructions were that I'd be met on arrival by the Czech scientist. I was not unduly concerned as I knew which hotel I was staying at in Prague and if he did not turn up I could always take a taxi to the hotel and wait for him there.

Fifteen minutes passed and I occupied my time by scrutinising every new person who entered from outside. In most cases they went directly to the barrier, others looked round the hall first and none of them showed the slightest interest in me. Being dressed in typically English Harris Tweed jacket and grey flannel trousers, I realised that I probably stood out like a sore thumb. It was still summer here in Prague and virtually everybody else was lightly dressed. I heard myself humming *Mad Dogs and Englishmen* as beads of sweat stood out on my brow, and I smiled wryly as I reminded myself that I was not known for working undercover unobtrusively, especially out in the midday sun!

I was then further amused by a man who must have entered the hall by a door on my left. He was rather tall, dark and balding and appeared to be in a hurry. It was the couple of windscreen wiper blades that he was clutching in his right hand that riveted my attention! It tickled me and I was chuckling to myself when the man turned round and walked up to me. The wiper blades were swiftly transferred to his left hand, leaving his right free to be extended towards me as he spoke in impeccable English.

'Mr Brittain? I'm Peter Svoboda, I'm very sorry I'm late, please excuse me.'

I shook his hand firmly and hurriedly composed myself, being somewhat taken aback by this turn of events. So this was Dr Peter Svoboda of the Brno Institute, who was evidently well enough thought of by the Institute to be offered a year's secondment to do research. On closer inspection, I saw that he had high cheekbones, indicating a Slavic origin, and was probably approaching forty, although it was difficult to be precise due his baldness, which could loosely be described as a very wide parting! He seemed to be somewhat agitated, as if he were suddenly becoming unsure of himself.

'Mr Brittain, could I perhaps look at your passport?' he asked hesitantly, at the same time fumbling in his pocket and producing his. 'Here, this is mine,' he indicated, opening the passport deftly with one hand to show his picture and name.

'Of course, no problem, Dr Svoboda,' I said, doing the same.

He relaxed visibly, grasping my elbow and steering me expertly and swiftly towards the exit. We hurried to a car park where he held open the door of a battered beige Skoda for me to get in. He then affixed the two wiper blades to the holders on the windscreen and got in beside me. I doubted that we were going to need them as the sun was now virtually cracking the flags and the heat which had built up in the closed car hit me akin to opening an oven door! Fortunately the good heat protective qualities of wool serge trousers prevented my behind from being scorched on the hot seat.

Peter Svoboda appeared to be immune from the heat as he rapidly started the car and clumsily slammed the gear lever into reverse before jerkily exiting the car park and heading for the main road into Prague. The only effect of the heat appeared to be on his vocal chords as he commandeered the conversation all the way into Prague.

'I am late because I am being followed by the StB secret police! I explain details later but I want to meet you without bastards seeing you!' Peter Svoboda announced vehemently.

'Yes, but...' I started to say.

'No you don't understand, they stop me coming to England next year if they get breeze of what I know!'

I was distinctly puzzled; I'd understood that since the *Prague Spring* there was new hope of freedom and democracy sweeping the country, but what Peter was describing was a lurch back into the old communist ways! Dubcek was the breath of fresh air that was in the ascendancy. I was getting the vibes that this trip wasn't going to be a breeze after all!

'But, I thought...' I tried again.

'No, you haven't clue to what they can do!' Peter gripped my arm in a vice-like grip, fixing me with a stare while blindly overtaking a lorry one-handedly, as if on autopilot.

'You stopping at the Constans Hotel?' Peter suddenly queried.

I nodded, at least he couldn't cut me off if I didn't speak!

'We go for meal and beer at the U Sedmi Svabu Inn, which is near hotel and I meet you my colleague,' he announced, his English regressing markedly.

He was silent for a short time as he negotiated a tricky turn against oncoming traffic into a side road and pulled up at the U Sedmi Svabu Inn. I was racking my brains as to what he was going to tell me which merited close scrutiny by the secret police; my bet was it wasn't anything to do with wool research.

We got out of the car after Peter belatedly decided to park it round a corner to partially obscure it behind a large van. He then removed the windscreen wipers and I followed him down into a cellar, which was a dark, medieval, subterranean wonderland! I became more determined to find out what was special about Peter's wipers, maybe they were gold-plated, but now was not the right time!

He quickly led me past a display of suits of armour, swords and weapons of all description, to an area which contained large wooden tables and benches of extremely solid construction. My eyes were now becoming more adjusted to the low lighting conditions, compared to the brightness outside. A number of benches were occupied, but we were apparently heading for one in an alcove at the far end. There was the faint but unmistakeable sound of Roy Orbison's *Pretty Woman* coming from a juke box at the far end of the room, which seemed incongruous in the surroundings!

As we passed one table, occupied by three men, my attention was drawn to a particular suit of armour just as one of the men stood up and I walked into him, making him spill some beer!

'Goddammit! You son of a… James, James Brittain!' said the man in astonishment, and I found myself looking into the familiar face of Rod Trask, the American security agent I'd worked closely with five years ago during JFK's visit to the UK.

'How you doing, buddy? What you up to now?' he said warmly.

'I work for a wool research institute now; I'm involved in technical service, trying to interest the Czechs in new technology and processes,' I said cagily, aware that Peter Svoboda was hovering immediately behind me. 'What about you, Rod?'

'Oh, I'm with the US Embassy here in Prague,' Rod replied with a sly wink, which was on Peter's blind side.

'Let's have a beer, how about tomorrow lunchtime?'

'Unfortunately I'm flying back tomorrow morning. It'll have to be later on at my hotel, the Constans, do you know it?'

'Sure, it's close to the US Embassy, we put a lot of folk up there. Eight pm OK by you?' Rod asked, checking his watch. I nodded and we parted with a nod and a grin.

Peter seemed to be a bit nervous again. I explained that I knew Rod from a few years back when he visited the UK, which seemed to satisfy him for the present. We arrived at the table in the alcove, where I was surprised to see a slightly built lady already seated, elegantly drinking a small beer.

'This is my colleague, Irena. She understands and reads English well and she welcomes the chance to speak — as practise, that is.' Peter reverted to almost full fluency again.

'You must be very pleased to meet me,' Irena said confidently, looking at me for the first time, with incredibly big pale blue eyes, just as *Pretty Woman* ended, leaving an awkward silence. Under normal circumstances I would have taken this as an obvious jest, but not this time. Peter said something quickly under his breath, which I did not understand, and those incredible eyes took on an instant look of embarrassment and briefly released me from their hold.

'I am very pleased to meet you too, Irena,' I responded, trying to defuse the situation. It worked.

Peter went up several points in my estimation. I did not know what the relationship was between him and Irena but, whatever it was, they were an unlikely couple. Still, they say opposites attract!

The music had changed to *Blue Bayou* which inevitably brought me back to those mesmerising blue eyes. Dammit, I would be prepared to reveal all under interrogation from Irena; they didn't mention anything about this in the training manual!

Meanwhile, Peter had ordered up a couple of Czech beers and confirmed that, since it was warm, sandwiches would be the most appropriate. We all agreed. The beer was cold and excellent and I soon realised that I was hungry, having had only coffee and biscuits on the flight, and it was now mid-afternoon. The sandwiches were thick bread rolls filled with salami and gherkins, quite spicy but delicious. Peter attacked his sandwich as if he hadn't eaten for a fortnight and was way ahead of Irena and me. I'd anticipated correctly that he'd 'got the niceties out of the way first' and was literally chomping at the salami bit to divulge the reason for bringing me here to Prague.

'I was nine when war broke out and my father managed to get us out of the country the day before the Germans walked into Czechoslovakia. I probably wouldn't be here today if we hadn't gone, as we're Jewish!' Peter said emphatically. 'We emigrated to

Brazil, where my father got a job as Professor of Chemistry at Sao Paolo University and my mother taught English at our local school. After the war, in 1946 my mother and I returned to Czechoslovakia. My mother was very worried about her family and she and my father broke up, I don't know why!' Peter continued.

Maybe it was Peter's idea of small talk, but as far as I could see, none of this had anything to do with why I was there; it just goes to show how your mind wanders when you're nervous. How wrong I was!

'My father and I wrote to each other quite often, despite not having seen one another for a long time. Just recently he wrote that, on one of his field missions, he was sure that he had seen Josef Mengele and, having discovered where he is living, he wants me to get this information to Simon Wiesenthal as quickly as possible!' Peter was becoming quite agitated, as he added, 'I've not heard from him since this letter and I now know that my mail is being opened by the secret police!'

Mengele was the Nazi doctor known as *The Angel of Death* who was being hunted for his horrific medical experiments in Auschwitz.

The expression on my face must have shown my disbelief, for Peter said, 'Yes, I give you his letter, to prove what I'm saying.' He handed me the letter, which meant nothing to me as it was written in what I presumed was Czech.

'You want me to get this to Simon Wiesenthal in Vienna?' I repeated, trying to grasp the enormity of the facts.

'You can show it to the authorities in UK, they can approach Simon Wiesenthal so it is taken seriously. It's not easy for me to go to Vienna at present and I don't want to miss my chance to work at your Wool Institute,' he added.

Peter did not know I was working for MI6. I was not sure how the news would be received in the UK, but anticipated it would be a great coup if they could manage to target Mengele's whereabouts and help bring him to justice. I said I would do as he wished and try to get the authorities in the UK to forward the information to Simon Wiesenthal, the most prominent Nazi hunter, at his offices in Vienna.

Peter looked relieved and then added that Irena knew nothing of this. She nodded and looked as surprised as I was with the news, her eyes reflecting total compassion for Peter.

'I wanted you to meet Irena, since she also wants to come to Wool Institute. She works very closely with me on number of projects; here is list of papers she published. She is 'shit-hot' protein chemist!' Peter announced, almost breaking into a smile.

'I'm not sure whether there will be enough budget for the two of you but I will certainly try,' I agreed. Irena's eyes had taken on a mild look of pleading which almost had me under their magnetic spell again, until I forced myself into suggesting that we should all have another beer.

I gave them a rundown of the Wool Institute, which was situated in the quiet country town of Ilkley in Yorkshire, and said there were scientists from all over the world there, the most predominant being from UK, Australia and New Zealand. The reason it was there was because it was close to the Universities of Leeds and Bradford, where a lot of the wool science was centred. They were especially interested in my role as technical service expert, trying to introduce new wool technologies into different countries. I suspected that they were envious of my freedom to travel, which they were unable to enjoy. However, with the coming of the *Prague Spring*, things might now improve for them. I passed over the glossy literature I'd brought with me to give them an idea of the facilities and projects we worked on; these were eagerly accepted.

Peter insisted on paying and we left the cellar. Rod and his two companions had already left. It was 5.30pm local time and still very warm outside but the car seats were almost bearable now. The ritual refitting of the windscreen wipers was accomplished once again and we set off. It was only about half a mile to the Constans hotel so we were soon there. Both Peter and Irena got out of the car and shook me warmly by the hand to say goodbye. I allowed myself the luxury of wallowing in Irena's blue eyes before I took control of myself again and waved them off.

I checked in and found my room, refreshed myself by having a shower and sat down on the bed to mull over the day's events. But for the fact that I was meeting up with Rod at 8.00pm I could almost have returned to the UK on an evening flight; nevertheless, it would be good to catch up with him. The day's events must have caught up with me, for the next thing I knew, I woke up with a start and looked at my watch — 8.00pm! I dressed hastily and almost ran to the lift down into the foyer of the hotel. Rod was not there, he hadn't been in asking for me, neither was he in the adjacent bar.

I felt better about this as I hated to be late for any meeting. It was now 8.15pm, so I settled myself down on a stool in the bar, from where I was able to see the foyer, and ordered a beer.

I began to enjoy the beer and easily got through three glasses while thinking over the things Peter had said, it was certainly turning out to be more interesting than I'd expected. I did not fancy another beer and the bar was virtually empty, apart from what looked like a couple of business men huddled over a table studying a file of papers. I began to feel drowsy again, the effects of the alcohol and heat, no doubt. I left word at the foyer that if Rod arrived I'd be in my room. It was now 9.45pm.

I did not undress but lay on the bed just to rest. I was awakened by violent banging on the door. 'Steady on, Rod,' I thought, as I jumped up and caught a glimpse of my watch which said 2.15am! Feeling irritated, I opened the door and was amazed to see Irena standing there alone, tightly clutching a pair of windscreen wipers in her right hand!

'Russians have invaded, tanks on street!' she shouted hysterically.

'Steady on there,' I said, trying to comprehend the situation and calm things down.

'Peter shot dead by Russians!' said Irena.

CHAPTER 2
WHEN SPRING TURNED TO WINTER OVERIGHT!

Angela Jones was in the middle of a bitter argument with Nigel, her boss. These rows were becoming increasingly frequent and acrimonious. The phone carried on ringing but Nigel just continued his diatribe. *Why the hell doesn't he answer it?* thought Angela, furious. In the end she snatched up the phone from Nigel's desk and mimicked his secretary by informing the caller that 'his high and mightiness was too busy to talk to them at the moment!' The phone continued ringing to Angela's incredulity. Finally, the penny dropped! It was a dream and she woke up with a jolt, realising it was her own phone ringing on the bedside table.

'Hello,' she said croakily down the telephone.

'Oh, sorry to disturb you, Ma'am, there's been a development which you ought to know about. Can you come into the office right away?'

This was thinly-coded talk to indicate that there was a problem with one of her operations which she immediately suspected was James Brittain's mission to Prague. She was highly irritated with James, he had shown remarkable resourcefulness in the past but she wondered whether he possessed the necessary skills to operate successfully abroad, since he seemed to attract attention to himself without even trying!

Angela and James had had a fling. It had lasted for about eighteen months but they had drifted apart, mainly because Angela had been promoted and was now based in London and James was recruited into MI6 to train up as a wool technical expert, based in Ilkley, Yorkshire. They still enjoyed one another's company on the odd occasion they met up, but neither of them wanted to give up their careers which they were both passionate about.

Yes, she was intensely annoyed at being woken up! She hastily dressed and ran out of her flat to her Mini. She drove quickly to the operation's offices in central London and was admitted by the gateman, who was expecting her.

'Right! What's wrong?' she demanded as she walked into the duty office.

'It's all still confused at the moment, but there's no doubt that the Soviets, or more precisely the Warsaw Pact, is invading Czechoslovakia, as we speak!' said David, the duty officer.

'Shit!' said Angela, with real feeling. Her somewhat irrational irritation with James was at once transformed into concern and she switched into problem-solving mode. After all, even with James's perceived flaws, it was unlikely that he was responsible for his current predicament!

'There are reports that at 2300 hours Central European Time, that is last night, 20th August, Soviet special forces landed and occupied Prague airport, where, at 2311, NATO radar screens went blank, preventing observation of what is happening,' added David.

There had been a build-up of Warsaw Pact forces observed in Eastern Europe throughout the summer but the speed of intervention was unexpected, and unconfirmed reports were coming in that Czechoslovakia was currently being invaded from the North, East and South.

'I don't suppose we've any news of James Brittain, have we?' Angela inquired hopefully.

'No not a thing. We've not been able to contact our embassy either, all lines are dead or constantly engaged,' David volunteered.

Angela looked at her watch. It was 3.00am, so 4.00am CET, and therefore unlikely that they'd learn anything more for a few hours. She went to her office and in the file for James's Prague visit, looked up the name of his hotel — Constans. She rang the number but the line was dead. She checked with the British European Airways desk, who confirmed that his flight had arrived on time in Prague, and yes he was on it. The flight had returned to the UK before the airport was closed down, so James was still in Prague!

She decided there was nothing else useful she could do at present and informed David, on her way out, that she'd be back about 9.00am, unless there were further developments, in which case he should contact her. On her way back to her flat she tried to put herself in James's position. On the face of it he would have to keep his wits about him and try to leave the country overland, via either Austria or Germany, without getting shot! It all depended on how much resistance the invaders met with and how trigger-happy they became. Her priority, as she saw it, was to try to contact the British Embassy later on in the morning and get an on the spot assessment of the situation so they could plan to spring James from Prague.

'God!' she shouted to herself, as she realised the unintentional pun. 'Prague Spring! I'm even beginning to think like James now!' This irritated Angela no end and she wondered if it were possible for the mind to become infected by this way of thinking. Pun virus or contagion perhaps? The latter was more likely as she had certainly been in close intimate contact with James a few times, though not recently she admitted. The recollection of this calmed down her irritation and a hint of a smile flickered across her face as she let herself into her flat.

*****

I woke to the noise of what sounded like distant fireworks, then realised it wasn't bonfire night, it was gunfire! I was stiff, mainly because I had spent an uncomfortable night in a chair in the bedroom as Irena had crashed out exhausted on the bed and was sound asleep in a foetal position, just covered with a sheet. I immediately recalled what she had told me of the events leading up to Peter being shot. They had visited an old colleague in Prague and spent longer than anticipated in his company but still planned to drive back to Brno afterwards. They had no idea that they had been invaded until, just as they were leaving Prague, they were stopped and ordered out of their car by an advance party of soldiers. Peter attempted to reason with them but his instinctive action in attempting to remove his windscreen wipers, in the darkness, was misinterpreted as hostile and he was shot by a nervous soldier. Why Irena had brought the wipers with her was still a mystery to me!

I looked at my watch, it was 9.05am. I opened the curtains and it was already a fine morning; it was going to be another hot day, probably in more ways than one! I noticed for the first time that the bedroom seemed old fashioned to British eyes, with rather ornate furniture, probably the Czech equivalent of Victoriana, which was systematically being discarded at home in favour of the clean cut, mass produced look, regarded as 'with-it'. I decided to investigate downstairs and on seeing that Irena was stirring, I told her I'd be back in five minutes and we'd both have some breakfast. She was fully awake now and she nodded and fixed me with those hypnotic eyes again as she let me out of the room. I heard the lock being turned again as I made my way to the staircase.

At first glance, the hotel's reception area seemed deserted and the place was decidedly untidy. I then realised that there appeared to be no staff on duty at all. Surely they all hadn't been shot! A man came hurrying through the door with a stern expression on his face.

'Guten Tag, Mein Herr, leider das Frühstuckzimmer ist geschlossen!' he said and then realised that I was probably English. I'd understood his announcement that breakfast was not going to take place; he then explained he was the manager and that virtually all his staff had fled home and he was terribly sorry that he didn't know when normal service was going to be resumed!

I asked him if I could make myself an omelette in his kitchen. He nodded and said they had good stocks of provisions for the moment. He pointed me in the direction of the kitchens and I said I would be back in a couple of minutes when I'd fetched Irena from upstairs. Irena dutifully followed me downstairs and into the kitchen where I gingerly lit a gas-fired hob about three times the size of a household appliance and asked Irena to find some eggs. I selected a medium sized pan which I judged to be suitable. I was no Fanny Craddock but reckoned I could make an edible attempt under the circumstances — my jokes were decidedly better than hers anyway!

'Right, Irena, get cracking!' I ordered. She was holding a bowl of around a dozen eggs, and was, in contrast to last night, very quiet and subdued, no doubt reflecting on the mess we were all in. She did not understand my instructions so I qualified it by adding, 'We can't make an omelette without breaking eggs!'

'Me shit-hot protein chemist, not bloody cook!' she said angrily. Her reaction surprised me so I moderated my approach by relieving her of the eggs, cracking two of them into a bowl, adding an equal volume of water and seasoning it with salt and pepper. This was followed by a brisk whisk with a fork and then the pouring of the mixture into the hot oil which was beginning to sizzle in the pan.

After two to three minutes cooking I folded the omelette over on itself and, almost in the same action, deposited it on a plate which I presented to Irena, together with a fork.

'Here, Irena, try this! As an expert protein chemist you're well-qualified to judge it.' The plate was immediately seized and the contents rapidly disappeared, right before my very eyes!

'You shit-hot cook!' she announced whilst licking her lips. A hint of a smile crossed her face and I realised she was hungry too. I cooked myself an identical omelette and she watched me devour it with the same relish. Invasions make you hungry, I thought to myself, as I noticed that we now had two more people in the kitchen, no doubt attracted by the smell of cooking.

'Anybody else for an omelette?' I inquired generously — after all, they were not my eggs! They said something presumably in Czech and Irena immediately copied my actions in cracking the eggs into the bowl and preparing the mixture before handing it to me to do the cooking. For the next half hour, at least, we provided what seemed like an endless stream of omelettes, and variations, as one of the new 'guests' found some cheese and ham, so the menu was extended to include, plain, ham, cheese and even ham and cheese omelettes. By this time, the kitchen was full of people chattering in different languages, in all of which Irena seemed able to converse, much to my admiration. We Brits are pretty poor in the linguistic department, I thought to myself.

Just then, I heard a familiar voice.

'Can you do me a fried egg over-easy, James?' I looked round into the face of Rod Trask.

'No, just joking, James, I've had one of your excellent omelettes. Can we go somewhere to talk?' Rod said, becoming more serious. I looked at him, he was decidedly dishevelled and there were bloodstains on his jacket. It looked as if he'd also had a run in with soldiers.

'Yes, let's go into the bar, I can probably do a good impersonation of a barman as well, if there's nobody there!' I said, judging that no more omelettes were required at present. I guessed that everybody was going to be bound over, probably until the invasion ended, at least! Irena noted my move and made to follow us out of the kitchen. Rod said something to her which I did not catch and she looked at me with those pleading blue eyes again, as if to say, 'Can't I come too?' I explained we were just going in the bar for a chat. I nearly added 'man-talk' but thought better of it! She nodded and watched us leave the kitchen.

'Sorry to stand you up last night, I'll give you the low-down in a minute,' Rod said, as I poured two large lagers from the bar; it was a little early to start drinking but it's not every day that you're caught up in the middle of an invasion!

'Look, James, what the hell are you really doing here in Prague?' Rod said aggressively.

'As I told you yesterday, I'm here to meet up with the Czech scientist who was going to be on secondment to our Institute next year,' I began, taking a good draught of the strong lager.

'What do you mean, was going to be seconded? Is there any doubt?' he quizzed me sharply.

'Well, he was shot dead last night by soldiers as they were preparing to leave for Brno, so yes, there is definitely some doubt!' I countered sarcastically, staring at him hard, indicating that I did not care for his tone.

'Sorry, buddy, I'm all shook up right now! I need to know if you're still with the service?' Rod said, with a definite change of manner.

'Yes, I'm with MI6 now. I've been training for the last four years to become a wool service technologist and this is my first solo overseas mission. It was supposed to be straightforward and I should have been almost on my way home now!' We both looked at one another and burst out laughing at the irony of the situation.

'Yeah, tough shit, but it's not a patch on what I've gotta tell ya!' Rod's face took on a hard look again, as he braced himself to launch into his saga.

'OK, James, I gotta trust you, we're still on the same side and you did a great job back then with President Kennedy. I was almost shot last night!' he confided quietly, pausing to let his words sink in.

'So, you ran into the Ruskies too?' I volunteered the obvious question.

'No, not by the Ruskies but by my own fuckin' side!' he erupted, almost apoplectically.

I just did not get it! This must have shown in my amazed expression which encouraged Rod to continue.

'The two guys with me yesterday said they were US government officials, but they were here to rub me out, presumably to tie up loose ends. I was driving through Prague when one of them pulled a gun on me and then we almost ran into a tank in a roadblock! He got out and the Ruskies shot him, then the other man got out, and while they were all standing over the shot guy, I drove off under a hail of lead!'

'Why did they want you dead? What are you doing at the US Embassy? What are you going to do now?' I shot off a series of questions, which turned out to be more of a volley!

'I've gotta get out of the country someways, maybe I'll hitch along with you, James? I've always been a loyal Kennedy man, but what did they do when we got back to the States in '63? They took me off the President's detail about a fortnight before Dallas! Some of my buddies were saying JFK had dangerous enemies in high places, pulling strings. He was not popular with certain people in the CIA over the 'Bay of Pigs' disaster in Cuba in '62, and wanting to pull out of Vietnam was the last straw with some who were cashing in on the war! They had too much to lose. The fact is that Robert Kennedy was a presidential candidate this year and making the same noises as his brother Jack over withdrawing from 'Nam. It's my belief that Bobby Kennedy was killed for the same reason as his brother! My mistake was to try and warn another buddy who was involved in his security. He died mysteriously two months ago as well! I applied for, and got, the job at the Czech Embassy since my family emigrated from Czechoslovakia in '38 just before the Anschluss and I speak Czech. I've been here about six weeks.'

Rod answered all my questions, not necessarily in the same order as I asked them but his answers raised still more questions as far as I was concerned. I took time out to digest the implications by reprising my barman impersonation and pouring four more lagers, the extra two for two satisfied omelette customers who, by now, were convinced I was on the hotel staff and were starting to order me about. I put them in their place by stating that it was their turn to do the omelette and barman rotas later on in the day, and they soon shut up.

Robert Kennedy's assassination in early June this year was still fresh in my memory. It had never occurred to me that Rod was Czech born and the irony that he'd fled back to Czechoslovakia to avoid almost certain death in the 'Land of the Free' was not lost on me!

'You could transfer some information to Vienna, if you want?' I said tantalisingly. I then went on to fully explain the reason Dr Peter Svoboda asked to see me before he came to England, including all the details about Dr Mengele and the information he wanted Simon Wiesenthal to have in Vienna. I finally produced the letter from Peter's father which Rod read avidly in amazement!

'You see, Rod, if we copy the letter, there is more chance of it finding its way to Vienna in the present volatile circumstances.' It was Rod's turn to be almost lost for words.

Just then, the hotel manager swept into the bar and came up to our table, beaming, closely followed by Irena, who sat down next to me.

'Thank you for your cooking expertises, you are very good cook!'

'No, James shit-hot cook!' announced Irena with pride to all in the bar, which was now filling up.

'We have staff returning now, you must have dinner on house tonight as our guest,' said the manager, still beaming.

I muttered that I would be honoured and suggested that Irena and Rod should be allowed to participate too. After the manager had left the bar I formally introduced Irena to Rod and explained that Rod and I had worked very well together in the UK a few years ago. I suggested that he might take a copy of Peter's letter directly to Vienna as a safeguard in case I did not make it. Irena looked uneasy, before announcing, 'Me leave country now.'

'Perhaps you and Rod could go to Vienna and deliver Peter's letter together?' I suggested helpfully.

'No, I want to go with you to UK Institute, James. I can do job instead of Peter now,' she said forcefully, focussing the full power of her hypnotic blue eyes on me from an uncomfortably short distance. What chance did I have? I looked helplessly at Rod for support.

'Gee, James, sounds like a good idea to me, most sensible people will want to try and get out now if they can, you could help her do this.'

So between us, we'd sorted out the strategy we wanted to follow; there remained only the small inconvenience as to how we would carry it out! It was now approaching 11.00am on Wednesday 21st August and it seemed to me as if I'd already been abroad for a week! I was trying to understand why time appears to pass slowly when you're abroad and fully occupied, but flashes by when you're involved in routine tasks at home. Perhaps Einstein's theory of relativity applied in this case too? Rod suggested he wanted to go back to the US Embassy, which was close by, before troops arrived and made things more difficult. He would have to be careful to avoid running into the other US gunman, and I'd had similar thoughts about trying to reach the British Embassy.

Rod had no sooner left when the phone on the bar counter rang. Irena and I looked at each other in surprise as the manager dashed into the bar, still beaming, and picked up the receiver.

'It's your wife on the phone for you,' he said, handing it over to me.

'Hello? Yes, this is James Brittain... Oh it's you, Angela... Yes, I'm OK... No, I don't know what the situation is right now... What am I doing? Well I've just made omelette breakfasts for twenty to thirty people actually! No, I'm not yolk — joking! — and I'm not being flippant, the kitchen staff fled and we were hungry!... Yes, had the meeting yesterday but will fill you in with details later... Yes, I'm planning on trying to leave ASAP, going to try and contact the embassy shortly... Looks like I'll have extra baggage on way home!... You're going to have to leave it to me, I'll try and ring you from the embassy if I'm successful... Bye.' Thus ended a rather stilted conversation, both Angela and I being conscious of not divulging too much on the phone, which may have been tapped.

'You married?' said Irena, as soon as I sat down again.

'Actually no, it was my boss and the manager obviously mistook her for my wife,' I explained rather hastily. It was the first time the conversation had strayed onto a personal level, so I thought I would try and clarify for myself the relationship between Irena and Peter.

'You and Peter were close?' I inquired. Irena looked puzzled.

'Peter was your boyfriend or companion?'

'Peter my brother! My name is Irena Svoboda,' she announced to my amazement!

CHAPTER 3
ESCAPE ON THE *GOODSHIP LOLLIPOP* CONVOY

Rod left the Constans and turned right, rather than taking the most direct route to the US Embassy, which was located in the Schönborn Palace just down the road to the left. He wanted to visit the small pension where he was staying to check on his VW Campervan which was parked close by. Everything was in order both in his room and the van. He reflected briefly on the break-up of his marriage which was due to his wife's inability to adjust to living in Czechoslovakia, but consoled himself by thinking that at least he didn't have to worry now about getting her out of the country. It was relatively quiet and there weren't any soldiers about, although he noticed that the people he passed wore worried expressions. The brief detour only delayed him by about fifteen minutes and he headed to the US Embassy via a lower route past the Prague Royal apartments, patting his pockets to assure himself that his van keys and passport documents were secure. As he headed for the embassy entrance, a thought struck him — could the sudden appearance of two US officials obviously sent to rub him out have anything to do with his wife's premature return to the US? He couldn't be sure but did not rule it out.

The American Embassy was a hive of activity when Rod arrived. As it turned out, several US civilians were already there seeking refuge and Julien Niemczyk, a military attaché who Rod knew, was dashing around trying to reassure the civilians that all was being done to secure them safe passage out of the country. Rod learnt from Julien that he had been tasked with trying to organise a car convoy to Germany, but it might take a day or so to finalise things. Also, one of the other attachés was investigating the possibility of hiring a train with the same objective but lines of communication with rail transport authorities were proving difficult, if not non-existent!

Rod immediately decided that the car convoy option was probably the better bet and his VW Campervan would be ideal for carrying himself, James and Irena, as well as several other civilians. Julien was appreciative of an additional vehicle and asked if Rod could assist in liaising with the civilians as more were expected to arrive as the day wore on.

Rod was pleased to help out; in truth, it took his mind off his own predicament. As he went out into the extensive grounds of the embassy, he realised the scale of the civilian refugee problem; they stood, sat or paced in various states of dress, surrounded by their belongings. It was unlikely he was going to be able to return to the Constans for the meal with James and Irena that evening. He was pleased to note that there was no sign of the other hitman at the embassy; hopefully he had been 'detained' by the Soviet soldiers and wouldn't reappear anytime soon! On one of Rod's frequent trips back into the embassy building to ferry out refreshments, he stopped briefly at his office to ring James at the Constans. He managed to get through, conveyed the news of the potential escape and told James to remain close to the hotel, which would be more comfortable than roughing it at the palace, and await further news as to when the exodus might occur.

*****

'Rod says we could possibly leave the country in a car convoy being organised by the US Embassy,' I volunteered as I returned to the table where Irena was seated.

'When it happens?' she asked expectantly. I explained it was not clear when but we should remain in or around the hotel to hear the latest developments. After my several abortive attempts to contact the UK Embassy, this latest news came as a great relief. I had considered making the journey to the UK Embassy on foot, but Irena didn't like the idea as the sporadic gunshots, audible in the city, appeared to be increasingly near and I was not sure whether I could make the return journey before the curfew came into force.

Just then, the manager rushed into the lounge and announced to all present that dinner would be served in the next fifteen minutes since the chef would like to return home before the curfew. The time was 5.00pm and everybody in the room looked surprised since the curfew was from 9.00pm till 4.00am! I thought, either the chef was using a slow cooker or he lived a hell of long way away!

I followed the manager out of the room just as an announcement interrupted the music on the radio. This was not of immediate interest to me as it was in Czech, but the manager stopped in his tracks to listen. I inquired if it was possible to stay for another night and did he have another room for Irena? His reply was somewhat off hand as I could see his mind was more on the radio than me. The gist of his reply was yes, I was free to stay another night, but as I might have noticed, they had been invaded, they had an influx of people and all the rooms were now full. Amongst the new arrivals were a number of foreign journalists, who had commandeered his telex machine to send their stories out of the country, much to his irritation.

Why hadn't I thought of using telex? Probably because I didn't have the number of my office in London, was the obvious answer. I wandered into the foyer and saw two men, who I took to be journalists, queuing up to use the occupied telex booth. One of them turned out to be American called Neal who was only too happy to chat. He was a mine of information as he'd obviously been out all night observing the invasion at first hand. Communications didn't seem to be a problem; telephones were not reliable, which was my experience, but telex was the best option. He also told me that all the street signs were being rapidly pulled down to confuse the Soviet military. This settled the question as to whether I should attempt to reach the UK Embassy today, as I might get lost before the curfew came into force.

I returned to the lounge and found Irena in animated conversation with a group of people. She took me to one side to explain. They had been listening to a clandestine radio broadcast which said that the small Czech army had been ordered by the government not to fight the invading troops as they were completely unprepared for invasion! The broadcast called for passive resistance and denounced violence. Even at this early stage, it appeared that this tactic was wrong-footing the Soviets who were well-prepared for any military resistance but not for the passive type they were encountering. The broadcasters promised to help coordinate civilian resistance against Soviet control and to keep information coming for as long as they could.

It was no wonder that people were excited, as this was almost the first coherent information they had received so far in this conflict. We went into the dining room and were shown to a table for three; I told the waiter that Rod would not be coming and he immediately removed the cutlery and rearranged the table for two.

'The manager says the hotel is full and there isn't another room available for you,' I informed Irena apprehensively.

'I sleep with you!' she said, matter of factly.

I avoided her gaze and fumbled with my napkin clumsily, thinking over the various connotations inherent in her response. Fortunately the starter arrived, defusing the situation. I was now feeling tired, the uncomfortable night spent in the chair was catching up with me and I was in need of a good night's sleep. The starter was a soup, which could be loosely described as cheesy, with garlicky croutons. It was actually delicious and beads of sweat were rapidly forming on my brow by the time I had finished it. I avoided looking directly at Irena but I could tell she was appreciating it as well. The main course was pork with dumplings and sauerkraut, which Irena mentioned was considered a typical Czech dish — no concessions had been made to the fact that it was still summer and this added further to my perspiration problem! This was partially solved by the quenching effect of a cool Pilsner Urquell beer, which, by now, was becoming my standard tipple.

Everybody in the dining hall was more or less at the same stage and numerous people lit up cigarettes as an accompaniment to the lager. Irena did the same and I watched her discreetly as she drew deeply on the cigarette, the smell of which I did not recognise. I could not weigh her up; she seemed to me to have erased the shooting of her brother, Peter, completely from her memory in less than twenty-four hours. Perhaps she should apply to go to RADA, rather than the Wool Institute, as she was giving a consummate performance! What did I know about women anyway? I'd never been able to totally fathom, or predict, their thought processes in my limited experience.

'Cigarette bad for my body.' Irena suddenly announced, bringing me back to reality. 'I gymnasium!' she confided, looking me directly in the eye, which brooked no argument.

'Oh, so you're a gymnast, are you?' I asked. She nodded and I could see she was mentally taking note of the correct English words.

'I shit-hot on floor, second in Czech championship,' she continued with pride.

I looked impressed and mentally made a note to mention to her, when the time was right, not to use this particular phrase, especially in polite English society! The knowledge that she was a highly trained athlete explained her posture; I'd half thought she might have had some ballet training. My imagination was beginning to run wild and I had to kick myself to concentrate on our current situation, which was still very uncertain. The relaxing effect of a second Pilsner was no doubt a contributing factor in this respect.

The Czech speaking guests congregated again after dinner to continue their speculations as to what would happen next. I caught some of the drift but after another beer I was ready for some shuteye. I told Irena that I was going back to the room to freshen up; she nodded and carried on with her conversation.

I sat down on the bed and closed my eyes for a short time. I was jolted awake by Irena bursting into the room, eyes shining, no doubt fired up by the conversation she had just been having downstairs. I thought it was almost time to bite the bullet and suggest we should toss a koruna to see who should have the bed when she emerged from the bathroom completely naked! I was suddenly fully awake, my mind was racing and, despite my strong Catholic background, the only thing that I was thinking of was 'chapel hat pegs'! Her eyes were decidedly fixed on me, with that hypnotic look again.

'Oh God', I thought to myself, 'what am I getting into this time?' You're right! Talk about leading a lamb to slaughter, I willingly crumbled and I knew I was going to be putty in her hands. I tried, in vain, to invoke the traditional British stiff-upper-lip but found that feeling migrated elsewhere! The rest was an enjoyable blur which revitalised me totally. It certainly was a new experience for me; I would never be able to hold my face straight in future if anybody used the phrase, they would bend over backwards to please you! Anyway, it solved the awkward question of deciding who was going to occupy the bed.

The last thing I heard before dropping off was, 'You shit-hot fuck, James!' I really must remember to mention to Irena not to use that phrase too often in future, especially in public!

I woke up the next morning totally refreshed. It was 8.30am and it was partially cloudy outside but it had the promising appearance of another fine day in the making. Irena still had her eyes closed and it momentarily crossed my mind that a strenuous matinee encore performance might be required from me? Apparently not, she stirred and in almost one movement she was out of bed and disappeared into the bathroom. Ten minutes later, she emerged fully dressed and immaculately groomed and announced, 'Me hungry.'

It turned out it was only for breakfast. Somewhat chastened, I carried out my ablutions in quick time realising that I too was feeling somewhat peckish.

Breakfast was a serve yourself affair, after being led to a table by the single waiter on duty and a choice of tea or coffee poured. I soon realised that there was no point in looking for Weetabix or cornflakes, instead there were lashings of dark sliced rye bread, Irena called it rohlik, with a choice of jam, honey, cheese slices, salami or ham. I settled for buttered rye bread and honey. Irena looked surprised when I didn't follow it up with the cheese or meat. I did, however, indulge in three cups of coffee which I found very satisfying. I'd learned on my previous trips abroad to Germany and France to avoid tea, since it usually consisted of a glass jar, held in a wire holder, containing lukewarm water and a floating teabag on a string, with a disappointing taste for my palate to boot.

Rod rushed into the breakfast room, his face showing gratification when he saw us.

'Right, you guys, we're getting outa here *today*!' he announced forcibly.

'What, right now?' I said, draining the last residue of my third cup of coffee.

'Yeah, right now, buddy! The VW's outside, I couldn't get through on the phone so I've come to get you. Here's a 'spare' US passport for Irena, the photo's nothing like her but it'll have to do.'

Rod and the US Embassy certainly had come up trumps. I hadn't expected to leave this early but it was welcome nevertheless.

'I'll go and pay the hotel bill and get a copy of Peter's letter for Simon Wiesenthal,' I said as I left the room in search of the manager, indicating to Irena that she should get her things together.

Eventually I located the manager and duly paid the bill with travellers' cheques. I realised I didn't have a lot of spare money with me, and made a mental note that I should try and arrange some extra funding when we reached Germany. I watched the manager as he placed Peter's letter against a sheet of heat sensitive paper and fed it through the 'burn machine', as the American's call it, to produce a copy. I watched him carefully in case he attempted to read the sensitive letter, but he didn't.

After collecting my few belongings from the hotel room, I waved cheerio to a few bystanders in the lobby and climbed into Rod's VW Campervan.

'I'm going back to the embassy to pick up some of the other guys who haven't got wheels. The convoy is setting out from Rudna, a little village about 7–8 miles from here, so you'll have to make your own way there,' Rod told us, pointing in the opposite direction to which we were travelling.

'What do you mean, you'll have to make your own way? Aren't you coming with us?' I queried.

'No, I gotta try to get the folks without wheels on a train to Vienna, which we've been able to set up. It'll give me a head start at delivering Peter's letter to Wiesenthal, and I don't plan on returning to Prague afterwards so I'd like you to take my VW to England,' said Rod unexpectedly.

I hadn't planned on driving back to England from Southern Germany, more like taking a train to an airport and flying back! Rod then reached into his jacket pocket and produced a thick envelope. I looked inside and found close to 500 US dollars — my money concerns had been solved.

The VW bumped along a cobbled road aggravated by tram lines as we neared the US Embassy. I glanced at my watch; 10.15am and Rod had said the convoy was due to leave Rudna around 11.00am. Rod got out and ran into the embassy, returning a few minutes later accompanied by five elderly people. I guessed they were in their mid-sixties, presumably two married couples and a single man, all American and all carrying luggage. Rod attempted to bundle them as quickly as possible through the VW doors onto the seats in the back and stuffed their luggage after them as best he could.

'The others have left. Here's a rough map showing the way to Rudna. Good luck! If you're stopped by soldiers, show your US passports.'

I let the clutch out and the VW lurched forward jerkily, a result of my inexperience of left hand drive and a rather temperamental gear shift.

'Goddammit! Have you got a licence, young fella?' shouted one of the American passengers from the back testily. I ignored his comment to concentrate on making sure I was driving on the right hand side of the road. Irena had the rough map Rod had given us, and pointed to the road she thought we should take. There was a choice of three, and there were no road signs! I remembered the reporter telling me earlier that the Czechs were taking signposts down to confuse the invaders. It was not only the Soviets it was confusing!

Irena had her window down and shouted to a walker, 'Rudna?' He pointed to the middle road — the one we wouldn't have taken!

'You'd betta get a move on, young fella, the convoy leaves at eleven!' continued the back-seat-driver.

'Hush, Bud dear, he's doing his best,' said his wife, trying to calm things down.

We passed a few military vehicles going in the opposite direction, but fortunately they took no notice of us. We seemed to be making good progress; it was now 10.50am and I guessed we had travelled three to four miles but it was going to be touch and go whether we made it for 11.00am. I realised that we were all really tense and I was beginning to sweat profusely as the sun had now come out and it was hot. Up ahead, I noticed a line of stationary cars, the jam being caused by two tanks, each with a white cross marked on top, blocking the road!

'Shit!' said Bud, now virtually apoplectic.

Having stopped, Irena and I jumped out of the VW and approached the car in front of us. The occupants turned out to be Czech and said that the tank commander wanted everybody to turn around and go back. Irena sprinted ahead of me and engaged the commander in an animated discussion in Russian, whilst waving a false US passport at him. The commander was not budging and repeatedly indicated that he wanted everybody to turn round and go back. Dejectedly, Irena retreated and we returned to the VW. I remembered passing a side road about a mile back and suggested we might try that to bypass the roadblock. Irena agreed but Bud said we were wasting time, although he did not offer any alternative suggestion.

I turned the VW round jerkily, to Bud's disgust, and headed back to the side road. I noticed we were now being closely followed by four of the cars from the line-up. We all turned into the side road, and had only travelled about a quarter of a mile when I realised it was a cul-de-sac!

'Shit,' I said, before Bud could say it for me.

Irena tugged frantically at my sleeve, pointing to a field on the right, where she had just seen a motor cycle heading for what appeared to be a road at the other side.

I turned into the field and followed the motor cycle over the uneven ground, demolishing a series of rows of well-cultivated cabbages. Eventually we reached the road and realised that we had bypassed the block, the white crosses on the tanks clearly visible about half a mile away. We were now in the lead of our own small convoy of vehicles hopefully heading towards Rudna. We were stopped only once by soldiers, but on seeing our US and British passports, they waved us through.

We arrived at Rudna just in time to see the tail of the convoy leaving the village; we were stopped by US Embassy staff who asked us if we'd enough gas. There was a truck by the side of the road still half full of five-gallon gas cans, so we took one on board just to be on the safe side. I could see by the fuel gauge of the VW that the tank was virtually full, another reason to thank Rod for his excellent preparations. We were urged to set off and catch up with the convoy, which we did. In my rear mirror, I could see the embassy official offering gas to the cars behind and finally jumping into an American car, bearing a large US flag, which brought up the rear of the convoy. We were hopefully heading towards Germany and, for the first time, I realised what it was like to be invaded by a foreign power, as we passed a seemingly endless series of tanks and armoured vehicles, all marked with white crosses which I realised was to differentiate them from the identical Soviet made Czech models. Soon after passing through Pilzen, we crossed the border into Germany, and sighs of relief were heard as we entered Waidhaus.

We followed the convoy into the grounds of a school where I realised the size of the convoy for the first time; there must have been at least sixty cars of European and American origin.

'Well done, young fella!' conceded Bud with a grin, as we helped him and his wife out of the VW with their luggage. In the gymnasium, where the Americans had laid on refreshments, there must have been four hundred people milling around excitedly, relating their experiences to one another.

'Me hungry,' announced Irena, eying up the extensive array of refreshments on offer.

I hadn't quite realised the extent to which I was relieved to leave Czechoslovakia.

'I think the wurst is now over,' I confided to Irena as I espied some white sausage, a speciality in Bavaria. Irena looked at me, puzzled. I chuckled to myself — it was the first pun I had come out with in ages.

Just then, an almost reverent hush descended on people close by.

'It's Shirley Temple!' said one man in awe. Sure enough, a striking looking lady, probably in her early forties, was passing through the crowd chatting to people, shaking hands as if she'd been doing it all her life, which was true!

The buzz in the crowd was electric and the word was that Shirley Temple Black, as she now was, the world famous child movie star, had insisted on being in the lead US Embassy car. She had been visiting Prague in an attempt to get Czechoslovakia to be the 20th country to join the International Federation of Multiple Sclerosis Societies. It had been really bad timing! No wonder we had been allowed a relatively easy passage through into Germany. I was highly amused and watched her, as did the whole of the crowd in the gymnasium, with delight.

I excused myself and left the gymnasium, in the best humour I'd felt for some days, in search of the toilets. I was washing my hands when I heard the swing doors open behind me, I looked up into the mirror to see a podgy man staring at me and pointing a large gun at my back.

'Where the f... f... fuck's T... T... T...' said the man with an American accent, which could have been straight from a George Raft, Bogart or Cagney movie.

'Trask?' I said helpfully, volunteering this information out of self-preservation as I'd noticed his trigger finger turning increasingly white with each stutter. I didn't want his speech impediment to increase the pressure on this important digit!

'Yeah — T... Trask, 'ure in his VW.'

In an instant I knew exactly who this podgy American was!

CHAPTER 4
FERRY GOOD!

Rod was relieved to see his VW, containing James, Irena and their passengers, disappear into the distance towards their rendezvous with the convoy in Rudna. He could do no more for them and it was up to them now, but he was confident that James would find a way to get through. His mind and efforts were immediately re-focussed on the next task, which was to contact as many Americans in Prague as he could in order to inform them that a special train would be leaving at 7.00pm this evening for Vienna. His job was to ring round the hotels and boarding houses; he also had a list of American personnel who were long-term residents, like himself, who should be given the choice to leave if they wanted. He definitely counted himself in this category and he already had his bag packed and was ready to go. He was in awe of his colleagues at the embassy who had managed to spirit-up a special train, almost out of thin air, in such a short period of time. He was pleased with himself in that he had volunteered to accompany the American refugees on their journey. No doubt his Czech linguistic skills were a major contributing factor here, but his German was very limited, which he would worry about if and when they reached Austria safely. The train journey was likely to be more of a risk than the car convoy, since it would be travelling mainly in the dark and it would not take much to spook a trigger-happy soldier if things went badly for them. All these negative thoughts were pushed to the back of his mind as he concentrated on his contacting duties. The time flew by as he passed on the same information time after time.

At 5.30pm he was interrupted by Joseph, one of his colleagues, who was also going on the train, and informed that it was time to leave since they had to ferry about thirty remaining American refugees from the embassy to the station. Joseph also reminded him that they had to negotiate their passage across one of the bridges over the Vltava River to get to the Prague–Vršovice station, and this might take some time. Rod remembered having been told that Prague's main railway station was a no-go area since it was occupied by Russian troops. He handed over his duties to one of the secretaries, picked up his bag and dashed outside where he boarded a coach toting prominent 'Stars and Stripes' flags from each of two open windows. The coach was crammed with anxious looking people, mainly Americans, who were the unlucky left-overs from the earlier exodus. They soon reached the bridge, which was guarded by two machine-gun-wielding soldiers and a tank parked about twenty yards away. Joseph did the talking in fluent Russian. One of the soldiers appeared nervous but the other one visibly relaxed when presented with a stack of US passports. From what Rod could understand of the conversation, it appeared that the Russians were keen to get rid of foreign tourists and so were cooperative in allowing them across the bridge. At the other end they were waved through by two fresh-faced soldiers, who looked to be about fifteen years of age, each with identical machine guns.

Despite the lack of street signs they managed to reach the Vršovice station without problem. Rod felt pleased with himself, as the throng of people already there showed that his earlier efforts had been successful. Even more interesting was the presence of a train with eleven carriages attached. Over the next hour or so, Rod, Joseph and other colleagues from the embassy busied themselves answering questions and assisting refugees onto the train, which, at 7.20pm, left Vršovice station heading south towards Austria and Vienna. The journey was relatively uneventful apart from major delays at the Czech/Austrian border, where officials from both countries asked endless passport and visa questions. The train finally pulled into Vienna at 4.45am on 23rd August.

Four hundred and twenty-six passengers got off the train, of which two hundred and forty-five were US citizens.

US Embassy staff from Vienna were on hand to meet the train and Rod and Joseph briefly made themselves known to them, then left it to them to organise the processing of all the refugees. Rod enquired from one of the US Embassy ladies present the whereabouts of Simon Wiesenthal's office; he was in luck, the lady he asked knew Rod from speaking to him on the telephone, and volunteered the information, as, she said, she'd just given the same information to a Czech man the day before. She added that Wiesenthal's home and office addresses were restricted information as there had been a number of threats on his life from his many enemies amongst the ex-Nazi regime.

It was still too early in the morning for Rod to go to the Wiesenthal Documentation Centre so he offered his help in the processing of the train's refugees, which was gratefully received. Two and a half hours later, he completed his task and made his way to the station's refreshment bar where he ordered a well-earned breakfast of black coffee and bread rolls. This was about the first time he'd had the luxury of sitting down to contemplate what he was going to do next; in fact, he was still torn between following his VW and heading for the UK, or making his way back to the USA in the hope of perhaps resurrecting his marriage. Three cups of coffee later, he was still undecided but there were still two things that worried him greatly; who wanted him dead and why?

It was turning 9.00am now so he followed the directions he'd been given and headed for the U-Bahn, adjacent to the main station. There he bought a ticket for the Old Jewish Quarter of Leopoldstadt where the Documentation Centre was situated. He emerged from the U-Bahn station into a perfect Viennese summer morning. For the first time he appreciated the feeling of freedom and the difference between Prague and Vienna was palpable. He soon located Rudolfsplatz 7 and wondered if he had been given the correct address as he was in a nondescript run down area. Nevertheless, he went in, found the correct door and knocked; his knock was answered by a solidly built man, who had evidently ducked out of charm school. Rod explained in his best Czech that he had come from Prague specifically to give Herr Wiesenthal important information. The man looked on impassively without saying a word, either he hadn't understood or was playing for time.

'Come on, Bud! You gotta let me in!' Rod said, beginning to lose his temper.

Just then, a door opened and a small, dapper, middle-aged man with a moustache emerged,

'What's this important information you have?' he said.

The doorman surprised Rod by frisking him to see if he was

armed and then ushering him rather forcibly into a sparse office lined with metal filing cabinets, a desk and two chairs.

'Here's a copy of a letter I promised a friend of mine I would deliver only to Simon Wiesenthal in person,' Rod explained, realising he was now talking to Wiesenthal. The letter was handed over and was scrutinised carefully for a few moments.

'This is second time I read this letter since yesterday. Who asked you do this?' said Wiesenthal forcefully.

'James Brittain,' said Rod.

'He's OK!' said a voice from the doorway. Rod turned round to see a balding man framed in the doorway, grinning at them.

'Meet Peter Svoboda!' said Simon Wiesenthal to a speechless Rod.

*****

Angela answered her phone in her London office at 10.05am.

'Hello, Ma'am, I have an American on the line from Vienna. He asked to speak to Nigel but since he's not here perhaps you'd care to speak to him? Said his name was Rod Trask.'

Angela, somewhat surprised and intrigued, agreed to accept the call.

'Say, Angela, nice to speak to you again. I'll come right to the point; I got some important info for you. I got out of Prague last night, by train, James Brittain should have joined the US Embassy convoy to Germany and be there by now... No, I don't have any information if it arrived safely, but he has Peter Svoboda's sister with him. I'm here in Vienna with Peter... James has a letter detailing the whereabouts of Josef Mengele in Brazil, which is why Peter wanted to meet up with him. I'm lying low here in Vienna for a few days; maybe we could talk again when James arrives in the UK. Right now I'm at Simon Wiesenthal's office.' Rod ended the conversation by giving Wiesenthal's number to Angela and wishing her good day.

Angela did not have much time to say anything. She formed the distinct impression that Rod was giving her information on a need to know basis and that he was not alone whilst he was talking. Nevertheless, it was more than she'd been able to obtain from the UK Embassy who hadn't heard from James at all. She felt slightly better at hearing the news, but did not see how Rod fitted into the picture at the moment. She expected James to ring in as and when he could to inform her which flight he would be on, so she was resigned to waiting. She was well aware of who Josef Mengele was and thought at this stage she would wait to hear the full story from James before she went off at 'half-cock', so to speak.

*****

'Yes, we used Rod's VW to travel here,' I said nervously, confirming what the podgy American had just said.

'Where the f... f...' stuttered the American again, becoming increasingly more agitated.

Just then, the swing doors opened to reveal Irena carrying a baseball bat.

Our attention was immediately diverted as Irena swung the bat at the American's gun arm, connecting with a home-run accuracy and timing. The gun exploded, shattering the mirror I was looking into, and clattered to the floor, coming to rest, still smoking, against my foot. The second home run hit the American in his nether region. He doubled up and fell, hitting his head on the hard floor. He was out cold.

I picked up the gun and stepped over the substantial body of the American, taking the baseball bat out of Irena's hands, in case she was considering a third home run on me!

'Let's get the hell out of here fast, Irena!' I said, taking her hand and leading her through the swing doors into the corridor. From there, we made our way outside to the car park, hopefully without drawing undue attention to ourselves. I put the gun and the baseball bat in the back of the VW and we momentarily drew breath as we decided what we should do next. Irena was visibly shaking; not surprising I suppose, as it's not every day that you escape from an invaded country and tackle a gunman.

'You certainly cream-crackered him!' I remarked, as I drove out of the car park and headed towards Nuremberg, which was clearly signposted and which was, I believed, the final destination of the US Embassy convoy after the pit-stop. Irena looked puzzled at my remark and didn't reply. I realised that it was probably too soon to start explaining the technicalities of Cockney rhyming slang so I concentrated on trying to decide which channel port we should head for. Thanks in the main to Hitler's Third Reich, Germany was blessed with an extensive motorway system which I hoped to join close to Nuremberg, from where it should be relatively straightforward to head north past Frankfurt am Mein towards Düsseldorf and Köln. My inclination was to head for Rotterdam's Europoort and pick up the overnight ferry to Hull. The other option was Zeebrugge, which also ran a ferry to Hull. I had recently used both these ferries and my experience was that there had been less hassle with Dutch border officials than with their Belgian counterparts. Also, the boat from Europoort was bigger and therefore more comfortable if the North Sea crossing was rough, a possibility at any time of the year. It was now 3.00pm and we should be able to travel a good way towards Frankfurt today, completing our journey to Rotterdam tomorrow in time to catch the evening ferry.

The motorway was soon picked up once we came close to Nuremberg and we headed towards Frankfurt am Mein which, according to the signs, was a further 250km. The VW was made for motorway cruising, a bit underpowered uphill but streaking away on the downward stretches. Irena was still hunched in the corner of the seat, preoccupied with her own thoughts, watching the road. I let her be, trying to imagine what it must be like, having lost your brother a few days earlier, to leave your homeland not knowing whether you'd ever see it again. I passed the time by mentally working out the German equivalent of 'eating up the miles'. The most plausible I could come up with was 'Kilometerfresser.' I thought I would run it across some unsuspecting German at the next opportunity. We made good time and Irena was becoming restive. The motorway was quite busy now and it seemed that it might be a good time to take a break at the next service area. Irena agreed and I turned off onto a slip road which conveniently presented itself as if on cue, leading to the services.

I felt tired now, as if the events of the day had suddenly caught up with me. We'd been travelling for roughly four hours since escaping Fats Domino, as I'd affectionately begun to think of him! No doubt he'd have both a sore head and a badly bruised wrist. I found myself humming *Ain't That a Shame*! At least I was sure nobody had been following us since we'd made our escape. We reviewed our progress over refreshments; it seemed that we had made good time and had managed to reach Frankfurt. At a rough guess we had about another 500km to go to reach Europoort, which, barring unforeseen holdups, we should be able to cover in around six hours the following day, leaving us plenty of time to catch the ferry.

The services did not have any accommodation on site but the VW would serve as a good alternative. A quick inspection of the layout in the back of the VW showed that the three-seater settee was easy to convert into a full width double bed with sleeping bags and some bedding stored underneath it. Despite having probably another two hours of daylight left, we decided that we could afford to rest up here tonight and make a prompt start early the following day. I was ready now for a decent meal; Irena, on the other hand, still seemed out of sorts and said she was not interested in anything to eat. I noticed she still shivered on occasions even though it was a pleasantly warm summer's evening. Perhaps she had caught a summer cold, I thought to myself.

I slept rather fitfully, partially rerunning the day's events through my mind and half conscious of Irena's twitchings and occasional incomprehensible mutterings to herself. I got up early and dashed to the service area's washroom. On returning to the VW I was reassured to see Irena up and dressed, apparently feeling somewhat better. After the mandatory Continental breakfast, we stopped to fill up the VW with fuel and rejoined the motorway, making our way towards Düsseldorf. The journey was thankfully without incident and became easier once the morning rush-hour traffic subsided, so for the next four hours we kept up our steady progress towards the English Channel.

We were now well on track to make Europoort in good time. The only concern at the back of my mind was the German-Dutch border crossing at Venlo, which was coming up ahead. I was well aware that we did not have any VW vehicle documents and would have to rely, in the main, on bluffing our way through, which was why, learning from previous experience, I'd chosen the Dutch border crossing.

I needn't have worried. We queued for a short time to be inspected by the border guard, who looked carefully at my British and Irena's Czech passport, and then at the VW, with its distinctive CZ sticker on the rear. I explained that we'd managed to escape from Czechoslovakia the previous day in the US organised convoy with Shirley Temple in the lead! This did the trick and the guard cheerily waved us through as he passed on our story to his colleague nearby. The *Welkom in Nederland* sign duly announced our arrival into Holland; nevertheless, we still had a further two hours' drive to get around Rotterdam and approach the massive Europoort complex, at the far end of which was the North Sea Ferry terminal.

Using the same story I'd employed at the border crossing, I

mesmerised the booking clerk in the North Sea Ferry booking office with our exploits and paid for the passage and cabin in American dollars, which raised a few eyebrows but were accepted nevertheless. After leaving the VW in the designated car assembly area to be subsequently driven onto the ferry, we explored the terminal building and I found Irena standing transfixed in front of a sign which said 'Ferry Good'.

'Ferry Good,' she repeated several times, nonplussed. 'What it means?' she said, exasperated.

'It's a play on words; it sounds like 'Very Good'! The Dutch have a similar sense of humour to us,' I explained, and she snorted in disgust. Just then, an announcement came over the loudspeaker system requesting us to return to our vehicles as embarkation would commence very shortly. It had just occurred to me that I really ought to have contacted Angela to inform her of the situation now that we knew how we were going to enter the country, when Irena suddenly collapsed in a heap on the floor in front of me.

She came round quickly, she was evidently running a temperature and her hands and face were clammy to the touch. She refused to be taken to seek medical attention so I helped her to the VW and we waited our turn in a line of cars to drive into the bowels of the Norwind Ferry, which was flying the Dutch flag. The overnight crossing under different circumstances would have been very pleasant, as there were good restaurants and entertainments on-board. The North Sea was, on this occasion, as flat as a pancake, but I was duty bound to keep a close watch on Irena who was confined to her bunk in our cabin, now running a significant fever and sweating profusely. It looked like 'flu to me.

The morning arrived with a tannoy announcement that breakfast was being served. Irena's fever had subsided and she managed to get herself together enough to have coffee in the dining area upstairs. I did the same but looked longingly at the 'full English' breakfast which was available from the hot meals' counter; I decided against it as the sight of it might turn Irena's stomach. We were now passing Spurn Point and entering the Humber estuary. The Norwind's speed had been reduced and it wouldn't be long before we were preparing to enter the King George Dock. The tannoy announcement came to return to our cars as the car decks had been opened for access. We drove off the ferry with relief and queued up to pass through passport and customs control.

'Have you anything to declare, sir?' asked the customs man, as he eyed first me and then the Czech registered VW with suspicion.

'No, nothing, officer,' I replied, somewhat quickly, as I was anxious to get under way as soon as possible.

'Let's have a look inside the van, sir,' the official announced ominously.

I pulled open the van door and the first things we both saw were the baseball bat and the gun, lying on the floor! The official immediately slammed the door and faced up to me squarely with a smugly satisfied look.

'You'd both better follow me!'

Over the next forty-five minutes we were bombarded by a series of questions. Who had we shot at? Who was Irena? Then there was the VW, the lack of a driving licence and insurance, and the four hundred and twenty-five US dollars. Our explanations just didn't seem to make sense to them. Didn't they know Czechoslovakia had been invaded by the eastern bloc countries? Yes, but it was no concern of theirs! They were not buying the Shirley Temple routine either, so it evidently was not going to be 'The Good Ship Norwind', was it? I didn't want to inform them of my MI6 connections in front of Irena at this stage, but it was becoming increasingly clear that I needed outside help to cut through the bureaucracy crap. In the end I convinced them to let me make a phone call; it was time I finally spoke to Angela.

'Hello, Angela… Yes, I'm sorry I've not rung sooner but there's been a series of events… Yes, I'm OK but I'm at Hull customs offices… They don't seem to want to let me and Irena Svoboda in! OK, I'll let you speak to them.' I handed over the receiver to the officer who was hovering in the background.

'Yes, Ma'am, I understand but I'll need further confirmation, can you arrange that?' responded the officer, handing me back the receiver, a little more graciously.

'Oh, James, by the way, Rod Trask rang from Vienna. He was in Wiesenthal's office, having delivered the letter you got from Peter Svoboda… Yes, he got out OK by train… Peter Svoboda was also there!' Angela informed me.

'What! He was shot dead in Prague by the Russians, Irena told me,' I yelled, totally confused.

'No, it was Peter Svoboda, he'd delivered the letter to Wiesenthal just before Rod arrived!' said Angela calmly.

CHAPTER 5
EMERGENCY IN WARD 10

A ngela sat for a few moments after putting the receiver down, going over the details of her conversation with James and the customs officer. She realised there was a hell of a lot more to know than she'd been told and, true to form, James had landed himself in the middle of something big. She, like James, was livid over the customs hold-up, and the usual stereotypical male response she got from those who couldn't accept that some women were capable of holding down responsible jobs. She normally just got on with it but occasionally she looked on the dark side and seriously questioned whether women's rights had advanced any further since Mrs Pankhurst's time. She did take some crumbs of comfort from Barbara Castle's successful intervention this year in the Dagenham Ford sewing machinists' strike over 'equal pay for women', securing 92% parity with men for doing a skilled job. There was also Mrs Castle's promise to put forward an 'Equal Pay Act' which would be significant, but Angela wasn't counting her chickens just yet! Her dark thoughts were partially lifted as she smiled at the thought of the fiery Mrs Castle, Harold Wilson's Secretary of State for Employment; yes, some progress had been made, but there was a lot more still to be done. Maybe one day we'd have a woman Prime Minister? Angela's final thought on the subject before 'getting on with it' was to remind herself that it was one of James's strong points that he treated women as equals and was prepared to share things fifty/fifty, and he didn't believe in man's work or women's work.

She picked up the phone again and made a series of calls which would result in James and Irena being released very shortly!

*****

I was stunned at the news that Peter Svoboda was alive and very much kicking in Vienna! Naturally I was pleased for Irena, but she must have known all along, so what was the charade all about? That was what stuck in my craw. I looked across the room at Irena and saw she was in a shivering mode again and obviously suffering. She'd heard my outburst to Angela and she now presented a rather pathetic figure, expecting my wrath to descend. I could not question her in front of the customs officers so I resigned myself to bide my time.

'Looks like you got friends in high places,' the customs man conceded reluctantly. 'Off you go.'

We were let out of the locked office without the gun, which was retained, and the VW, which was impounded as we didn't have insurance for it. I phoned for a taxi and we finally set off towards Bradford. By this time Irena was very ill and in no fit state to discuss anything. It was clear that she needed medical attention and I did not have the facilities, or time, to look after her, so when we reached Bradford I instructed the driver to head for the Bradford Royal Infirmary, saying that I would direct him as we got nearer. She was eventually admitted (and assigned to 'Emergency Ward 10'!) after being seen by one of the doctors on duty in the casualty department, to whom I had explained the circumstances. There was not a lot I could do for her at present, so I arranged with the ward sister who admitted her to visit her the following afternoon. It also became evident that since it was a weekend, apart from making her as comfortable as possible, nothing would really be done on the treatment side since the consultant physician would not visit her until Monday at the earliest. I'd almost lost track of what day it was and completely overlooked the fact that it was Saturday!

Somewhat deflated at the turn of events, I travelled back by trolleybus to the house I was renting, close to where I'd been brought up. It was a semi-detached, pre-war house, far too large for my needs, but it had become available a few years ago and had been convenient for travelling by bus to my workplace in the centre of Bradford. Now that the Institute was moving to new, purpose-built premises in Ilkley, where there was an on-site car park, I had invested in a cream coloured, four-year-old Hillman Imp which was parked on the narrow drive just outside the side door of my house.

'Nah then!' boomed a voice from behind me as I put the key into the door. I looked round and saw, on the other side of the privet hedge, Stanley Robinson, my next door neighbour. We'd become quite friendly whilst I'd lived there. 'Nah then' was one of his favourite phrases which could mean anything, depending on the intonation — 'Nice to see you, what've you been up to?' 'You've arrived just at the right time.' 'I need you to do this for me!' Stan was a newly retired tax inspector, who lived with his long-suffering wife, Edna.

'Yes, Stan, I'm back!' I volunteered, somewhat superfluously. Stan knew very well I'd been abroad, since he was 'minding' my house for me. In truth, he 'minded' the whole road we lived on as he was fast becoming the local busy-body; rather taxing might be an apt description of him at times.

'Yorkshire's done it again!' Stan said, ignoring my comments about my trip, referring to the County Cricket Team which had just won the County Championship for the third year in a row, beating Kent into second place again. Normally I would be happy to chat for a while over the privet hedge but I was desperate to ring Angela again as soon as possible. Stan was not going to be denied, and waxed lyrical over the team's performance. Cricket took precedence over world affairs in his eyes; he only ventured out of Yorkshire when the team was playing an important match away from home. I managed to extricate myself by lying that I was desperate for a leak, and I'd catch up with him later!

'What do you think is wrong with her?' Angela said, when I had recounted my Czechoslovakian escapade in detail. Well, not quite all the details, as I didn't think Angela would appreciate all the areas wherein Irena deemed I was 'shit-hot'!

'I'm not sure, but it's 'flu-like, and she's really ill now... No, I feel OK, let's hope it's not catching,' I said, thinking that I probably would be a strong candidate if it was infectious. We agreed that I should visit Irena again tomorrow and get her to translate the letter from Peter's father more fully if she was up to it and Angela would try to speak to Rod again to see if more information was available from Peter.

Unfortunately my visit to Irena on Sunday was unsuccessful as she had had another poor night and was asleep at visiting time. I was advised not to disturb her so I returned home, rather worried about her condition. The outing did, however, serve one useful purpose in that it allowed me to give the Imp a run and to familiarise myself with the handling characteristics associated with its rear-mounted engine, to which I was not accustomed.

Presented with more time on my hands than I was expecting, my mind wandered over my previous existence as a priest. My change of career had been determined five years ago by Bishop Brennan, a 'black-sheep of a bishop' if ever there was one! He'd managed to flee the country on his diplomatic passport after the unsuccessful attempt on President Kennedy's life by his henchmen, and I'd heard that he was now holed-up in Vienna. He'd effectively organised my defrocking from a distance and the church had closed ranks, making it clear that I was persona non grata, even in my own parish. I'd already arrived at the conclusion that the priesthood was not for me and was preparing to resign owing to irretrievable doctrinal differences, but had been beaten to it!

I smiled inwardly over my seminal meeting in '63 with Bertrand Russell at the Ritz Hotel, which was instrumental in changing my career path. The furious debate over David Steel's private members' bill which resulted in the Abortion Act 1967, coming into force on the 27th April this year, reinforced my opinion that I'd made the right choice. The Act made abortion legal in the UK up to 28 weeks gestation, and was specifically aimed at reducing the amount of disease and death associated with illegal abortion. A very practical solution to a serious problem which had been swept under the carpet! Pope Paul VI's response was predictable. On the 25th July he issued an encyclical 'Humanae Vitae', forbidding abortion and most forms of birth control. I toyed briefly with the puns available to the word 'issue', but settled for thinking about the harassed midwife involved in a multiple birth, who kept instructing the father to bring the light closer, 'because there's another one on-the-way.' The father was reluctant to conform as he was sure 'it was the light that was attracting them'. You're right, the old ones are the best!

On Monday morning, after my usual breakfast of cornflakes, two slices of buttered toast with honey and a pot of tea, I ventured out into an overcast day to travel to the Institute's offices in Bradford. It was only about a ten minute journey, on the blue and white number 40 trolleybus. Downstairs was already quite full so I chose to go upstairs to be sure of getting a seat.

I was looking forward to the move to our brand new premises in Ilkley rather than working in a series of unconnected buildings, mainly in the area known as *Little Germany*.

Only Angela and Dr Hamish Finlay, the Institute's Director, knew of my dual role with the Institute and MI6. Hamish was an amiable Australian with an easy going manner which belied a formidable scientific intellect and shrewd man-management skills. Until now, I'd had minimal contact with him as I was still getting up to speed with the various wool technologies I needed to absorb. From the MI6 side, my secondment to the Institute seemed to be a godsend in the cash-strapped government circles of the day since they had a resource to call on in me, when needed, which was paid for by the Institute. My guess, knowing Hamish, was that there would be some significant benefit in it for the Institute as well! I did now wonder how I should handle my immediate boss, Tony Pickard, who was about as subtle as a ram, 'on a promise', and had an ego the size of Yorkshire. I'd managed to co-exist with Tony fairly easily so far since we were in different buildings, but I knew this would change once we moved to Ilkley. Tony's favourite phrase, which only he found amusing, was, 'Look lad, I may have my faults but being wrong isn't one on 'em!'

The trolleybus soon reached Bradford where I alighted in Forster Square and walked quickly past the post office to the bottom of Church Bank, directly opposite the building I was heading for. I pushed open the right hand swing door and chose to ascend a helical flight of steps, instead of using the lift, up to my office on the second floor. While climbing the steps I always meant to check whether it was an α–helix construction as I got a crick in my neck looking up; in which case, Crick & Watson might be more appropriate! I met nobody on the way up and pushed open the door into the office to find Tony Pickard seated at one of two desks with a file of papers in front of him.

'Ah, Jim, they let you out then?' Tony said snidely. I nodded. He appeared somewhat rattled and I realised that he was reading one of my files which had been taken from the shelf behind him, where I'd left it. He quickly recovered his composure and stared directly at me with his beady eyes.

'What the hell did you really go for?' he probed; this was about as subtle as Tony ever got on one of his better days. I took my coat off and hung it on a wooden peg near the door, while Tony re-lit his pipe clumsily with a Swan Vestas match, depositing the spent match on the desk, two inches away from the ashtray. I was temporarily distracted by the shape of the hat peg which brought back certain memories for me.

'Eh?' said Tony forcefully, through a smokescreen. He was beginning to get under my skin. I hadn't expected him to be around so early and obviously he had thought the same about me! I decided I'd better feed him a plausible line as he was nobody's fool, but the fine details were only for Angela and the Director.

'Dr Svoboda wanted me to meet his sister, Dr Irena Svoboda, who's apparently a shit-hot protein chemist,' I volunteered breezily, picking up the still-smoking used match and dropping it neatly into the ashtray, grimacing as I braved the cloud of tobacco fumes.

'Peter Svoboda says she'd be invaluable in the work he's going to do with us, wants me to recommend her to Hamish,' I finished, looking him straight in the eye.

'Bloody hell, do they think we're made o' brass?' Tony countered, as if it was coming out of his own pocket.

'She's highly qualified and got some good points.' I responded, wishing I hadn't used the last phrase!

'Well, I'm against it; we've got enough foreign blokes as it is,' Tony said weakly, quickly getting up and leaving the room under another tobacco cloud. After a couple of minutes I opened the door to let some of the smoke escape as I preferred a cleaner atmosphere. I knew the real reason for Tony's objection, he was narked that I'd gone to Czechoslovakia instead of him. He'd come to regard his section's travel budget as his own. Hamish had insisted that I went, mainly because I spoke German; Tony's German was limited to *Ein Bier — bitter*!

From my desk I picked up the closed file which Tony had been reading and quickly flicked through the pages. It was obvious from the trapped ash residues in certain pages what he'd been looking at; Peter Svoboda's letters and my comments in the margins. 'Check with Angela' was the one which stood out and would have had Tony puzzled, since we didn't have anybody called Angela in the Institute. I would have to be more careful in future.

I looked at my watch. It was 9.15am, and I decided to let our secretary know I was back. I walked down the corridor, turned left, and entered the typing pool, which consisted of four girls, all chattering away discussing the previous evening's escapades. My appearance caused a stir, they were all eager to learn of my adventure and I was made to feel like a VIP for a change. When I'd managed to satisfy their curiosity I concentrated on Joan, our secretary, a platinum blonde girl of about nineteen, incredibly tall, with legs right up to her armpits and a pelmet skirt to match! Despite this initial off-putting appearance, Joan was diligent and efficient and unfortunately not going to make the move to Ilkley, due to travel problems. She informed me that Tony had decided all his section was to be moved into Ilkley by the end of next week, and this was going to be her last week here. I thought it odd that Tony had not mentioned anything about this to me. Hamish, the Director, had phoned on Friday from Ilkley to see if there was any news about me, so I should probably contact him ASAP, but not today as he'd gone to London.

I actually did very little that morning, for, as news went round the building, I had a stream of visitors, making it seem almost as if I were 'holding court', which was not how I wanted to spend my time. As lunchtime approached I decided to make an early exit and head towards the hospital as I was anxious to see how Irena was faring. I left word with Joan that I would be out until the following day.

After leaving the building I walked across the centre of Bradford, picking up a small pork pie for lunch from Philip Smiths at the bottom of Ivegate. I was reminded, as I sank my teeth into the pie, that my mother always regarded this butcher as the best in Bradford, so much so that we always had a big stand-pie from them at Christmas, which fleetingly brought back happy memories as I travelled towards the hospital on a trolleybus.

I entered the hospital through the main entrance and turned left along a large corridor whose marble-like floor acted as an echo-chamber for sounds of all kinds. Ward 10 was conveniently situated halfway down this corridor on the left. I'd visited people here before and had always, on entering the corridor, been transported back to my childhood when I would have loved to have been given the chance to roller-skate up and down on this magnificent surface! As always, I didn't have any skates with me and thought that the hospital probably now had rules forbidding this type of practice anyway — shame! I quickly put this trivia to the back of my mind as I pushed open the door into Ward 10. Just outside the main ward I spotted the ward sister talking to a nurse.

'Hello, Sister, how is Irena Svoboda doing today?'

'Ah, Mr Brittain, please come into my office,' said Sister Farthing. 'Dr Nightingale wants to speak to you about Miss Svoboda.'

We went into her office and she picked up the telephone. A couple of minutes passed and then there was a knock on the door and in walked Dr Nightingale.

'James! I thought it must be you!' said Dr Nightingale. To my amazement, I was looking into the familiar face of Sally, one of the three girls I'd briefly shared a flat with in Leeds at the time of President Kennedy's visit to the UK in 1963. Sally was now Dr Sally Nightingale, the house doctor for Ward 10. She immediately got down to the business in hand regarding Irena. She was no doubt conscious of Sister Farthing's presence and probably very busy to boot!

'Miss Svoboda is quite ill, but she's young and fit and should pull through; it appears to be a 'flu-like illness and I'd like to know if she'd been in contact with anybody from Hong Kong recently?'

'Now you mention it, I think there was somebody in the hotel we were staying in who had been there in the last week. Why?' I said, still perplexed.

'Well, it may be a new type of 'flu, Hong Kong 'flu, which has been identified earlier this summer. This is why we've put Miss Svoboda in isolation in a side ward, just as a precaution.'

'Is she well enough to see me today?'

'Well, for a short time. You'll need to wear a mask to go in there and not stand too close, we're all taking this precaution. Miss Svoboda has had a high fever for the last couple of nights and was delirious for a time so she's very tired now,' Sally said. Sister Farthing produced a white face mask from a drawer and handed it to me to put on and then we both followed Sally out of the office, down the corridor and into the side ward where Irena was. She was awake and, on seeing me, she smiled weakly.

'Hello, Irena, are you feeling a little better?'

'At moment a little better but tired,' was the response.

Sally felt Irena's pulse whilst looking at her medical temperature chart, nodded and said I'd got fifteen minutes. Both Sister and Sally then left the side ward and left us alone.

'If you're up to it, Irena, I'd like you to read and translate Peter's father's letter for me.'

'This is first time I read this letter,' she announced, to my surprise.

Irena read the letter out loud and then did a disjointed translation which I pieced together into a coherent story as she went along. The gist of it was as follows.

The usual opening remarks were made hoping both Peter and Irena were doing well at the Brno Institute. Then followed details about the sighting of Josef Mengele, which closely matched what Peter had told us in the pub in Prague, namely that he was sure he'd seen him on one of his field missions in Brazil and that Simon Wiesenthal should be informed. The next paragraph was apparently news to Irena, as well as me, in that their father was being blackmailed into doing drugs research and development by a man in Bolivia. The task was twofold; to improve the process of converting coca into cocaine and then to scale this up for factory production. Their father had evidently accomplished the first part and was now overseeing the setting up of a factory in the jungle in Paraguay. He believed the drugs were intended for the US market. No names, apart from Mengele, were mentioned but it became clear now why their father needed to make field trips.

The letter urged Peter to take Irena with him to England. Until they were out of Czechoslovakia he could not attempt to leave Brazil, as his blackmailers had threatened that unless he cooperated with them, his children would be killed. He concluded by saying he was sending a package of process/factory details to the usual contact.

'What does 'usual contact' mean?' I interrupted sharply.

'No know, Peter will know.' Irena suddenly looked exhausted and became quite agitated at the implications of the letter's contents.

'You must get Peter out of Vienna, he not safe now,' she croaked.

I nodded and said I'd let her rest now, and I would ask the authorities to try to get Peter on the first plane out of Vienna. She smiled weakly and waved limply as I left the side ward.

I left Ward 10 through the main door, turned right into the corridor leading to the outside and met Sally Nightingale just returning to the ward.

'Got what you wanted?' asked Sally cheerfully.

'Yes, but you're right, she's quite weak and needs to rest,' I replied seriously, still thinking of the contents of the letter.

'Is there anything that you're not 'shit-hot' at, James?' said Sally, with an impish grin on her face.

I realised, to my embarrassment, the extent of Irena's delirious ramblings the previous night!

CHAPTER 6
ALL AT SEE

Bishop Brennan paced agitatedly up and down his apartment in the Opus Dei centre in Vienna. He'd just put the phone down on one of the American operatives he had hired to carry out a routine elimination procedure on Rod Trask in Prague. Three things had gone wrong:

1) Czechoslovakia had been invaded; an irritation which even he had to admit wasn't foreseeable.

2) One of the operatives had been shot by invading troops and in the confusion Rod Trask had escaped; inexcusable and careless.

3) The remaining operative had subsequently located RT's campervan and followed it out of Czechoslovakia into Germany. The operative now had a throbbing swollen testicle the size of a Jaffa orange after an encounter with a deranged female baseball player and an intensely irritating Limey! Bishop Brennan couldn't care less about the operative's scrotal elephantiasis. Unbelievable but true, but the worst part was that this Limey was James Brittain. Brennan was sure it could only be the same loathsome James Brittain who was the cause of his virtual side-lining after his failure to eliminate President Kennedy in the UK in 1963, with the intention of causing a major world crisis by putting the blame on the Soviets.

He desperately wanted to be able to prove he was still the 'go-to' man in Europe, especially for the branch of the CIA he dealt with. He had all the necessary connections but was beset by fools who kept failing him.

It was obvious to him that Brittain was still in league with Rod Trask who had smuggled him and his female companion out of

Czechoslovakia. Brennan suspected they were heading for the UK, and the thoughts of revenge spurred him on. *La vengeance est un plat qui se mange froid.* He began to feel really pleased with himself now, he was so much smarter than anybody could possibly imagine. It would be easy for him to locate where Brittain was living, probably in the Leeds/Bradford area. He would get an 'out-of-town' contractor to do the job properly this time! Kill three birds with one stone. Yes, he was feeling supremely confident to the point of smugness; it might even be possible that the contractor could be ready and waiting when they arrived home, and with this he picked up the phone again and made a series of calls to the UK.

*****

Less than two miles from Bishop Brennan's apartment in Vienna, Rod had done what he'd promised and delivered the letter to Simon Wiesenthal. In fact, he still had the letter in his pocket since Peter Svoboda had beaten him to it! He was somewhat confused as he was sure James had said Svoboda had been killed by invading troops — obviously not, as he'd just met him and had recognised him from the inn where he'd bumped into James. He put it down to his memory playing tricks; so much had happened in the last couple of days that it seemed like a dream.

Rod had been given the address of a modest hotel called the Hahn Apartment, two streets away from Wiesenthal's office. In truth, to US eyes, it was poor in all respects apart from it being out of the way and could therefore be considered a safe house for a limited period of time. He had agreed to meet up with Svoboda the following day at Wiesenthal's office so he now had some time on his hands to reflect on his predicament and try to understand what was going on.

Often, when trying to solve a problem, switching off and doing something completely different for a period of time can help; the brain seems able to continue to work away on its own in the background, making connections which indicate a way forward. This happened to Rod as he had a glimmer of an idea forming at the back of his mind which now appeared to be making sense to him. His decision to accept this mission to Prague was, he had to admit, a gut reaction to events which could have been no more than a series of coincidences. Robert Kennedy's decision to adopt an anti-

Vietnam war stance, as his brother had done five years earlier, was almost certainly the reason for his assassination. Rod's friend, who was on Robert Kennedy's security detail, had died mysteriously very shortly after Rod had told him of his concerns over Kennedy's safety. The actions of the two Americans who had tried to kill him in Prague were pretty unequivocal — somebody wanted him out of the way, period!

His brain was now telling him that there could be another reason for him to be targeted and it all seemed to revolve around his elder brother, Joe, who was a history professor at Wisconsin University. They were close but only really contacted one another on birthdays, Thanksgiving, etc., so Rod had been surprised when Joe had called him out of the blue in October last year. Joe chewed both his ears off over the Wisconsin University Dow riots in which he had been inadvertently caught up. The growing unrest in the US over the Vietnam War boiled over at Wisconsin University when Dow Chemicals, who manufactured the Napalm used in Vietnam, were trying to hold a job fair on campus. This caused a student demonstration and Joe, whilst attempting to mediate between the riot police and students, was viciously beaten up with billy clubs, along with his students, requiring hospital treatment. Joe, a proud American and supporter of the Democratic process, was incensed at the State's overreaction. He was determined to find out more about the government's involvement with Dow Chemicals and the only government employee he knew and trusted was Rod. Joe knew his students weren't commies; they were just kids trying to make a peaceful protest against the use of Napalm in Vietnam. Joe wanted Rod to attend the Russell Tribunal in Denmark to get another view of it; he knew Rod was due to go to Europe around that time.

Rod was against it at first but was persuaded that it was a democratic right to know all the facts. He also remembered Bertrand Russell's invaluable help in getting vital information from Soviet Premier Khrushchev, which averted the assassination attempt on Kennedy in the UK. This had been hushed up, so Rod did not regard Russell as anti-American, just anti-war. Rod knew that the CIA had been given the green light by President Johnson to carry out investigations into domestic dissidents (independently of the FBI's ongoing Counter Intelligence Programme). Operation MHCHAOS was the code name for the CIA's domestic espionage project with a worldwide remit. It was dawning on Rod that he and Joe could be regarded as being subversive suspects after he had attended the Russell Tribunal in Roskilde, Denmark, in late November 1967! He even vaguely remembered seeing someone who was obviously American, and whom he half recognised, taking an interest in him.

The Russell Tribunal, also known as the International War Crimes Tribunal or Russell-Sartre Tribunal, was a private body organised by British philosopher Bertrand Russell and hosted by French philosopher and playwright Jean-Paul Sartre. Bertrand Russell justified the establishment of this body as follows: *If certain acts and violations of treaties are crimes, they are crimes whether the United States does them or whether Germany does them. We are not prepared to lay down a rule of criminal conduct against others which we would not be willing to have invoked against us.*

After attending the tribunal, Rod was in no doubt as to the horrific effects burning Napalm could have on the human body. The USA mainly ignored the tribunal and reporting of it in the USA was sparse, to say the least, but people attending it were taken note of. The incontrovertible truth, ludicrous as it may seem, appeared to be that he was now regarded as being expendable by this arm of the CIA, and there was nothing he could do about it! He just hoped that Joe was OK.

It was vital to contact Angela again to warn her against passing on any information about him to the CIA in London. He opened the letter he'd taken to Wiesenthal and reread the last part which contained disturbing information about drug-trafficking to the US. Something told him that this could be his key to salvation if he could get more details to the US authorities of the factory set up Paraguay where drugs were being manufactured. Never mind Josef Mengele, he'd leave that to the Brits, Wiesenthal and Svoboda! His meeting tomorrow with Svoboda took on a greater significance as he needed to learn more about the information alluded to in the letter.

*****

On leaving the hospital I made my way back to the house with the intention of phoning Angela as soon as I was able, hoping she was still in the office. As I turned the corner on to my road I spotted two police cars and an ambulance. A sense of foreboding told me that somehow they involved me.

'Sorry, sir, you can't go in there,' said a young constable from behind the privet hedge in Stan's garden, where he was having a crafty smoke.

'But I live here! What's happened?' I responded.

'What's your name, sir? I'll have to see the Inspector first.'

'James Brittain,' I volunteered, becoming more concerned with every second.

'Mr Brittain, I'm Inspector Button. When did you last leave the house?' The Inspector suddenly appeared from behind another part of the hedge twenty feet closer to Stan's house. He was quickly followed by another uniformed policeman and an ambulance man.

'Eight fifteen this morning,' I replied as I walked up to Stan's gate. Stan's body was lying close to the hedge where he used to stand when we had our 'nah-then' conversations.

'I'm afraid your neighbour, Mr Robinson, has been savagely attacked and this is now a crime scene.'

Over the next half hour I filled in the Inspector about my relationship with Stan and how he'd 'minded' my house while I'd been away on a business trip. I omitted, at this stage, to mention where I'd been and he didn't ask. The Inspector was also economical with information about the attack; it was only later when I paid my respects to Edna Robinson, Stan's widow, that she said she'd heard Stan yelling and screaming with pain as he was being attacked. Stan had gone outside after lunch to finish trimming the privet hedge, which was his pride and joy, and must have seen two men trying to open my back door. Edna Robinson disturbed them just in time to see them run away, jump into a big black car and speed off. Not only had Stan been stabbed in his chest but two of his fingers had been severed using his hedge shears! She had told the Inspector that they were both smartly dressed in suits and one had shouted to the other in what she believed may have been a Cockney accent.

It was clear to me that I was the object of their visit and poor Stan had paid the price for his neighbourly diligence and inquisitiveness. The fact that they were prepared to torture Stan, probably to try and extract information about me, both incensed and terrified me. I quickly ran through in my mind what I'd told Stan about my trip abroad — yes, I'd said I was visiting Czechoslovakia, and since I got back I hadn't mentioned Irena by name but had told him I was visiting a friend in the BRI — Irena could be in danger too! I was really confused and at a loss to explain why I was being targeted. Who knew enough about me to organise this sort of outrage? I hadn't a clue but I was sure that my house and car were not safe now. I must be on my guard at all times and find another place to stay, at least in the short term. I decided to stay overnight, as I judged the two men would not return so soon, especially with so much police activity in the area.

Eventually, at about 6.30pm, I made a telephone call to Angela, not expecting that she would still be in the office, but she was.

'Hello, Angela, yes I've seen Irena... Let me speak. It appears I'm high-up on somebody's elimination list, I'm going to have to lie low for a while... No, I haven't a clue what's going on.'

'Maybe it's something to do with Rod, he rang me again from Wiesenthal's office this morning; he and Peter Svoboda intend to go to Munich to pick up some important information from a left luggage locker at the railway station. He told me not to share this information with anybody else apart from you and particularly not with the American Embassy; I'm not happy about this but I agreed,' Angela said.

This tied in with Irena's translation of her father's letter and her certainty that Peter would know how to obtain the additional information relating to the drug factory in South America and presumably Mengele's whereabouts. I also updated Angela about the attack on me in the Waidhaus School gents by the podgy American gangster I'd labelled Fats Domino. He'd been looking for Rod and was obviously prepared to use whatever force was necessary in order to find him. Luckily for me, Irena rearranged his itinerary and I surmised that any future rendition of *I'm Walkin'* might be in a higher key now. I didn't share this with Angela though!

We still did not understand why Rod was being targeted and from what Rod had told me in Prague, neither did he! It was also clear that Rod was not prepared to divulge everything over the phone to Angela, but he and Peter intended to make their way to the UK after their mission to Munich. I told Angela that I would drop in on Irena tomorrow, after which I'd go on to Ilkley, see Hamish Finlay and find another place to stay for a while. There was not a lot we could do until Rod and Peter arrived in the UK.

I spent a rather fitful night listening for odd sounds and going over the previous day's events in my mind. Eventually I got up about 6.00am, hastily threw some clothes into a suitcase, bolted a breakfast of cereal and toast and then left to travel by trolleybus to the infirmary. Reluctantly, I decided to leave the car in the drive as it might be recognised by Stan's attackers and lead them to me and Irena.

I arrived at the Infirmary at around 7.30am and entered through the main door as usual.

'I'm sorry, sir, this is a restricted area at the moment. Do you have any identification on you?' said a policeman, who was blocking my way as I turned the corner towards Ward 10.

'It's all right, officer,' said a voice behind me. It turned out to be Sally, approaching from the other direction.

'It's OK, James, Irena is safe. Fortunately she was down in the X-Ray department when two men posing as window cleaners tried to climb into one of the side wards through an open window. Both fell off the window ledge — one impaled himself on the iron railings below and died instantly, the other fell on the path and has a broken leg and collar bone. He's helping the police with their enquiries as you might say!' said Sally, as we walked towards the entrance to Ward 10.

'Does he have a Cockney accent?' I queried, as we met the Ward Sister at her door.

'Yes he does!' said Sister Farthing fiercely. 'Look here, Mr Brittain, I don't know what trouble you're in but I don't want it in my ward, do you understand?'

She then marched swiftly into the main ward and started barking orders at two bewildered nurses who were attempting to make beds. Sister Farthing was one of the old school and did not like her routine being disturbed for anything or anyone!

'I think you'd better buzz off until she calms down a bit,' Sally said under her breath. 'By the way, James, we're pretty sure it is Hong Kong 'flu that Irena has. She had a better night and her temperature's back to normal so it looks like she's on the mend.'

'That's the first bit of good news I've heard today. Can I see her?'

'They've kept her in X-Ray for the minute until the Police say it's OK for her to return to the ward, I'll show you the way,' Sally said helpfully.

'You seem to turn up everywhere there's trouble, don't you, Mr

Brittain?' said Inspector Button, suddenly appearing from behind a curtain in the X-Ray department.

'I was just checking on my friend, Dr Irena Svoboda, Inspector.'

'You didn't tell me you'd both escaped from Czechoslovakia, did you?'

'I didn't think it was relevant to my neighbour's murder,' I muttered, somewhat irritably. I was keen to see Irena and head off for Ilkley.

'I think you and I had better have a little chat at the station, if you don't mind?'

'I do mind, Inspector, I've got to be in Ilkley by lunchtime.'

'All right, Mr Brittain, I'm arresting you for obstructing Police business,' said Inspector Button sharply, indicating to a constable to take me away. Sally and Irena looked on in amazement as I was led away.

CHAPTER 7

HOT ROD!

Rod had left Wiesenthal's office alone, feeling that his presence was not required further until he was to meet with Svoboda and Rudy, Wiesenthal's sullen doorman, at Vienna's main railway station at 3.00pm.

It seemed rather opportune that the key to a left luggage locker at Munich's railway station should arrive in the morning post from Germany. Rod was not complaining, at least it meant he didn't have to hang around in Vienna any longer than necessary. He did, however, have four hours to kill; after a coffee in a café, he made a phone call to the American Embassy and spoke to an ex-colleague from his JFK protection days.

'Hi, Kathryn, it's Rod... Rod Trask... You gotta few minutes to talk?'

'Hi, Rod, yeah but not on the phone. Can you make it in thirty minutes to the place where we originally met?' Kathryn said mysteriously.

He confirmed that he could and hung up, as Kathryn had cut him off. He paid for his coffee and made his way in the direction of the American Embassy.

'You seem t've gotton yourself into the shit!' greeted Kathryn, as Rod joined her in a quiet café, close to the American Embassy.

'Go-on, give it to me straight.'

She gave Rod the bad news that he was now wanted for questioning over the attempted murder of a US official in Prague, this was the line that the CIA office at the embassy was taking. The CIA knew that Rod had been on the train out of Prague and were now searching for him in Vienna. Kathryn had been questioned and had admitted that Rod had been helping out with the processing of the refugees, but had no idea of his present whereabouts. She was risking a lot to talk to him now but felt she should warn him that he was in danger, for old times' sake. Rod filled her in with the true facts, that the two Americans sent to talk to him in Prague were bent on taking him out but, as luck would have it, they'd run into some trigger-happy Soviet soldiers who had shot one of the men, allowing Rod to escape. She accepted his version and told him to 'get the hell out of here, pronto!' With that she wished him luck and left the café by the back door.

Rod was now in a dilemma, since he was sure the railway stations would be staked out and that he was almost certain to be spotted as he met up with Peter and Rudy. What to do? From the telephone kiosk in the corner of the café he rang Wiesenthal, who answered immediately.

'Simon, it's Rod... I gotta problem... Can I come round?' He could, and set off immediately via the same exit Kathryn had used.

*****

Bishop Brennan's mood was still good, but not quite as chipper as it had been three hours ago. He'd just had a conversation with his CIA contact at the American Embassy and the wind had been taken out of his sails by the news that Trask was in Vienna, having escaped on the refugee train from Prague. Apparently he'd been heard asking for directions to Wiesenthal's office, but he wasn't there now. The CIA man was confident that they had all major exits from Vienna covered, such as the airport, bus and railway stations. This let Brennan off the hook and he didn't share any information he had from his 'Fats Domino' operative in Germany regarding Trask's escape. He couldn't understand why Trask had not gone to Germany in his VW with Brittain and the woman unless it was a bluff to throw them off the trail. And what did Trask want with Wiesenthal? Maybe he had underestimated him? Nevertheless, he was still supremely confident that he could get rid of Brittain and the woman by the measures he had just put in motion. This brought a smile to his face again; it would be nice to finish with Brittain for good!

He mused over his past successes; wasn't it he who had helped set up the 'Ratlines' to aid fleeing Nazis escape to Argentina? Sure it was! Hadn't he 'oiled-the-wheels' to get ex-Nazi gold from the Swiss bank accounts he'd set up and have it smuggled into Vatican City for 'safe-keeping'? OK, he'd skimmed some off the top into his own Swiss account to help keep his mistress of twenty years in comfort in a villa in Portugal and to pay for his son's education in the UK, making sure there was always some left for a rainy day. He'd joined Opus Dei at an opportune time and had had a meteoric rise, partly due to his financial acumen, but mainly through his connections with the Nazi hierarchy and subsequently acting as go-between with the American army and then with the CIA, who gave him virtually carte blanche to help ship gold and drugs (morphine) to Argentina, along with the human cargo. The CIA also conveniently used the Ratlines to spirit useful ex-Nazi scientists and others out of harm's way, regardless of their war crimes record, eventually providing them with new identities to start life again, some in the USA. They were all fighting the same enemy, the communists, and the end justified the means as far as he was concerned.

But times were a-changing! Gone were the days of Pope Pius XII, who gave Opus Dei complete official approval in 1950; things were satisfactory with Pope John XIII, who lauded them but was a little too cosy with the Soviets for his, and the CIA's, liking. A downward shift in their relationship, which could now only be described as stormy, had occurred since 1963 when Pope Paul VI took office. The time was rapidly approaching for him to retire and take a back seat, but he needed a final push to 'top-up' his cash reserves to a more substantial level, which was why he was keen to do extra errands for the CIA. The phone rang, it was his CIA contact again; Trask had just been seen entering Wiesenthal's office, could he help in supplying a tail? This was his big chance.

*****

Against my better judgement, I drove to Ilkley in the Hillman Imp, but needs must and I was late for my appointment with Hamish. I had finally got the police to see sense and they had released me after I had given them a run-down of my Czechoslovakian adventure minus my 'shit-hot expertise'. After making my way up Hollins Hill, I was passing Harry Ramsden's fish and chip emporium at Guiseley when I suddenly realised that Hamish did not fit into any of the stereotypical pictures I'd formed of the Australian male. I hadn't ever heard him humming 'Tie me Kangaroo down, Sport', or greet anybody with 'G'day, mate'. In fact, apart from the obvious 'Strine' twang, he could easily have been taken for the average middle-aged Brit! I put it down to our over exposure to their sportsmen, cricketers and tennis players who, in the main, were larger than life characters with egos as large as their sporting talents. Hamish could have been forgiven any of these foibles, since he was right up there in the talent department in his own field! From what I'd read, his wool research record was impressive, but, crucially, his ability to convert this research into marketable processes was outstanding. This was why, in my opinion, he had been made Research Director of the Wool Institute to roll out these ideas on a much larger scale, worldwide. Wool products were currently being viewed as old-fashioned, mainly due to the introduction in the market place of the new synthetic fibres such as nylon, polyester and acrylics which had 'washable, easy-care' virtually written all over them. A large amount of the Institute's efforts were now being channelled into producing 'washable wool' from jumpers to trousers in order to counter this synthetic threat. Hamish was astute enough not to put all his eggs in one basket and had recognised that more research effort should be focussed on enhancing wool's inherent natural properties where synthetics could never compete. One such area was wool's natural flame-resistance. Peter Svoboda had patented a process for treating wool, similar to dyeing, which would significantly improve its flame resistance without affecting its normal properties. It was my belief that Hamish now wanted to extend this work, in order to see if it could be rapidly commercialised, using the second-to-none resources available at the Wool Institute.

This was the first time I'd visited the new Institute and as I approached Ilkley, with the River Wharfe on my right, I saw the old iron bridge I'd been told to look out for. I followed the directions I'd been given until I came to a newly planted hawthorn hedge behind a wire mesh fence, with a sign which identified this as my destination. I parked in the massive but sparsely occupied car park and walked towards the entrance. This proved to be a large glass walled atrium jutting out from the main building. An upper floor featured a sculpted ram's head across the front wall. It was evident that no expense had been spared; there was a bob or two here! I also noticed that a large marquee, which would have been more at home at Kilnsey show, had been erected alongside the reception area. This must be for the opening celebration bash I'd heard about.

'Is it Mr Brittain?' said a pleasant looking receptionist who was new to me. She was seated behind a desk in the vast reception area, which was dotted with potted plants which wouldn't have been out of place in Kew Gardens. I nodded as I completed the signing-in procedure.

'You're to go right in, Dr Finlay and his guest are waiting for you,' she said, ushering me through yet another glass door into Dr Finlay's outer office where his secretary, Mavis Johnson, sat at her desk.

'Hello, James, welcome to our new building. Go straight in, they're waiting for you,' she said.

'There you are, James,' said Hamish, somewhat impatiently. To my surprise, Angela was here with one of her, 'What's happened now?' expressions on her face.

'Sorry I'm late. I got arrested again!' I explained, deciding that honesty was the best policy in this case.

'OK, Hamish, I'll put James in the picture straightaway,' Angela started, completely ignoring my excuse. 'The Americans are causing us some problems regarding Rod Trask. They think we know more than we are telling them, which is quite true, but I promised Rod not to divulge any information until he arrives in the UK.'

It was clear that Angela had taken Hamish into her confidence regarding Rod, and it then became evident that she hadn't trusted Nigel with the details.

'Rod believes it's vitally important that he and Peter Svoboda retrieve the information from the left luggage locker at Munich railway station as soon as possible and they should be on their way there now.'

I actually knew most of this after talking with Angela the other evening, so presumed it was a recap to ensure we were all up to speed.

'Hamish informs me that the Institute has good connections with South America, Uruguay and Brazil in particular, Argentina to a lesser extent. This might come in handy regarding Peter's father and the Mengele question,' she continued.

'Don't forget I'm due to visit SA in a couple of weeks' time to discuss possible projects we might cooperate on,' said Hamish helpfully.

I could see now why Angela thought it necessary to get Hamish on board since it might be necessary for me to spend a larger amount of my time on MI6 business for the foreseeable future. It was also sensible to tap into Hamish's extensive knowledge of countries where the Institute had good contacts so that any future undercover activity could be organised legitimately, without suspicion.

'I foresee some difficulties with my immediate boss, Tony Pickard, especially if he's not in the loop; he's already grilled me as to why I went to Czechoslovakia instead of him,' I said seriously.

'Don't worry about Tony; I'll keep him out of harm's way,' Hamish reassured me.

'Nigel's very excited about the possibility of locating and bringing Mengele to justice. His minister wants to be kept informed on a daily basis as to the progress, so as you can imagine, Nigel's on my back daily! I'm not sure if the Americans have been informed of this development yet. There is nothing we can really do until Rod and Peter pick up the information and arrive in the UK, which should be in the next day or two. Can we all arrange to meet in my London office when they arrive?' said Angela.

'Yes, providing it doesn't clash with the grand opening ceremony next weekend,' said Hamish.

'Irena Svoboda is on the mend now; it looks like it was Hong Kong 'flu which was pretty nasty while it lasted. We seem to be the target for a London gang, don't ask me why. It may all be connected with Rod, so you're right, it'll be good to pick his brains as soon as he arrives. I was thinking I might lie low in the Ilkley area for a while but after what happened to the two hoodlums this morning we might have got a reprieve for a day or two,' I volunteered.

'I didn't realise we'd employed the real James Bond at the Institute!' quipped Hamish.

'Well, I knew I wouldn't be able to pull the wool over your eyes, Hamish!' I retorted.

Angela's face took on an expression, which I knew from experience meant, 'For God's sake, don't encourage him'. Fortunately Hamish appeared to enter into the spirit of it. I'd already realised my new career with the wool industry opened up an almost endless stream of pun-possibilities but at this stage I thought it best to go easy on him and spin things out a bit.

I decided to jump the gun and ask Hamish if there was a possibility of employing Irena as well as Peter Svoboda at the Institute.

'We'll have to see, James. I'll look at her publications and talk it through with Peter when he arrives. We're already interviewing new graduates to start in the next month or two so if she has the right experience it could be possible,' said Hamish.

The phone rang. It was Mavis to inform Hamish that his next appointment was waiting for him in reception.

'I'm sorry but we'll have to leave it here for the minute. We can keep in touch and I'll try to keep some time free at the end of the week,' Hamish said.

Angela and I got up and instinctively made our way into the reception area before speaking. I had intended to see Angela off and then investigate the new building and report in to my boss Tony Pickard. Angela had other ideas.

'I have to return to Leeds now to tie up some loose ends at the Mill. You know it's going to close down in the next six months, don't you?' she said.

I nodded. The Mill was the victim of the latest series of government cost-cutting exercises which were being increasingly felt by all the services.

'I've got about forty minutes before the next train, so let's get a coffee in Ilkley and you can update me on your eventful trip to Prague,' said Angela, as we nodded goodbye to the receptionist.

I drove the short distance into Ilkley and headed for the Grove with its long parade of shops on the right hand side. I spotted Betty's Tea Rooms and found a convenient place to park almost outside. Going through the door was like stepping back in time some thirty years at least! Near the entrance hovered a smartly dressed middle-aged lady, who ushered us to a table for two and allowed us a few minutes to study the menu card. Angela had already decided what we were having and summoned a waitress to our table.

'Two coffees please and perhaps a scone. What do you think, James?'

'I think I'd like to try a 'Fat-Rascal' with clotted cream and jam if the budget will run to it?'

She grimaced and nodded in agreement. The waitress disappeared swiftly with our order. I glanced around the tea room, which was almost full with, I assumed, the genteel ladies of Ilkley and district. I realised I was the only male present and we were the youngest people by far, apart from one of the waitresses.

'Why did you have to bring Irena Svoboda back with you?'

Angela said, getting down immediately to brass tacks.

I'd been aware that Angela had been unusually quiet during the ride into Ilkley town centre, as if preoccupied by something; I found it difficult to interpret the signs so I chose my words carefully in response.

'It's difficult to explain the emotions you experience of being in a foreign country when it is suddenly invaded; for me there was a sense of helplessness and uncertainty in not being in control of things, and, of course, a certain amount of fear. For Irena it must have been many times worse as it was her country and she thought she had also just lost her brother, Peter; so I guess I felt a sense of responsibility towards her. Peter, after all, was trying to secure a position for her at the Institute. It was a decision we discussed with Rod in the hotel and he thought it was a good idea too!'

I could see Angela was not totally convinced so, in order to avoid her gaze for a moment or two, I concentrated on taking a large bite of my 'Fat-Rascal' scone which had now arrived.

'I've got the unenviable task of informing the remaining staff at the Mill that they are going to be made redundant,' she said.

The Mill was now run on a skeleton staff but, like Nigel and Angela, they had also been transferred from MI5 to MI6, some three or so years ago. The Mill, which had remained open for historical reasons, was now to close in the constant search for economy.

It became clear that this was the main reason Angela was in her present mood. I grimaced to commiserate with her position, while at the same time being relieved that she had not got wind of the fling I'd had with Irena!

'It's probably just as well you're working for the Institute as Nigel still seems to have his knife into you, and would have loved to let you go as well!' Angela said forcefully.

'What is it with him? My face has never fitted and he got more of the credit for the Kennedy visit than we did, didn't he?' I spluttered, projecting a number of 'Fat-Rascal' crumbs across the table onto the floor, much to the amusement of two elderly ladies at the next table, who were obviously earwigging.

Angela glanced at her watch and summoned the waitress for the bill as she decided it was time to go. We left rather hurriedly and I could feel eyes following us as we reached the door. I was tempted to utter 'Floor show's over for today,' but could only offer a weak smile to the manageress as she ushered us out.

I dropped Angela off at Ilkley station. I'd always wondered how this relatively small branch line had evaded the 'Beeching-Axe' in '63, and wondered if there had been some judicious lobbying on behalf of the Wool Institute to indicate they wouldn't build in Ilkley unless they kept the branch line open?

'Right, James, we'll meet up at my London office as soon as Rod and Peter arrive in the UK and I'll keep in touch with Hamish. Unfortunately Nigel is keen to be in on this, he sees it as his next step up the ladder.' Angela closed the Imp's door with a flourish and waved as she disappeared into the station.

It was still only mid-afternoon so I had time to return to the Institute, report in to Tony Pickard, and have a look round to see where my desk was likely to be. The Institute was less than five minutes' drive from the station so I was soon back in reception.

The pleasant lady on reception, who I learned was Irene, told me, 'Go past Hamish's office, and Tony's is the fourth or fifth on the right, you can't miss it.'

This time, as I walked down the grey vinyl tiled corridor, I got more of a feeling for the new Institute building; offices and meeting rooms were to the right and laboratories to the left, all spanking new, bright and airy, very impressive. I was going to enjoy working here after the drab facilities in Bradford. As Irene had said, Tony's office was the fifth door down the corridor on the right, his name clearly marked on the door. Through a vertical narrow slit window in the varnished wooden door I could see Tony seated at his desk, enveloped in a haze of smoke. I knocked and entered. There was a pause as Tony registered my presence with a sharp intake of breath.

'Bloody hell, you kept this to yourself, didn't you?' he said aggressively, pushing a piece of paper across the desk towards me. It was a memo to all staff dated today, announcing my transfer from the International Technical Service Department to a newly created role of International Liaison Manager, responsible directly to the Director, Dr Hamish Finlay!

CHAPTER 8
A MUST-SEE FILM!

Rod Trask and Peter Svoboda both gave a sigh of relief as the train they were on pulled into Munich's Hauptbahnhof. Rod's opinion of Wiesenthal's odd-job man, Rudy, had been changed by the latter's expert driving of his battered VW Beetle through the backstreets of Vienna, avoiding the obvious route to Munich via Salzburg and taking them into Germany at the Wegscheid border crossing, and then on to Passau railway station some twenty miles or so further on. Rudy was sure they had not been followed and saw them onto the Munich train. After an uneventful journey they followed directions to the left luggage office, Rod following Peter as they jostled their way along a crowded platform as a train was approaching. Rod felt a tremendous push in his back and fell headlong into Peter who, caught off-balance, could not prevent himself rolling off the platform onto the track just as the train arrived! There were horrified screams from bystanders. Rod rose quickly to his feet and motioned to a rail official to move the train on a bit so they could see what had happened to Peter. Miraculously, he had managed to slide himself into the void under the platform edge to avoid being totally crushed under wheels, but the bad news was he hadn't managed to get his left arm fully out of the way in time. His shoulder was dislocated and the wheel had severely crushed three of his fingers. Help quickly arrived and he was taken by ambulance to the nearest hospital, Rod managing, despite his lack of German, to make the ambulance driver understand that he wanted to go with them.

Rod knew that he had been deliberately pushed, meaning that somebody clearly knew he was on his way to Munich and was waiting for him. He had to stay with Peter who had the key, in more ways than one, to solving both their problems and who may not be fit to travel to the UK for some time. As far as Rod could read the situation, both police and railway officials seemed to assume that Peter's injuries were an unfortunate accident and not foul play. Rod was not going to raise his profile by telling them otherwise as he did not want the US Embassy involved at all. At the hospital, as soon as he got the chance, he telephoned Angela in London. She was not in but expected to be back in her office later that afternoon, so there was nothing he could do but wait.

*****

Bishop Brennan got word that Rod Trask had visited Simon Wiesenthal's office and left with two other men in a VW Beetle. They had been followed through the back streets of Vienna and, rather than taking the Salzburg road, were heading towards the mountains. It was assumed they were going to Munich airport. There were two main possibilities; they would be driven directly to the airport or dropped off over the border to catch a train into Munich before heading to the airport. Brennan covered both options; his American (Fats Domino) operative was assigned to cover the railway station and one of his German contacts to watch the airport.

The phone rang and he answered it immediately; Fats Domino reported stutteringly that he'd pushed Trask, together with his companion, in front of a train — bliss! There obviously was some justice in this world and Brennan couldn't wait to report his success to his CIA contact at the US Embassy in Vienna.

*****

Back in London, after giving the remaining staff at the Mill in Leeds their redundancy notices, Angela decided to call in at her office to see if there had been any messages. There was just one from Rod, no details but it was important and he would ring back later, so she had to wait. She could do with some good news. She had not enjoyed giving out the redundancy notices, she knew all the staff at the Mill very well and she thought this such a waste of fine talent. The phone rang.

'Hello, Angela, it's Rod.'

'Where are you, at the airport?'

'No, I'm at a hospital in Munich, Peter's been injured, there'll have to be a change of plan as he's going to be here for some time — can you get James over here?'

Angela realised immediately that Rod could not go into details but she recognised from the tone of his voice things had gone badly wrong and he needed help PDQ. She phoned the Institute, where fortunately Hamish was still in his office, entertaining some guests before taking them out for a meal. James had left, so she told Hamish the gist of Rod's call and agreed that they should talk again tomorrow. There was no answer from James's phone in Bradford, so on an off chance she phoned the Bradford Royal Infirmary and asked to be put through to the ward Irena Svoboda was in.

'Hello, Ward 10, Sister Farthing speaking.'

'Good evening, Sister, I just wondered if James Brittain is visiting tonight?' said Angela as tactfully as possible.

'He is, but we don't allow personal phone calls from the ward, Madam!'

'I realise that, Sister. This is Angela Jones from the Department of Overseas Aid in London, it's a matter of National importance, please bring him to the phone.' Angela's tone brooked no nonsense, even from Sister Farthing!

'Hello, Angela, what's wrong?' said James.

'Just spoken to Rod, Peter's been injured and is in a hospital in Munich. Rod wants you over there ASAP; can you get on a flight tomorrow? I've OK'd it with Hamish. No, I don't know any more details except the plans have been changed — speak to you when you get there, bye!' she said, matter of factly.

'I hope you're not going to make my ward part of your office, young man!' said Sister Farthing scathingly.

'Of course not, Sister, you've been most helpful,' purred James, tweaking her chin on the way out which brought a hint of a smile to her face — mind you, it could have been wind!

*****

It was turning out to be one of those days! I'd visited the new Institute, experienced the delights of a 'Fat Rascal', learned I was still persona non grata with Nigel (no change there then), been summarily promoted to manager — working directly for the Director, though my guess was there would be no extra money in it — and found Irena to be much improved and beginning to eat like a horse again, doubtless she'll be back to her old nagging ways shortly! On the down side, there was the unsettling news that Rod and Peter were in trouble in Munich and I had to go over there and try to help out. Obviously they hadn't retrieved the information from the left luggage locker yet.

I managed to get an early flight to London from Leeds-Bradford airport and found myself waiting to check in for a Lufthansa flight to Munich. I rang the Institute to speak to Hamish who was incredibly informative and helpful.

'G'day, James! Angela's been on the phone this morning. She'd just had another chinwag with Rod; Peter's in the University Hospital in Munich and I've arranged for Hans Klein, who's been visiting firms in South Germany, to meet you at the airport. If you give me your flight number I'll pass it on to him; he doesn't know any details but he knows the area well and could be very useful.'

I now appreciated one of the advantages of working for an international organisation with good connections on the ground. In the time it took to make a short phone call, I'd found out which hospital Peter was in with the added bonus of having 'our man in Germany' meet me at the airport. I'd met Hans a few times before; he was the main technical service man in West Germany, a jovial blond man with a build to rival any sumo-wrestler! He must be six feet four at least; Klein was most inappropriately named, I likened it to our ironic custom of calling very large, well-built men 'Tiny'! You would want him on your side in any fight.

The flight was uneventful and I found myself in a queue to pass through passport control.

'Your passport is not in order, Mr Brittain,' said the officer who was examining my passport. 'See, you do not have an exit-visa-Stempel from Czechoslovakia, how do you explain this?' he said, triumphantly waving the document at me. I'd obviously brightened up his day. This type of man was probably originally responsible for putting the Sauer into Kraut!

'If you look at the entry date into Czechoslovakia you'll note it's the day before the Soviets invaded, stamping of passports on the way out was quite low on their priority list. I was lucky to escape in the Shirley Temple Black-led American convoy into

Germany.' I added ironically. Once again this explanation got me out of another pickle, much to the officer's chagrin.

'Velkom, Mr Brittain. How can I help you?' said Hans Klein as I finally cleared customs.

'Please call me James,' I said as we shook hands, mine disappearing almost completely in his massive paw. Thankfully it wasn't the start of round one and the best of three falls, or there would be only one outcome!

'Can you take me to University Hospital, please? Dr Svoboda, who was on his way to our Institute, has had an accident and Hamish thought we should give him every assistance,' I explained, as we walked from the airport building, heading to the car park. We jumped into Hans's BMW and he expertly negotiated a series of complex road junctions as we headed for the centre of Munich. The hospital had LMU signs everywhere, which I learned stood for Ludwig Maximillians Universität. We were directed towards the reception desk by a wizened man who looked as if he might have been around at the opening in 1472.

'You are family of Dr Svoboda?' enquired a nurse as we approached Peter's room.

'No, but we are colleagues and would like to see him if it's possible?' I said.

'Dr Riemenschneider needs to speak to you, a moment please.'

'I am Dr Riemenschneider and Dr Svoboda is under my care. As I was telling your other colleague this morning, he has had an operation on his hand and this went well. Unfortunately he hit his head in the accident and there has been a delayed reaction to this. We are carrying out tests but he is now in the moment in a coma, I'm sorry to say,' said the Doctor, in almost perfect English.

This was not what I wanted to hear and was much worse than expected.

'There is another point I would like to mention; we have not been able to talk to Dr Svoboda about the costs of his treatment. Are you able to pay for this?' said the Doctor, trotting out a well-rehearsed spiel!

I decided to refer this to Hamish and get an official Institute opinion. Dr Riemenschneider ushered me into his office from where I rang Hamish. He said he would pick up the tab but wondered if there were any cost advantages if it was handled by our German branch? I put Hans Klein on the phone and there then followed an animated discussion between the good Dr Riemenschneider and Hans in a German dialect I could not follow. Just then, Rod poked his nose round the door.

'James, am I glad to see you buddy!'

I walked over to the door, blocking Rod's entry and indicating that we should talk outside while the two Germans were still in conversation. He nodded in agreement.

'The Doctor says Peter's in a coma; did you manage to get the key from him after the accident?' I said, as soon as the door was closed behind me.

'No, it was no accident, James! I was deliberately pushed from behind and unfortunately fell into Peter... It's me they're really after, not Peter... They now know I'm in Munich, that's why I asked Angela if you could come. Who's the big blond guy?'

'Right, I understand now. Hans is our technical man in Germany. Hamish, the Institute's Director, thought he would be useful... He's dealing with the question of fees right now, he doesn't know the full story, only that Peter was in an accident on his way to our Institute... We'll keep it that way.'

'The hospital's been cagey with me since I could not pay the fees. They don't understand my tie-up with Peter, anyway. Peter's been under sedation after surgery and now the complication with the head bang,' Rod added, pre-empting my next question. I must admit the question of fees had never occurred to me, as people of my generation in the UK took free-NHS healthcare for granted. It was an eye-opener for me.

Rod and I agreed that I should try to gain access to Peter's room and look for the left luggage locker key in his belongings, which we assumed were stored somewhere inside the room. I would then go alone to the station to retrieve the documents in case there was somebody still on the lookout for Rod. Hopefully they would not recognise me.

'We go now to administration office to deal with Dr Svoboda's fees, we meet again in reception, yes?' said Hans, as he and Riemenschneider came out of the office and disappeared down the corridor.

'OK, James, see if you can find anything in Peter's room. I'll keep watch outside and tap the wall with my heel if anybody arrives.'

I opened the door to Peter's room. The bed was empty and I

quickly looked round to see if I could see any of his belongings. The locker next to the bed did not contain anything remotely like keys, just a jug of fruit juice and an upturned glass on top. The only other possibility was a cupboard close to the door. I opened it and thankfully I found Peter's clothes neatly folded inside. In a jacket with bloodstains on the left sleeve I felt some loose coins through the fabric. I put my hand inside the pocket and pulled out a handful of Czech coins, and a key with the number 89 stamped on it. I'd found it! There was no key in any of the other pockets of the jacket or trousers. I quickly replaced the coins in the same pocket and closed the cupboard door before leaving the room. The look on my face told Rod I'd been successful.

'Well done, James, here comes the nurse.' I deliberately asked the nurse where Peter was as I said I had looked into the room and found it empty; apparently he was undergoing further tests to investigate the head trauma, but she said we could come back in a couple of hours' time to sit with him for a short while. We headed down the long corridor following the exit signs. As we went along, Rod explained that the station must be close by and within walking distance. He would make excuses for me while I carried out this important mission.

Sure enough, on reaching the street, the Hauptbahnhof was clearly signposted and I set off at a brisk pace to find it. I guess it took me ten to fifteen minutes to reach it and I walked round keeping my eyes peeled. Fortunately I seemed to blend in with the people there, looking like a typical traveller with small case and jacket. The left luggage area was clearly marked on a separate floor and I examined the key again to confirm the number. I could feel the hairs on the back of my neck standing on end as I put the key in the lock of locker 89. It opened the door, and there inside was a small, plain, oblong cardboard box. Not what I'd been expecting at all! I'd been expecting a substantial envelope with papers in it. I picked up the box and carefully removed the lid while it was still inside the locker; it contained a few rolls of 35mm Kodak film, a sub miniature Minox camera and some small cassettes which I took to be Minox films. Underneath there were some $100 travellers' cheques. It was now clear that all the information was on film. I transferred the cardboard box to my case before closing the locker door. I left the area by a different exit and studied the train departure board as a ruse to check if I was being watched. I left the station and made my way back to the hospital by the same route.

'It's all on film, Rod,' I said, as I found him hovering close to the reception area.

'Goddamit!' said Rod, clearly disappointed. Hans had been back but Rod had deflected him by saying I'd gone to the men's room.

We headed back to Riemenschneider's office but there was no one there, so we moved on to Peter's room. I opened the door and he was there in bed, a bandage round his head, lying still with his eyes closed. As I approached the bed his eyes opened and he recognised me immediately, I bent down to whisper to him and he clasped my arm with his right hand in the vice-like grip I remembered from our first meeting.

'Get key from my jacket... Go to left luggage... Hauptbahnhof... Take it to England,' he whispered hoarsely.

'Done it, Peter! Irena is safe in England now,' I said triumphantly. Peter smiled weakly and closed his eyes.

CHAPTER 9
A WUTHERING DISCLOSURE

Angela had just put the phone down after a long conversation with James, who was now at Munich airport waiting to board the flight back to London. She was going over the details in her mind; he had picked up the information from the locker at Munich station. It was all on film, 35mm and evidently sub-miniature Minox film; therefore it needed to be processed as soon as James arrived. She made a mental note to contact the relevant department to arrange top priority. She finally had something positive to report to Nigel, who, as usual, was making her life a misery on a daily basis.

James had already given her the latest news of Peter; despite the complication of the head trauma, it seemed hopeful that he was responding to treatment and should make a full recovery. Angela wondered if James was being too optimistic at this early stage. She would ring Hamish with the details and also thank him for providing the Institute's German technical man to help out. Interestingly, James had arranged for Hans to take Rod by car to Düsseldorf, where the German branch of the Institute was based, thus avoiding the use of public transport in Munich which may be under surveillance.

There was a potential problem looming for MI6 when Rod arrived in the UK; what to do with him? She had agreed verbally with Rod not to pass on any information about him to anybody, especially the US Embassy and her CIA contacts. It was going to be more difficult to keep things quiet once he was actually here. Rod and James had talked for most of the night trying to figure out why Rod should be targeted by a branch of the CIA. Angela was not familiar with all the details as James did not have time to fill her in, but it was clear that determined efforts were being made to eliminate Rod by his own side. She was doubtful that the information which Peter's father had sent from South America would help to clear his name.

One thing they were all agreed upon was that it was vital to establish the identity of the contact who had deposited the films in Munich. Probably only Peter and his father knew this.

The other thing that was worrying both James and Angela was the two Cockney accented hit men who had tried to eliminate both James and Irena. How was this related to Rod? Somebody knew a disturbing amount about James's background and his movements in Yorkshire! She wondered if it could be linked to the Institute or his severance with the Catholic Church. She was keeping an open mind on this.

*****

Rod waved goodbye to Hans Klein at Düsseldorf airport after the drive from Munich. The long chat he and James had had the previous night was very useful and he was interested to learn how James and Irena had made their way back to the UK in his VW Campervan. He needed somewhere to lie low, as far away from the US Embassy in London as possible. James had suggested he take the same route as they had and he could then pick up his campervan from the customs vehicle pound at Hull ferry terminal. He had all the papers with him to prove it was his and crucial for him was the fact that the campervan contained, hidden in a dummy exhaust system, large amounts of American dollars and German marks, set aside for a rainy day such as this! He went from Departures into Arrivals and made his way towards the Avis Rent a Car desk. After arranging to leave the car at Rotterdam Europoort Terminal, he studied the map and estimated he had plenty of time to travel there before the boat left and set off on his way.

*****

I was keen to drop the films at Angela's office and get on my way back to Bradford. It was Friday 30th August and I could hardly credit that it was only ten days since I'd set off on my journey to Prague. Rod should be well on his way to Rotterdam and the Europoort Terminal, and if things went to plan he would pick up his Campervan tomorrow morning. I'd arranged for him to make his way to Ilkley and book himself into the central Crescent Hotel where I would meet him when I got home. The tube from the airport seemed to take forever and I counted off every station but eventually it reached my destination and I legged it, for all I was worth, to Angela's office.

'Here they are, at last!' I said triumphantly, plonking the innocuous looking cardboard box in the centre of Angela's desk with a theatrical flourish of which Sir John Gielgud would have been proud.

Angela managed a smile and picked up the phone to inform the technical department that she had the films. Despite the fact that we were not going to learn anything really useful, she removed the three 35mm Kodak cassettes, the Minox camera and its sub-micro cassettes. Finally, with metronomic precision, she counted out ten unsigned $100 travellers' cheques.

'Let's hope it's all worth it! When's Rod arriving?' she asked.

'He should arrive in Hull tomorrow morning, he's taking the overnight Rotterdam-Hull ferry. I've agreed to put him up at my place until things quieten down a bit,' I replied

'Interesting, you didn't mention this when we spoke earlier. Anyway it's good he's out of the way.'

'Rod thought the fewer people who knew his travel plans the better as he's getting twitchy at the moment, and I don't blame him.'

A technician arrived to collect the films saying that, depending on what they found, they should have something for us to look at by lunchtime tomorrow.

I was just about to get up and leave when Angela said ominously, 'Nigel wants to see us both before you go.'

'Shit! Has he changed his mind about letting me go?'

Unfortunately Angela now worked in the same building as Nigel, just down the corridor, in fact.

'Ah, there you are, have we got the documents relating to Mengele now?' said Nigel, eyeing us both with a little more enthusiasm than normal, as we entered his office.

'Yes, it's all on film, we should have something to look at by tomorrow,' Angela told him.

'See you got the timing of your visit to Prague wrong, James, eh?' Nigel smirked, unable to resist a dig at my expense. I nodded, not rising to the bait. He then assumed a more confidential manner and leaned towards us, encouraging us to do the same.

'It's not generally known, but earlier this year I was part of a mission sent to Buenos Aires for secret talks with the Argentines to explore the possibility of a deal to handover the Falkland Islands to them. Things went well but unfortunately the news of the talks was leaked to the bloody Falkland Islanders and they are claiming they are being sold down the river! You'll no doubt have read the press?'

We had no idea that Nigel was involved in this, but were well aware, of course, about the furore it was causing both here and on the Falkland Islands. Nigel continued, warming to his task.

'It's obvious that we're in the middle of an economic crisis in this country; the government sees that it has no option but to abandon its 'East of Suez' policy and wind up its residual empire for financial reasons; after all, it worked well with the island of Diego Garcia last year. OK, we forcibly deported and resettled a few inhabitants to Mauritius and the Seychelles, without much backlash, and handed the island over to the Americans for a strategic airbase — a good deal really! The same principle should have been possible with the Falklands, it's mainly full of sheep farmers anyway and you'd think they'd be happy to be paid to be transferred to New Zealand, wouldn't you? You ought to appreciate this, James; you work for this wool outfit now, don't you?' Nigel, typically, was totally unaware of the condescending manner in which he said this!

I could see the logic behind the argument but the way it had been handled — in effect, a fait accompli — going behind the backs of the Falkland Islanders, was bound to cause major resentment.

'Anyway, there's going to be another attempt in two to three months' time to persuade them to accept a deal and I'm going to be there to liaise in Argentina as well. Lord Chalfont, a minister at the Foreign Office, is going to lead this mission. It's important that I'm fully au fait with the Mengele case before I go,' he added pompously.

I didn't envy Lord Chalfont, or Nigel for that matter. From what the Foreign Secretary Michael Stewart had been forced to say earlier in the year in the House of Commons, no handover would happen, *unless it were clear to us... that the islanders themselves regarded such an agreement as satisfactory to their interests.*

'On another matter, Angela, the Americans are keen to get in touch with Rod Trask. He seems to have gone missing. I understand you have spoken to him recently? What can you tell me about him?' Nigel said inquisitively.

'Yes, he rang me out of the blue from Vienna to tell me he'd run into James in Prague just before the invasion, and had been involved in organising Americans who wanted to leave the country. He told me he had arranged for James to join the US convoy into Germany led by Shirley Temple Black. He had been on the train which ferried refugees from Prague to Vienna. I don't know where he is at this moment,' Angela said, being very economical with the truth.

'What about you, James?'

'As Angela said, I ran into him by chance in a pub where Peter Svoboda took me on my arrival in Prague. I arranged to have a drink with him later that night at my hotel but he never came. A couple of days later, he turned up and told me about the convoy the American Embassy had organised and suggested that we join it. It worked well,' I added.

'OK, I'll pass that on... It might satisfy them in the short-term. Let me know immediately if Trask communicates with either of you in the future,' Nigel said, standing up stiffly, which reminded me that his infirmity was no better. This was confirmed by the stick propped up in the corner of the room; it also signalled that the audience was over and we should leave.

'We make a good double act, don't we?' I said out of the side of my mouth as we scurried down the corridor, out of Nigel's earshot.

'Have you still time to make your plane connection? Do you want to stop over tonight?' said Angela unexpectedly.

'Nice idea, but with Rod arriving tomorrow and Irena's recovery making her discharge from the hospital imminent, unfortunately I feel I must decline,' I said.

'I thought it might be useful for you to be around when the films have been processed?'

'I know, but it's going to be mainly in Czech anyway, and we're going to need someone to translate which is going to eat up even more time,' I argued. Angela nodded and with that we parted. I picked up my case from her office and headed via the underground to the airport to catch the early evening flight back to Leeds-Bradford airport.

*****

Rod drove into Ilkley and found the Crescent Hotel just where James had described it, at the main crossroads right in the centre of the town. He'd just about got used to driving on the left hand side of the road again; it was five years since he'd attempted it. Goddammit! Why do the Brits always do things the wrong way round? Anyway, things had gone well for him on his arrival in Hull from Rotterdam; he'd had no trouble convincing the authorities of his ownership of the Campervan held in their vehicle pound. He was convinced that they were glad of somebody to take it off their hands. His only concern was that they might contact the American Embassy.

He'd checked in and decided he might as well have a look round this quaint little town while he waited for James to show up. His first priority, he'd decided when he arrived in the UK, was to ring his brother Joe to make sure he was OK and get an update from home, so he went down to the lobby to use the phone. He was just about to talk to the barman when the phone rang. It was James for him.

'Yes, James... I've arrived... Despite you all driving on the wrong side over here!... Sure, I'll be around when you get here in about an hour.' Rod put the phone down; it seemed James was keen to keep the talk down to a minimum. He discussed the possibility of ringing the States with the barman who took details of his room number and left him to it. Rod knew it was going to be very early in the morning in Madison, Wisconsin, but he didn't care; he had a better chance of speaking to his brother now than trying to locate him at the University during office hours. A few seconds after he stopped dialling he heard the phone ringing.

'Hell! This had better be important, you know what time it is?' bellowed an irate voice from the earpiece, almost deafening Rod! He smiled with relief; it was the familiar voice of his brother, Joe.

'Hi, Joe, it's Rod, gotta minute to talk?' he said sarcastically.

'Where the hell are you, Rod? I've been trying to get in touch with you for days now.'

'It's a long story. I got out of Czechoslovakia by train to Vienna and I can't tell you where I am at the moment in case your phone's bugged.'

'The authorities have repeatedly questioned me as to your whereabouts. First they told me you were wanted for shooting a US official but they've backed down on this as the slug they dug out of him was Russian! I told them it was me who convinced you to go to the Roskilde Tribunal last year on a fact-finding mission for me. You gotta give yourself up, Rod!' said Joe vehemently.

'What authorities — FBI? CIA? The US official who was shot by the Soviets was one of the two who were about to rub me out, so it's not that simple. There's been another attempt on me as well a couple days ago so I'm not going to make it easy for them. Listen, Joe, tell them I've been in touch and hope to have some information vital to our country in a couple of days' time, so it's in their interest to call off the cavalry.'

'OK, Rod, understood, goodbye.' Joe put the phone down first, but Rod kept on listening and heard a second click a couple of seconds later. He felt relieved that his brother was OK and was pretty sure his message had already been received by the authorities.

He decided he still had time to have a quick look-around before James arrived. Being just after midday on Saturday, people were dashing about finishing their weekend shopping in butchers' and bakers' shops across the road from the Hotel. He had some experience of rural life in England, having spent several weeks in and around the Chatsworth Estate, Derbyshire, in '63 when President Kennedy visited. People seemed to have more time to stop and chat to one another in small towns than in the larger cities; shopping was more of a social activity. He had some difficulty in understanding the local dialect though, and was quite taken aback when he bought a paper in a newsagents and the lady announced, 'Here's your change, luv!' He soon realised it was just a form of pleasant patter which was quite normal. This was obviously quite an affluent town as there were some fancy automobiles with which he was not familiar. He found the station — useful to know. He wandered along the Grove with its fine parade of shops on the right hand side, then realised that it was time to return to the hotel to meet James.

*****

I was relieved to see Rod entering the hotel as I parked my car on Brook Street, just a short distance away. The weather was gloriously warm and sunny for a change and I was uplifted momentarily to a level where I was tempted to break into song — *The sun has got his hat on... Hip-hip-hip-hooray!* — but pulled myself together quickly before entering the hotel.

'Want a warm beer, James?' said Rod, from the bar.

'Pint of Tetley's mild, please,' I said, realising it would refresh my vocal chords, the song in my mind having now played on to... *and is coming out to play!*

'Things have moved on a bit, Rod. Angela's had the films processed and there's a lot of information. As expected the written work is in Czech, so Angela's bringing it up to Ilkley tomorrow morning and she wants me to get you and Irena together to translate it so we can all understand it. I've arranged with Hamish for us to use one of the Institute's meeting rooms tomorrow, Sunday. The hospital is prepared to discharge Irena a day early, so I can pick her up tomorrow morning before collecting you here, around lunchtime. Is that OK?' I said, before taking a good draught of the beer.

'Sure, sounds great, James. What are we going to do till then?'

'What do you want to do?'

'Say, are we anywhere near Hayworth? I studied literature at school and we really got into the Brontë Sisters... If you know what I mean,' Rod said unexpectedly.

'Haworth, yes, it's only about twenty miles away, we can go this afternoon,' I said, warming to the suggestion. As is often the case, when you live close to interesting places, you only go there when you have visitors. I was also keen to have a look at the newly reopened Worth Valley steam railway line which was run by enthusiasts and had only been operational for around two months.

After a quick sandwich in the Crescent's bar, we drove out of Ilkley through the green landscape heading towards Keighley on the way to Haworth, some thirty minutes away. I realised that I could possibly kill two birds with one trip, so to speak, if we took the train from Keighley to Haworth instead of driving there. Steam trains were not Rod's 'cup of coffee' but he appreciated, nonetheless, the countryside and buildings which brought back vivid memories of the Brontë literature to him. I, on the other hand, was 'chuffed-to-bits' to experience steam travel again. Its strangely reassuring engine noises and the characteristic smell of smoke was immediately evident as we stepped onto Platform 4 where the train was situated, apparently straining at the leash to be off! We sat in a compartment next to the engine, a portly platform official blew his whistle, giving a passable impression of the 'Fat Controller', and we felt a couple of major jolts as the train slowly began chugging its way out of the station with a loud sigh of relief. Heading towards Oxenhope, we stopped briefly at Ingrow West and I was amused by an orange-yellow advertisement at the station announcing *Virol, Anaemic Girls Need It!* I remembered being dosed with it as a lad but didn't realise it was gender specific. A yellow Colman's mustard sign made a sharp impression as we left the station and entered a short tunnel, when we got the real benefit of the engine smoke which wafted into the carriage in ample lungsful through the open window! All too soon we reached Haworth station; we got out and began the increasingly steep uphill trek into the village. We reached the narrow cobbled Main Street, which had been virtually untouched for a century or more. Rod just couldn't believe what he was seeing and was transfixed. At the top, next to the parish church, we noticed The Black Bull public house, the favourite haunt of Branwell Brontë, the original cottages, shops, and finally, the parsonage. Haworth was busy with visitors doing exactly what we were doing on a pleasant Saturday afternoon. Rod said he would revisit it to spend more time looking round before he left.

On the way back, since we had full tickets, we took the train to Oxenhope at the end of the line, then travelled the full journey back to Keighley to pick up my car. After the momentous events both Rod and I had experienced over the past two weeks, the carefree jaunt was just what we needed to recharge our batteries for the days ahead.

At 11.00am on Sunday morning, I pushed open the swing doors into Ward 10 to collect Irena. I had not visited her since I returned from Munich but had arranged everything over the phone with Sister Farthing yesterday. I opened the door into her side ward and saw her fully dressed, sitting in a chair, obviously waiting for me to arrive. It was immediately obvious that she was not in a good mood for she gave me one of those withering looks women are so good at!

'Why you no visit me yesterday?' she greeted me angrily.

'I had to see Rod in Ilkley and arrange for us all to meet up this afternoon. Are you not feeling well enough to come out?' I said, worried that it might upset the proposed meeting arrangements in Ilkley.

'Course I'm OK, I have nothing to do here but wait for news!' she said, with another one of those looks. Irena picked up her few belongings and we called in at Sister Farthing's office to bid her farewell. Irena was gracious enough to hug the surprised Sister and express her thanks. We asked that Dr Sally Nightingale should also be thanked and with that we made our way out of the now familiar Bradford Royal Infirmary building towards my car parked outside.

On the way to Ilkley I updated Irena on Peter's condition. It came as a shock to her that Peter was also in hospital but I assured her that he was in good hands and didn't think the bang on the head was too serious. She was relieved to hear that he reacted very positively to hearing that she, Irena, was safe in the UK. It did mean, however, that we were relying on her to interpret most of the information sent to Peter. We picked Rod up at the hotel and drove into the Institute's car park a couple of minutes away. The security man in reception recognised me and said that Angela was already here waiting for us in the main meeting room, next to Hamish's office. It being Sunday, we were the only people there. Angela was sitting at a large, oblong desk which had about twenty chairs around it. In front of her was what looked like a stack of photos, and two piles of A4 papers.

'Angela, this is Dr Irena Svoboda of the Brno Institute,' I said formally. They shook hands and we all sat down except Angela, who asked if we would like any refreshments, tea, coffee, water, etc. We all declined. There then followed a brief discussion of Irena's health and Peter's condition. Rod then mentioned how he appreciated the outing to Haworth yesterday as a pleasant interlude to the serious work we were involved in. I could see out of the corner of my eye Irena bristling with indignation that I had left her out of this! Under different circumstances I would have quipped that her expression was a 'Wuthering Look,' but this was definitely not the time!

'What I propose is that we leave Rod and Irena to examine the information and do a translation for us. James and I will be in the office next door if you need us. Have you arranged anywhere for Irena to stay, James?' Angela said. It was something that had completely gone out of my head.

'It's OK, I sleep with James!' Irena announced.

'I mean hotel accommodation,' Angela clarified, looking bemused.

'No, OK, I sleep with James, he shit-hot in bed!'

CHAPTER 10
CZECHERED REPORT

Bishop Brennan had just boarded what was, in his opinion, a rather small turbo-prop 'plane at Amsterdam-Schiphol airport. Very shortly it was taxiing behind two other planes, waiting to take-off en route for Leeds-Bradford airport. Three days had gone by since he had been informed that Trask and his companion had been pushed under a train at Munich Hauptbahnhof. To his chagrin and extreme embarrassment he had subsequently learned that both had miraculously survived. It didn't seem fair to him as he was supposedly in charge of the miracle department! After swallowing a large helping of humble-pie with his CIA contact at the US Embassy in Vienna, he was told to keep in touch and wait for further instructions. Within thirty minutes of this conversation he received, out of the blue, a call from Johann Schmidt of the BND (West German Federal Intelligence Service). Brennan and Schmidt's association went back a long way; they first co-operated during the war when Brennan organised the transfer and safe-keeping of Nazi gold from Swiss Bank accounts to the Vatican. They had had little contact since but Brennan knew that Schmidt now worked for the BND whose headquarters were in Pullach, near Munich.

The nub of their talk centred around Peter and Irena Svoboda, who he learnt were the son and daughter of Josef Svoboda who had gone missing in South America. The BND had strong connections to South America through their chief contact there, Klaus Altmann, who was desperate to find the Svobodas as they had been under surveillance in Czechoslovakia by BND agents before the Soviet invasion, and it was known that Josef Svoboda had sent them damaging information jeopardising operations in South America.

Could Brennan help? It was vital that this information did not get into the wrong hands! The pfennig was slowly beginning to drop, so to speak, in Brennan's brain; could it be that Trask, the Svobodas and that irritant, Brittain, were all in it together? He thought it was too much of a coincidence. He agreed to do what he could and volunteered the information, that he believed the principal people involved, namely Irena Svoboda, James Brittain and Rod Trask, were now in the UK. He knew nothing about Peter Svoboda but had a hunch that he might have been one of Trask's companions when he fled Vienna. He suggested that he should travel to the UK to coordinate the search for them there, as he believed he could locate them more quickly if he was close to the action. He made a mental note before he set off to contact his 'Fats Domino' operative to investigate the identity and whereabouts of Trask's companion, who had also survived the train-crushing incident. Substantial expenses were agreed to cover this action. He was not sure how the authorities would react to his return to the UK, but thought he might gain precious time on the ground if he entered the UK by a regional airport rather than London; he still had his diplomatic passport as a safeguard. He would base himself in the Leeds area where he still had good people who were loyal to him. The flight was better than he expected and a car was waiting for him when he cleared customs.

*****

'I hope the pumping of Irena for information was carried out in accordance with the principles *laid down* in the MI6 manual!' Angela said provocatively, with as much emphasis on laid down as she could muster, as soon as I had closed the office door.

It had also occurred to me, more than once when I'd been in Irena's company, that MI6 training was deficient in advising the right course of action to take in 'close encounters of an amorous nature'. Before I could answer, there was a sharp rap at the door and Hamish bobbed his head inside.

'They said you were in here. I was keen to see Irena and Rod; I see by the stack of documents you've brought Angela they've started the translation, so they could be some time — anything to report so far?' said Hamish brightly.

Shit-hot timing, I thought, couldn't have organised it better myself! I could see it had completely taken the wind out of Angela's sails as I guess she had just been gearing herself up for the next sarcastic broadside!

'We're mainly relying on Irena to come up with the goods,' I said, filling in for Angela who had gone temporarily mute.

'Oh, I'm sure Irena's going to come up with the goods!' responded Angela, quickly regaining her voice.

'I was hoping to have a quick chat with Irena afterwards to see if she could fill in for Peter while he recovers. What do you think, James?' said Hamish, ignoring the obvious coolness between Angela and myself.

'I would think they've got a good couple of hours work ahead of them, don't you, Angela?' I said. She nodded so Hamish said he would leave us to it and come back about 4.00pm.

By now, Angela had composed herself and adopted a more business-like demeanour towards me, although she avoided eye contact. She quizzed me in detail about my trip to Munich; we went over every part of the visit to Peter and also my discussions with Rod since his arrival in the UK. One thing that we were both agreed upon, which we may have overlooked in our eagerness to retrieve the films from the left luggage locker, was that Peter could be in danger; especially if Rod's pursuers now transferred their attention to him. I said I would ring Dr Riemenschneider to get the latest information on Peter's condition. Angela wondered if we could consider having Peter removed from hospital in Munich as soon as possible. She would approach Hamish to see if he could offer any help in this matter.

The office door opened and Rod and Irena entered.

'Thought you might appreciate an update on where we're at. Dr Finlay said he was keen to have any news when he dropped in,' said Rod.

We nodded and followed them both back into the main conference room just as Hamish appeared, as if on cue.

'OK, we'll give you what we've got so far, there's a lot of detail but most of it is technical and Irena is best qualified to decipher this, so here we go,' said Rod, looking at a nodding Irena.

'First, there's no covering letter; if there was one it must have been removed by whoever the films were sent to before they were deposited in the Munich luggage locker. We still don't know who this is. Irena thinks Peter is the only one who does know.'

'Is there anything about Mengele?' asked Angela impatiently.

'Yes, luckily Josef Svoboda typed up a detailed summary of what he was doing and photographed them with the Minox camera. There are around sixty to seventy pages here about it! He'd carried out preliminary work in his university labs in Sao Paulo before organising large scale work in Paraguay. The factory is in a large estate in Paraguay, not far from the Paraná River and close to some German speaking communities, Hohenau and Colonias Unidas. He believes that Paraguay was chosen because President Stroessner is strongly anti-communist and pro-German and many ex-Nazis have found refuge here. The factory is not easy to get to from Brazil as it means going through a narrow band of Argentina which runs alongside the River Paraná before crossing it. Nevertheless, Josef Svoboda reports that the border crossing is easy and he had no trouble organising transport of necessary chemicals and equipment from Brazil, through Argentina and into Paraguay. It is anticipated that the transport of processed cocaine in the opposite direction will be equally easy; this has been proved by the already existing trade of marijuana into Brazil. It is on these factory trips that Josef Svoboda has come across Mengele, apparently working as a travelling vet in the various German speaking communities. There are some photos of a man in a white coat, supposedly Mengele, treating cattle in Cândido Godói in Brazil.'

We all stood up to examine the five or six black and white photos of Mengele carrying out some procedures on cattle, with the farmer holding a cow's head. The photos had obviously been taken clandestinely from some distance away as the face details were none too clear. The first photo was of Cândido Godói's sign. A lot of the others were of the factory in Paraguay, showing what appeared to be well-camouflaged buildings containing some substantial processing equipment; some of these were in colour.

'How did you leave it with Wiesenthal, Rod?' said Angela.

'In what way?'

'Well, did you agree to send him everything we find or just about Mengele?'

'I dunno! I did not discuss anything with Simon Wiesenthal, Peter was in control of that. They did not involve me in any discussions. We need to get Peter over here to get the full story. I got the impression that with Wiesenthal, you don't have a discussion with him, he tells you what is going to happen!' Rod said sarcastically.

'It'll be like going 'outback' in Aussieland. Any stranger will stand out like a sore-thumb and the bush-telegraph is going to alert Mengele long before you get anywhere near him,' Hamish chipped in.

'This is probably why Josef Svoboda wanted the information to go to Wiesenthal because he's in close contact with Israeli agents who successfully located and 'transferred' Adolf Eichmann from Argentina to Israel to stand trial,' I volunteered.

'OK; we've got a fix on Mengele in the German-speaking communities of Brazil, Argentina and Paraguay and he's working as a vet for farmers across these regions. It's not ideal but it's something to go on. James is right; Wiesenthal's agents have more experience in operating in South America and would have a better chance of finding him than us. However, I'll have to run it across Nigel first before we give any information to Wiesenthal,' Angela summed up.

I didn't say anything but I was disappointed with the preliminary information we'd just heard. I'm not sure what I was expecting but the build-up to retrieving the films from the left luggage locker had raised my expectations to a level which were probably unrealistic. I knew from the tone of Angela's résumé that she felt the same and was attempting to put a brave face on it. Nevertheless, it narrowed down the German-speaking regions in which Mengele was operating where he obviously felt comfortable and gave an insight into his thinking.

'OK, you guys are mainly interested in Mengele. I gotta say, I'm desperate to find out more details of this cocaine factory and how close it is to going into full production. The target market for this is the good-old US of A!' Rod said. 'I also gotta declare that I want to be in on any transfer of this information to US sources, it could get the cavalry off my back! Does Nigel know yet that I'm in the UK?' he added, turning to Angela.

'No, I haven't divulged anything about your recent whereabouts except that you escaped from Prague to Vienna by train. In fact, both James and I lied about you to Nigel, when James brought the films in,' Angela said.

Rod looked relieved and then suggested that he and Irena continue with the translation, concentrating now on the technical data about the cocaine research and production details. Angela said she had promised to ring Nigel at home when she had any information at all about Mengele as he had to keep his minister informed as soon as there was any news. I decided, even though it was Sunday, that I'd try to contact Dr Riemenschneider at the LMU hospital and ask if Peter's condition was stable enough for him to be moved to a more secure place.

Hamish led Angela into his office for her to ring Nigel whilst I returned to the office next door to the conference room to ring the LMU. I was informed by hospital reception that Dr Riemenschneider was not in at present but would be back on duty in two hours' time. I said I would ring back.

Angela returned to my office with Hamish after her brief conversation with Nigel.

'Nigel's been instructed by his minister not to divulge any information to US officials or Simon Wiesenthal until it's been thoroughly vetted here first!' she said.

'Well, that's plain enough,' I said, somewhat surprised.

'I told Nigel we wouldn't have finished the technical translations until tomorrow. It may give us time to sift through it so as to give Rod chance to decide how he wants it played.'

'Good idea, it looks like it's about to get political from now on!' I said.

*****

Bishop Brennan had spent a rather fitful night's sleep in the house where he normally stayed when he was in the Leeds area; it was not a patch on his quarters in Vienna but it would do for the purpose he had in mind and, crucially, the people he could rely on were close by. He was roughly a mile and a half away from the cathedral in the centre of Leeds, just off Headingley Lane, midway between Hyde Park and Headingley. The incumbent Bishop was not in residence so there would be no interference from that quarter, and he was held in awe by his subordinates who carried out his orders without question. His first request was to summon a trusty odd-job man, who would be ideal for the task ahead; his name was Mikhail Petrov.

He then rang his underworld contact in London, who had come highly recommended by Mafia connections in the USA. He needed an update on their progress in locating Brittain, the Svobodas and Trask.

He discovered that Brittain, now living in Bradford, was working for a Wool Research Institute with offices in both Bradford and Ilkley, which partially explained why he had been in Czechoslovakia.

Apparently the Institute's new facilities in Ilkley were being officially opened on Friday, no expense was being spared and all the local dignitaries were invited. There was even going to be a special train from London to transport some important people from the Institute's head office to the party.

The two men sent to deal with Brittain did not fare too well, they had been disturbed at his house by a neighbour from whom they had managed to extract information about Brittain and the foreign woman with him. She was in the local hospital and they had no trouble finding which ward she was on. Inexplicably, they had tried to pass themselves off as window cleaners and both paid the penalty. One with his life and the other with broken bones — pane-ful, as Brittain would no doubt have observed. Brennan, on the other hand, had always been oblivious to such comments.

The surviving hit-man was under armed guard in the same hospital, awaiting questioning. It was clear to Brennan that this was a loose end that definitely needed tying off. This was to be Petrov's first assignment. As he put down the phone, he was already formulating his next move. He had been right to come to the UK, he felt he had Brittain in his sights and this time he would do the job properly!

*****

Angela, Hamish and I listened carefully to Irena and Rod's translation of Josef Svoboda's research work on cocaine production and process refinements. I have to admit, I knew virtually nothing about drugs. The closest I'd been was at University when, in the labs for one of the practical experiments in organic chemistry, we had to extract caffeine from tea leaves, purify and crystallise it from a solvent before measuring its melting point. At the time I thought it was a waste of a couple of pounds of good tea!

We were getting a crash course into cocaine drug technology; it was evident that Svoboda had been very thorough in his work and it demonstrated what a good chemist he was in all respects.

Cocaine, we learnt, was an alkaloid substance extracted from the leaves of the coca plant, which is mainly grown in Peru, Bolivia and Columbia. Traditionally, local people dried the leaves in the sun and then pulped the leaves up in a 55 gallon drum containing water and an alkaline material (baking soda, for example), together with a solvent such as kerosene, benzol or gasoline. The pulping softens the leaves and the cocaine alkaloid is extracted into the solvent phase. The degree of mechanical action put into the pulping stage significantly influences the amount of cocaine released. The water and leaves are then discarded and acid (usually sulphuric acid) is added to precipitate the cocaine and allow the solvent to be removed before baking soda is added. It is then dried to produce a putty-like substance which is called coca paste, or 'basuco'. Josef Svoboda also carried out experiments without the use of an organic solvent and just used sulphuric acid, thus cutting out a step.

In South America, this crude coca paste is smoked, but for the USA and other outside users, the coca paste is invariably converted into the powder form by dissolving in dilute hydrochloric acid solution.

Josef Svoboda showed that this mechanical procedure could be standardised for both extraction techniques by using a simple concrete mixing machine for a certain time to optimise cocaine yields. This simple technique was aimed at the low-tech farms where the coca was grown. This part of the production has to be carried out in-situ on the farms or close to where the coca is grown to reduce transport costs. Typically, 114kg of dried coca leaves are needed to produce 1kg of coca paste, which can be then readily transported to the more high-tech cocaine hydrochloride labs.

Rod grimly reported that this method is currently being trialled at a number of selected sites in both Bolivia and Columbia in an effort to scale-up production. Josef Svoboda had also carried out significant work in investigating the purification techniques of converting coca paste to cocaine hydrochloride, but significantly mentioned that the factory in Paraguay was operating normally now and was ready and capable of supplying the USA with all it needs! Svoboda's need to visit the plant was not as important now. Rod had what he was looking for. This factory was geared up to be a major threat to the USA.

We had all listened avidly to this report and I had found it personally addictive! I chose, probably wisely, not to share this with my colleagues round the table. I then remembered that I should ring the LMU hospital again and try to speak to Dr Riemenschneider. After a brief phone call from the office next door, I hurried back to announce, 'Dr Riemeschneider has just told me that he discharged Peter Svoboda this morning and he left with people claiming to be from our Institute!'

CHAPTER 11
MINER STRIKES

Petrov was pleased to get a call from Bishop Brennan's office in Leeds inviting him to go and see the Bishop. Petrov was an ex-Russian soldier but passed himself off as a Pole in this country. After the war, he had avoided repatriation and certain death under the communist regime as a willing collaborator of the Nazis after occupation in October 1941. He was the youngest of five soldiers from the same region, who had stuck together throughout the war, and later in the UK. He had been very much the subordinate member of the group but was now the only one surviving; he now relished the chance to show that he could be trusted to carry out an important mission. They had handled several projects for the Bishop; he did not concern himself with the morality but enjoyed the practical nature of doing a good job. To him it was as if he was still in the army, it was an order.

As a sapper he recalled the last job he had done for the Bishop in 1963. The attempted shooting of President Kennedy in the graveyard on the Chatsworth Estate failed, yes, but not because he had done a bad job in concealing the marksman in an underground cache. On the contrary, he had done a magnificent job in its construction; it was just bad luck that it was discovered. Anyway, Kennedy was shot a few months later so it did not matter that much as far as he was concerned. It had caused him major trouble in avoiding detection though. The Bishop had used his connections to allow him to lie low for six months, and then he'd managed to secure a job with Middleton Broom Pit Colliery, just outside Leeds. He'd enjoyed that but the pit had been closed in May '68 and he was keen to find more challenging work. The Bishop had just offered that, and the pay was more attractive.

He stopped his daydreaming as the trolleybus reached its terminus outside Bradford Royal Infirmary. His mission there was to find the man under police guard and dispatch him immediately. He was to do the same with a woman called Irena Svoboda if she was still in the hospital. Unlike his ex-colleagues, he could easily blend into any background as he looked very ordinary and did not draw attention to himself. His loose-fitting, nondescript jacket masked a bodybuilder's physique developed over the years as a sapper and, more recently, a miner; he possessed abnormally strong upper-body power as a result.

He spent the next hour wandering along the long corridors of the hospital on each of the three floors looking for signs of police presence. He found it by chance as he almost bumped into a uniformed police constable coming out of Ward 9, and he followed as the constable went out of a side door for a smoke. He noted the time and then approached the reception desk just inside the main door and asked where he could find the policeman guarding an injured prisoner as he had a note for him. The busy receptionist naively gave him the ward number (9), and the name of the prisoner, Ronnie Ward. He was also able to learn that Irena Svoboda had been discharged yesterday. As he quickly walked back to Ward 9 he spotted a porter entering a lift with an empty trolley. The porter was roughly his own height so he stepped into the lift before it closed. The lift moved down towards the next floor but stopped halfway for around two minutes; when it started moving again and reached the ground floor, the porter pushed the trolley out into the corridor. It now contained what appeared to be a sleeping patient. Petrov had overpowered the porter, knocked him senseless and donned his uniform. He managed to deposit the unconscious man in a nearby toilet cubicle, with his head submerged in water. He then made his way towards Ward 9 and asked the first nurse he saw for Mr Ward, who was due in the X-ray department. The nurse said she would have to ask the policeman to accompany them, but Petrov cleverly countered that he'd just run into the policeman, who said he would join him on the way to the X-ray department after finishing his smoke.

On entering the empty lift, he stopped it halfway again between floors and surprised Ronnie Ward by swiftly and expertly breaking his neck as easily as snapping a brittle twig, before putting his original clothes back on again and leaving the dispatched patient on the trolley in the lift. He walked boldly out of the main door and jumped on the next trolleybus into the centre of Bradford; job done!

*****

The news that Peter Svoboda had been kidnapped came like a bolt out of the blue to all of us. Irena was particularly scathing towards me, as I'd flown to Munich specifically to help Rod and Peter, and then, in her eyes, been more concerned with retrieving the films from the left luggage locker than ensuring Peter was properly protected. Fortunately, I couldn't understand everything she said as she vented her feelings in a mixture of broken English and very fluent Czech! The look on Rod's face said it all. I was definitely not shit-hot at anything now, just shit!

Hamish tried to defuse the situation by suggesting that we adjourn the meeting for the present, and ushered both Rod and Irena out of the meeting room. He took them to the Crescent Hotel where he booked Irena in as a guest of the Institute, and once they were all seated in the bar, promised that the full resources of the Institute would be made available to find Peter. After a couple of large brandies, Irena's pent-up anger ebbed somewhat, tiredness took over and she went up to her room.

'I'd better get back to London and be ready to face Nigel tomorrow morning. Can you run me across to Leeds in time for the last train?' said Angela, as soon as Hamish, Rod and Irena had left for the hotel.

'Sure, let's go,' I responded, putting on my jacket, relieved to be moving again. 'Are you going to tell Nigel that Rod is now in the UK?'

'I'm not sure, I might play it by ear depending on what Nigel says,' said Angela thoughtfully, realising that she ought to have discussed it with Rod before he left.

'It's going to be difficult to keep it dark for much longer.'

'I know, but Nigel's under pressure from the minister and Rod's predicament is not likely to be of much concern to him,' said Angela. The journey from Ilkley to Leeds was straightforward since it was early Sunday evening and there was minimal traffic on the road. Angela was relieved that she was in plenty of time to catch her train.

She agreed to ring me after she'd spoken to Nigel the next morning. I said I'd learned that it was my neighbour's funeral later on tomorrow morning so it would probably be early afternoon before I got to the Institute.

Stanley Robinson's funeral was timed for 11.00am at Nab Wood Crematorium, which was just out of Bradford. I drove the Imp there and got caught up in traffic caused by road works on Manningham Lane, which meant it was 10.55am when I arrived. The driveway to the chapel was almost full with cars and I just managed to park in one of the last remaining spaces. As I left the car I could see that the hearse and accompanying cars had already arrived and were waiting for the last of the mourners from the previous funeral to depart. There was an incredibly large turnout, not surprising really as Stanley Robinson's untimely demise had rightly generated tremendous sympathy for the family. I looked around the crowd waiting to enter the small chapel and surmised that there must be many of Stanley's ex-colleagues from the tax office present; there were also quite a number of fit-looking, sun-tanned young men present who I recognised as Yorkshire cricketers. I knew Stanley had been very active in raising money for players' benefits, as I'd bought raffle tickets on more than one occasion for a cricket bat covered in signatures of Yorkshire players, England players, etc. — but never won one.

The funeral service was conducted very professionally by a Church of England clergyman, well versed in saying the right things and he had done his homework well on Stanley's background and interests. *Rock of Ages* was sung lustily by all, accompanied by an electric organ. A favourite song of Stanley's was also played. This, surprisingly, was *Big Spender*, but unfortunately Shirley Bassey was not present to belt it out. I inwardly appreciated the irony of an ex-taxman's choice of song, especially a Yorkshireman!

On the way out through the chapel's side door, after the committal, I paid my respects to Edna, Stanley's widow, who insisted I join them for a bite to eat at the nearby Bankfield Hotel. I had intended to give this a miss but felt I should attend, if only for one sandwich! As always, the relief at getting the funeral over with loosened everybody up a little, and good-humoured tales of Stanley's exploits were to be heard almost everywhere. The availability of free drinks from the bar had more than a little to do with this! I was just about to make my excuses and leave when I heard a familiar voice behind me.

'I thought we'd find you here, Mr Brittain.' I looked round into the sombre face of Inspector Button.

'Good to see you paying your respects,' I said diplomatically.

'Well, we'd planned to do just that, but we were called out this morning to an emergency at the BRI. The injured prisoner we arrested for murdering Mr Robinson had his neck broken and a porter was assaulted and died from drowning. The killer was also interested in Dr Irena Svoboda!'

'Was the assassin seen?' I asked.

'We've got a vague description from the lady at the reception desk who remembered a porter, or somebody dressed as a porter, asking her for the ward the prisoner was in. She was busy but said the man had an Eastern European accent, and apart from noticing he was middle-aged and of a stocky build, she could not remember any more about him. That description could apply to virtually all the porters in the hospital!' replied the Inspector gloomily. 'Where is Dr Svoboda now?'

'She's probably at the Institute in Ilkley; she stayed last night at the Crescent Hotel there,' I replied, getting the uneasy feeling I'd come to dread when danger was close by.

'I know you're something to do with national security and are reluctant to tell me everything, but I believe that both you and Dr Svoboda are probably in great danger. It would be in the interest of everybody concerned if we could cooperate,' said Inspector Button confidentially.

This was the first time that the Inspector had treated me with some degree of respect. He'd probably been checking up on me and was now also under significant pressure, since the injured prisoner in hospital was under police guard as well! I decided not to stir it by asking how the assassin had got past the police guard.

'I've always tried to cooperate fully with you, Inspector. I don't know who is trying to kill us, or why this assassin was sent to eliminate the remaining injured thug; I promise you that when I have any information, you'll be the first to know,' I responded helpfully.

This appeared to satisfy the Inspector for the moment so I volunteered the information that I was just about to leave for the Wool Institute.

*****

Bishop Brennan received the news from Petrov with great satisfaction. The police were not going to be able to extract any damaging information from this shoddy killer now! It was a pity the woman Svoboda had been discharged from hospital, but he was not too worried as he felt it was only a matter of time before he caught up with her, Trask and that irritant Brittain! He felt in control again and allowed himself the luxury of wallowing in the knowledge that he was so much cleverer than anybody realised. He also knew he had the element of surprise on his side which would tip the odds very much in his favour. He was pleased with Petrov. Although a little on the slow side compared with his ex-colleagues, he was a good, practical man who was loyal and would see the job through.

He had instructed Petrov to go to London in the next day or so to infiltrate the special train which was being arranged to transport special guests up to Ilkley for the official opening of the newly built Wool Institute on Friday. He suspected everybody was likely to be off guard, making it an opportunity for Petrov to use his skills and hopefully finish the job! He had no photographs of Svoboda, Trask and Brittain, but no doubt the informal situation at the Institute should make it relatively easy for Petrov to identify them. Since his conversation with Johann Schmidt of the BND, he'd decided that the chances of him now retrieving the information from his quarries was minimal, especially as they'd had a few days to deliver the information in the UK. Nevertheless, he saw it as a great opportunity for personal revenge and he was sure he could explain away their demise to Schmidt as necessary collateral damage.

*****

On my arrival at the Institute, I was informed that Hamish wanted to see me as soon as I returned so I entered his secretary's office and she said I was free to go in.

'Ah, James, Angela's been on the phone. Nigel said his minister is still adamant that neither the Americans nor Wiesenthal are to have any information at the moment about Josef Mengele! It's going to be discussed in a Cabinet meeting tomorrow. The official attitude to Peter Svoboda's abduction is that it's unfortunate, but since he's not a British citizen, there's nothing they can do.'

I was not surprised about this at all; it was very predictable, in fact. Before I could reply, Hamish continued.

'I, on the other hand, am of the opinion that Peter Svoboda risked his life to present this information to the UK. I told Angela that our conversation never took place; the Institute will use its resources to locate Peter, we have an obligation to help him since he could be a valuable member of our team. In fact, I've already asked Hans Klein to liaise with Dr Riemenschneider at the LMU hospital to see if he can come up with something.'

Hamish went up another two points in my estimation. I then told him of my encounter with Inspector Button.

'It appears that Rod, Irena and I are all in imminent danger from someone, or some organisation, prepared to eliminate even their own people if they get caught. It's more than likely related to Rod and Peter's experiences in Munich, but from what Rod said, he was the main target then. Unfortunately it looks as if they have transferred their attention to Peter. You had better warn Hans to be very careful now.'

'Let's talk to Rod and Irena, they're next door finishing the translation exercise,' Hamish said.

We outlined the latest news to Rod and Irena, Hamish re-emphasising that the Institute would do all it could to find Peter, omitting to say that the official UK government line was to do nothing at this stage. I said we would all have to be on our guard and perhaps I should consider relocating to the Crescent Hotel for the time being, where we could all keep an eye on one another.

Hamish then brought up the subject of the official opening of the Wool Institute on Friday, saying that Rod and Irena would both be very welcome. It might help take our mind off things for a short while. He said he planned on asking Angela as well, and she could take advantage of the special train as he was sure there was still room on it. I thought it would be a good idea.

'It don't make a lot of sense to me!' said Rod. He then went on to explain why he thought he was being targeted by a branch of the CIA, who wrongly believed he was involved in pro-communist (anti-American) activities after he had agreed to attend the Russell Tribunal in Roskilde, Denmark, to get information for his brother about the use of Napalm in Vietnam. He just didn't believe that Irena and I would be targets as well! There must be another reason, and it could be related to the information sent by Josef Svoboda relating to Mengele and the drugs work Svoboda was forced to do in South America. He also said he was sure his brother's phone was being tapped when he had spoken to him a couple of days ago telling him he had information of major importance to the US. He said he needed Angela to set up a meeting with US officials for him so he could put his side of the story to them as soon as possible.

I glanced at Hamish, who was seated almost opposite me, to see if he was likely to divulge the information that the Americans were still to be kept in the dark at the moment. Hamish ignored my look and nodded to Rod and suggested he discuss that with Angela directly. He then asked whether the latest translation exercise had thrown up anything vital of which we should be aware.

The answer was that Josef Svoboda had described the technical work he had done in improving both cocaine hydrochloride yields and cocaine–base, which is cocaine hydrochloride that has been reverse-engineered back to the chemical base state — and is smokable. This is chemically similar to coca paste but free from many of its impurities. The new technology was now being used in the Paraguayan factory, which was the most important point. Irena was prepared to go into the chemical details but we all agreed that, at this stage, we were satisfied with the fact that cocaine based drugs were now coming off the production line in frightening quantities, ready to cause misery to thousands, if not millions, of people worldwide.

Hamish then wondered if it was a suitable time for Irena to outline the work both she and Peter had done regarding the flame resist treatments for wool. I knew Hamish was itching to learn more about this work so he could arrange for lab facilities and other resources to be made available for Peter and possibly for Irena. Rod took the hint and said he would try to ring Angela to discuss his next move.

Irena was now in her element and began by informing us about chrome dyeing. Both Hamish and I were well aware that chrome dyeing was an economic and effective way of colouring wool black or navy blue and the dye fastness was very good. What I certainly wasn't aware of was that chrome dyeing increased wool's natural flame resistance. It wasn't ideal because the 'chroming' treatment discoloured the wool a dirty green shade, so it was only suitable for really dark shades such as black or blue. It could be loosely described as the 'Henry Ford' Model T treatment, in that you could have any colour you wanted, providing it was black or blue!

This had started Peter thinking that other metals might be used in place of chromium. He had managed to stabilise a titanium solution in strongly acid conditions by forming a complex with an α-hydroxy acid, such as citric acid, and applied it to wool under boiling conditions. The wool turned a light yellow colour but the flame resist effect was far better than the chrome dyed wool and had impressive washfastness as well. This was the basis of Peter's discovery and he had extended the work to include other α-hydroxy acids and established that it could also be carried out simultaneously with strong acid dyes as well. It was therefore a very cost-effective flame-resist treatment which could be exploited commercially. As yet, Peter had not carried out any commercial trials and was hoping to extend this part of the work when he arrived in Ilkley. For medium shades of most colours it worked very well. Peter was not sure how it worked, but chrome dyeing was known as a mordant dye (mordre meaning 'to bite' in French), in which it was thought the chromium formed a complex with the wool fibre before the dye was applied. The chromium metal was tightly bound to both the wool and the dye molecule, thus explaining the good washfastness. It was likely that a similar mechanism applied to the titanium complex.

Peter was also keen to investigate other metals, in particular zirconium, which was in the same chemical group as titanium, and therefore should have similar characteristics. It might be colourless, in which case it could be used for lighter dye shades without discolouration.

'And what was your involvement in this work, Irena?' asked Hamish pointedly.

'I carry out testing for Peter,' she said proudly.

'OK, Irena, the Institute is prepared to employ both you and your brother Peter, on the basis of what you have just described. I think this work is very important and we should try to exploit it commercially, as soon as is possible.' said Hamish.

'Thank you very much! It is very important now to find Peter, yes?'

'Yes, Irena, it's vital,' confirmed Hamish.

I too was tremendously impressed with the way Irena had presented their work. Peter was right; she was a shit-hot chemist and well worth a place at our Institute in her own right.

Just then, Rod came back into the meeting room with a curious expression on his face which I couldn't read.

'Angela's just told me Simon Wiesenthal's rung her. He announced that his contacts have 'rescued' Peter Svoboda from the LMU hospital and have him in safe-keeping. He will be released when Wiesenthal gets the information about Mengele that he was promised.'

CHAPTER 12
CABINET RESHUFFLE

This was turning out to be one of the worst days Angela could ever remember! The meeting with Nigel had turned into a bad-tempered spat when he ordered her to toe the line or be taken off the job altogether. The politicians were now very much in control of how the Mengele case was going to be handled; and he was determined that he was going to come out of it smelling of roses! This was on top of the uncharacteristic outburst she'd directed at James over his liaison with Irena; she bitterly regretted this now, regarding it as very unprofessional and vowing to avoid, if possible, getting involved with work colleagues ever again. It had, however, made her very aware that she still had feelings for James. She conceded that some men might be attracted to Irena, who she thought wouldn't have been out of place as a Mata Hari, femme fatale character in a spy novel, but she couldn't dispel the idea that Irena might have used James for her own ends in order to work at the Institute.

The phone call from Wiesenthal was almost the last straw; he was blatantly blackmailing the British government for the Mengele information before he would release Peter Svoboda. Her explanation that the information was all on film and had to be translated cut no ice with Wiesenthal. He said to pass it over — he would do the translation for them! There was a hint of menace in his voice as he informed her he expected to receive the information without delay.

She had blurted out the Wiesenthal news to Rod; this was done mainly so she didn't have to tell him that she couldn't set up a meeting with US officials at the moment. She now had to face Nigel again; she knew it was a no-win situation and Peter Svoboda's future was very much in the balance.

The other thing which worried Angela was Peter's present condition. The hospital had obviously been monitoring him closely after the bang on the head and it was unlikely that he would be under the same medical care wherever Wiesenthal and his cronies were keeping him! It was generally accepted that Wiesenthal had close ties with Mossad, the Israeli equivalent of MI6 and the American CIA. They had special responsibilities for hunting down Nazi war criminals and used whatever methods they thought fit to achieve their ends. Unfortunately, Peter was in the position of being a potential sacrificial pawn in a deadly game of chess if things turned nasty.

Angela was surprised that Rod had not quizzed her about whether she had set up a meeting for him with the US Embassy; she could only think that he was taken aback by the news about Peter and had forgotten. Nevertheless, he was going to ask sometime soon. It was also strange that the US Embassy had not been in touch for a day or two; she put this down to the bad news from Guatemala that their Ambassador (John Gordon Mein) had been assassinated on the streets of Guatemala City last Thursday, the 29th August. She decided that it was very important that ministers should have all the latest information about Peter before the Cabinet meeting tomorrow. She also decided she would tell Nigel that the Institute was prepared to go-it-alone and try to find Peter. It was very convenient that James had a dual role as part-time MI6 agent and wool technologist, as she could argue legitimately that this action would not compromise Nigel's orders to keep the Americans in the dark about Mengele and to withhold information from Wiesenthal. After all, the Institute believed Peter to be an important asset. She did wonder if she should have consulted Hamish first, but it might be in Peter's best interests. These were her immediate thoughts before she knocked on Nigel's door again.

*****

Rod put the phone down after speaking to Angela. He was not happy about the way things were going with Peter and wondered how this might influence the British government's handling of the situation. He had met Simon Wiesenthal and knew he wasn't going to be easy to deal with, but believed he was entitled to the information about Mengele. After all, Peter's father had intended him to have it. He could sense that Angela was under tremendous pressure now and he decided there and then not to involve the Brits as go-betweens. He would contact the American Embassy himself; he still knew a few people there who might talk to him off the record. He was unsure as to how Irena would react. In one way, it was good that Peter was relatively safe, but bad that he had been discharged early from hospital, in case he had a relapse. He knew Irena wouldn't understand why the Brits would want to withhold the Mengele information from Wiesenthal — neither did he! Rod found it surprising that he empathised strongly with both Peter and Irena Svoboda; it was as if he had known them all his life. He quickly decided that he should ring his brother again before he contacted the US Embassy; he would do it from the Crescent Hotel later that day when he knew his brother would be home. He then re-entered the meeting room and announced the latest news about Peter to Hamish, Irena and James.

'Hi, Joe, it's Rod. Are you alone?'

'Yea, glad you've rung; don't talk, just listen!' said Joe. 'You're dead right, Rod, we've both been under surveillance for anti-'Nam activities. It's OK now, they accept my explanation. You gotta contact our embassy in London and ask for Chuck Edwards, he'll explain everything. Gotta go, good luck.'

Rod put the phone down without another word being said, then was angry with himself for not waiting to hang up and see if the line was still being tapped. From Joe's manner, he guessed that it was.

*****

I was still persona non grata with Irena but she tacitly accepted a lift back to the Crescent from the Institute. I parked in the small car park at the back of the hotel which was accessed from the main road via a narrow cobbled side passage, a relic from when the hotel was a coaching inn, perhaps. I parked next to Rod's VW Campervan in which we had shared our Continental journey not so long ago. Irena still showed no interest.

She went straight up to her room as I was checking in at the reception desk, ignoring Rod, who was just putting the phone down. I needed some time to sort things out in my own mind. Rod put paid to this immediately.

'James, gotta few minutes?' he asked. Then, as I asked for two pints of Tetley's bitter without thinking, 'Do you Brits only drink warm beer?' The barman suggested a Skol lager as an alternative for Rod and we sat down at a table in the corner.

'Look, James, I'll come clean, I've gotta confession to make!' he said to my surprise. I almost switched back into priest mode but quickly checked myself.

'I know I can trust you now, I was on a mission in Czechoslovakia which partially involved your government.'

Rod went on to divulge some alarming information which, in some ways, I wished he had kept to himself. He had been sent to Prague to debrief a member of the Czech security service who wished to defect to America and, in return, was prepared to provide proof that a British cabinet minister was a paid informant supplying secret information to him about government technology plans, regarding the aviation industry in particular. The man named was the Rt Hon John Stonehouse MP, Cabinet Minister. The invasion had swiftly terminated further debriefings and there was an additional complication involving the two American thugs sent to eliminate Rod, which I will come to shortly.

The current CIA chief, James Jesus Angleton, was now virtually paranoid about moles, who were KGB agents inside the CIA, MI6 and foreign left-wing-leaning governments, such as the UK. This suspicion was partly fuelled by bad experiences he'd had with Burgess and Maclean's defection to the Soviet Union in the early fifties and, more recently, Kim Philby in '63. Philby had been a trusted confidante during his tenure as head of MI6 in Washington DC, and this stuck in his craw. There was a long-running suspicion, both within the CIA and MI5, that Prime Minister Wilson was a KGB agent; some thought it an unlikely coincidence that he became leader of the Labour Party, and subsequently Prime Minister shortly afterwards, following the sudden untimely death of Hugh Gaitskill. The current US President, Lyndon Baines Johnson (LBJ), had escalated the Vietnam War on taking over power after JFK's assassination and was sore that he could not get Wilson to agree to send even a token force to support him. To his disgust, all he got from Wilson was another peace initiative. Angleton fully supported the war and was happy to implement the covert domestic surveillance project (Operation CHAOS), ordered by LBJ to counteract the anti-war and civil rights movements, which were thought to be supported and funded from foreign communist sources.

This was when Rod and his brother, Joe, had come under suspicion after the Dow anti-war riot last year at the University of Wisconsin's Madison campus, where Joe had been beaten up by police. Rod's fact-finding visit to the Russell Tribunal in Roskilde, Denmark, on behalf of his brother, further implicated him as a communist sympathiser.

This was compounded by the fact that Rod had been told by a friend who was on Robert Kennedy's security detail that Kennedy had conducted a private investigation into his brother's assassination. The words used by his friend were that JFK was probably killed by a 'rogue CIA faction' and that Angleton probably knew about it! His friend had died under mysterious circumstances and Robert Kennedy was assassinated shortly afterwards. Rod had put two and two together and believed the same rogue CIA faction was responsible for his friend's and Kennedy's assassinations, and that he was next on the list to tie up loose ends! He had jumped at the chance to carry out the mission in Czechoslovakia to get out of the way. The two Americans he was with on the night of the invasion were, in his own mind, Mafia men sent to rub him out!

'Why haven't you told me the whole story before, Rod?'

'When I finally met up with you in Prague, you were with Irena. She could have been a Czech agent; they use gymnasts with bodies like hers as 'honey traps', James!'

It had never occurred to me that Irena might have been planted. It was unlikely, I thought, but I always did have a sweet tooth!

'Have you discussed this with Angela yet?' I asked.

'No, Angela's under enough pressure at the moment from Wiesenthal and her boss, Nigel; I thought I'd run it across you first. I'd also like to ask you a favour. Rather than involve Angela, I'm going to contact the US Embassy in London and ask for a meeting, but I want it to be on my terms and not in the city. The best place would be somewhere private and out of the way, can you suggest anywhere suitable?'

'Yes! The Institute's old offices in Bradford. There's only the caretaker in the building most of the time at the moment, and one of the railway stations is only two or three minutes' walk away. Get them to take a train from Kings Cross to Leeds and then a train to Bradford's Forster Square Station; we can meet them off the train there,' I said decisively.

'Great, James, I've just spoken to Brother Joe and he's told me to contact Chuck Edwards at our embassy. I might be in the clear but I want to make sure.'

Rod seemed relieved to have got this news off his chest, it had all the hallmarks of being a confession but I declined to instruct him to say three Hail Marys as I was now out of the habit, both from the dress and practice sense. It did give me a serious problem as what to do with the information that John Stonehouse might be a spy; governments have been toppled on lesser scandals. Rod disappeared to ring Chuck Edwards and arrange the meeting which was the most important thing for him at present.

'Chuck Edwards was expecting my call, he's going to come up to Bradford on Wednesday; I'm to give him a call tomorrow when he's sorted out the train schedules. Is that OK, James?'

I nodded and we both decided to return to our rooms.

*****

Bishop Brennan had just been mulling over his reduced contact and influence in America since the death of his mentor, Cardinal Spellman, last year. He had had the ear of the Cardinal ever since his very successful stint as Opus Dei's financial organiser in America in the early sixties. His relative side-lining since the foiled assassination attempt on Kennedy in '63 and his hasty departure from the UK was cushioned, to a degree, by Spellman's support for his appointment to his current position as Bishop in Vienna.

Cardinal Spellman had been an outspoken supporter of the Vietnam War describing it as a *war for civilisation*. The war had become known as *Spelly's War* and he was thought of in some circles as the Bob Hope of the clergy. It was unfortunate, in Brennan's view, that his finer points had been overshadowed by the reputation he'd gained as a homosexual; he recalled that he had been described by the journalist Michelangelo Signorile as 'one of the most notorious, powerful and sexually voracious homosexuals in the American Catholic Church's history.' Bishop Brennan was aware of many Catholic priests who had similar leanings but viewed it as an occupational hazard to be dismissed as irrelevant in the major scheme of things. If Brennan had had a more intimate knowledge of the British political scene, as well as a sense of humour, he might have appreciated Winston Churchill's biting comment against a current Member of Parliament, who he said 'was the sort of person who gives sodomy a bad name!'

A new Cardinal had not yet been appointed in America, but Bishop Brennan was not on especially good terms with any of the main contenders so had no expectations of ever having any significant influence there in the future.

His train of thought was brought swiftly to an end by an unexpected call from his main CIA contact at the American Embassy in Vienna who he'd kept informed of his movements. His immediate reaction was that he would be able to report some progress in his search for Trask, the Svobodas and Brittain. Instead, his contact was keen to pass on information from his opposite number at the US Embassy in London who was bemoaning the fact that he would have to endure the torture of British Rail to meet up with Rod Trask in some God-forsaken place called Bradford. Apparently he was booking a ticket to Leeds and then to Forster Square Station, Bradford. The visit was going to take place late morning on Wednesday this week. He also reported that the FBI in America had cleared Trask and his brother of anti-American activities and the word had gone out to 'lay-off him'. This news did not go down well with the two CIA men who agreed that they didn't want the drugs boat to be rocked in South America, amongst other things, and Trask would still be worth eliminating, in the interests of tidiness!

Brennan had to act quickly now. It was early Monday evening, and his main man, Petrov, was in London but he needed him back in Bradford to stake out the station to deal with Trask; this was the most promising lead they'd had so far and they must take advantage of it. Unfortunately, Petrov was not in the hotel he was told to stay at; he'd gone out, he was told. Brennan left a message for him to ring as soon as he got in. There was nobody else available he could trust at such short notice so he steeled himself for a long night waiting for Petrov to return to the hotel.

Tuesday morning arrived and there was still no word from Petrov. The hotel said they hadn't seen him and would give him the message as soon as he returned. Brennan, as well as being livid, was intensely worried that time was running out for Petrov to get back to Bradford for the rendezvous; he was even considering praying for divine intervention on his behalf when the phone rang. Yes, it was Petrov, and he was obviously blind drunk, babbling away in a European dialect Brennan couldn't understand. It was obvious that he wasn't going to be in a fit state until early tomorrow morning,

Wednesday. Could he still make it to Bradford in time? He hoped so!

Brennan had to resort to extreme measures to ensure that Petrov was put on the first train to Leeds from Kings Cross on Wednesday morning; he instructed the hotel receptionist to arrange for this to happen. A generous financial two-part incentive was agreed, the second part would be paid only if Petrov rang Brennan from Leeds on his arrival. He could only wait now!

*****

On Tuesday morning, Angela was on tenterhooks awaiting the outcome of the Cabinet meeting. Nigel rang her just before midday and summoned her to his office.

'The Cabinet puts a high priority on tracing Josef Mengele and bringing him to justice. My minister has put me in charge of expediting things, so if the Wool Institute wants to try to locate this Czech scientist, fine, they have no objections to them doing so, but our main priority will be to work out a plan to deal with Mengele. I understand the Czech scientist's sister, the one who James smuggled into Britain, carried out the translation. At this stage, we are not to communicate with Wiesenthal or the Americans,' Nigel concluded.

Angela nodded and remembered that she had purposely omitted to mention to Nigel that Rod had been actively involved in the translation as well — it was going to be difficult to keep the Americans out of it for much longer!

'You'd better get James involved in this as he has more of the background to it at the moment. Who do we know here who has Spanish and Portuguese? Probably not too important at this stage as our embassies in South America would be in on this as well, eventually,' said Nigel, thinking out loud.

'The Institute's going to want James's input into finding Peter Svoboda since they actually funded his trip to Czechoslovakia and have a vested interest in employing Svoboda over here,' said Angela bluntly.

'Yes, yes, but we must have first priority over James's time; I'll have to speak to the Institute's colonial director, what's his name?'

'Dr Hamish Finlay,' Angela replied, noting Nigel's typically condescending attitude and the smirk on his face when he heard the name; she was half expecting a jibe relating to 'Dr Finley's

Casebook' but suspected Nigel was not a fan of the TV programme.

'You'd better get me his telephone number; I'll give him a ring.'

Angela recited the number as it was fresh in her memory from her frequent talks with both James and Hamish.

'Oh, by the way, Nigel, who's the minister in charge of this exercise?'

'The Rt Honourable John Stonehouse.'

CHAPTER 13
BRIEF ENCOUNTER — US STYLE

Tuesday morning saw Irena and I back at the Institute, with Rod opting to stay behind intending to explore Ilkley and its immediate surroundings.

I would have appreciated putting some distance between myself and Irena until she got over her annoyance with me, but Hamish quashed that by instructing me to help her settle into a laboratory she'd been allocated on the top floor of the Institute. He was keen to get her installed so that she could start work on the novel flame-resist project she had described to us yesterday. Although I hadn't worked in any of the Institute's laboratories, I had the basic knowledge of how things functioned and I knew which people to ask. Helping Irena, I realised, would familiarise me with the new building and where people were now situated. The first stop was to introduce her to administration so they could put her on the payroll; I left her there for ten to fifteen minutes and went in search of the stores, which would be our next port of call to stock up on stationery, equipment and chemicals. This was situated on the second floor, manned by Harry, a jovial man in his fifties. He greeted me, as he did everybody for that matter, with, 'How do.' The intonation in his voice was always the same and just meant hello!

I explained that I was going to bring Dr Irena Svoboda to see him very shortly as she was going to be working in one of the labs upstairs and I suggested we could start to put together a few items she would need. Harry beckoned me through the door into the stores area, picked up an empty cardboard box and quickly put in a range of Biros, pencils and a ruler, together with notepads and the Institute's bound exercise books, all of which he'd done dozens of times before. He handed the box over to me saying that anything else she needed, she just had to ask. The apparent haste was excused by the fact that the whole of the building was now on countdown to the opening day on Friday. Most of the departments were frantically working on their displays and presentations for the important visitors who would be making a conducted tour of the Institute and its facilities. I had been insulated from these preparations which were now occupying most of everybody's time.

I went back to the accounts office just as Irena was about to leave; she seemed eager to look at her new laboratory, which was situated half way along the top floor corridor on the left. Each lab had two back to back desks situated near the window with benches alongside and behind, and masses of cupboards; there was a fume cupboard and a walkway running parallel to the main corridor joining all the laboratories. I deposited the cardboard box on one of the desks and asked if she wanted this desk as both were free at the moment. She nodded and, for the first time in a few days, I detected a slight thawing in our relationship. She was obviously highly impressed with the facilities and was keen to get started.

Just then, a smartly dressed young woman entered the lab door behind us and introduced herself as Joyce. She had been expecting us. She was to be Irena's secretary and asked if there was anything she could do to help. She had a notepad ready in her right hand and a pencil in her left — I noticed a gold band and diamond engagement ring on her ring finger. She was obviously a new recruit as I hadn't seen her at the Bradford offices and she was certainly very keen to be seen as being helpful. Irena indicated that she was still settling in for the moment and would get back to her when needed. Joyce retreated to her office just across the corridor from the lab.

What I hadn't realised was that we had achieved minor celebrity status within the Institute. Two escapees from communist Czechoslovakia. The in-house grapevine had been busy elaborating on our escapades and, like it or not, tongues had been wagging! Irena had noticed it too as she said, 'Why they look at me that way?' Every time we passed somebody new in the corridor we appeared to be the centre of attention.

'Word's got round that I'm James Bond and you're Miss Moneypenny!' I said, tongue in cheek.

'I no know these people!' Irena said curtly. It was obvious that she had some catching up to do when it came to popular Western culture.

Hamish breezed into the lab with a wry grin on his face.

'Settling in OK, Irena?' She nodded.

'I'm just going to have a walk round the pilot plant to see how the opening day preparations are going, want to tag along?'

We nodded simultaneously and followed Hamish out of the lab, along the corridor and down the steps to the ground floor where Irena excused herself as she had decided to investigate the ladies' toilet, leaving Hamish and I waiting close by.

'Angela rang this morning confirming that the Cabinet's decided, as we expected, that Peter's not their concern and the Americans are not to be informed of the microfilm translation yet. Oh, and John Stonehouse is the minister put in charge of the operation,' Hamish reported.

The first bit of news was expected but the second, naming John Stonehouse, came as a surprise. I did my best to not react to this but I'm not sure I succeeded, as Hamish added, 'Nigel apparently wants more of your time and is going to speak to me about this shortly. What do you think, James?'

Before I could answer, Irena re-joined us, curtailing further discussion on the subject. We quickly went out of the Institute's back door, across a narrow road between the two buildings and into the pilot plant's main building. It was an Aladdin's cave of wool processing machinery and equipment, with departments for carding, spinning, weaving, knitting and also dyeing and finishing, which was probably the most pertinent to Irena's project. We looked at a range of gleaming stainless steel side panels and dyeing winches, which could be used to scale up the flame resist treatments developed in the lab before commercial trials could be attempted in industry. This was the first time I'd seen it all together under one roof. Even I was impressed, and I was sure that the visitors on Friday would be too, as the staff would be laying on practical demonstrations, with samples of wool products produced in the plant as examples. Hamish seemed satisfied that things were coming along nicely; although he was not backward in coming forward to suggest alternatives when he thought fit!

As interested as I was in all this, I felt I needed to speak to Angela as soon as possible to discuss what Hamish had just told me regarding Stonehouse. Hamish and Irena had started to discuss wool dyeing treatment methods and I decided now was the ideal time to slip away back to my office and ring Angela. I was right;

they hardly noticed my departure as, after making my excuses, I hurried back to the main building.

*****

It was 10.30am on Wednesday and Bishop Brennan had just put down the phone after speaking to the hotel receptionist, who had confirmed that Petrov had been put onto the 9.00am train to Leeds City station from Kings Cross. Thank God! He thought maybe it was going to turn out right in the end. Depending on how many stops the train had to make, Petrov should be reporting to him around noon.

Petrov was not in a good mood. He had a splitting headache from a hangover he hadn't come to terms with yet. The movement of the train made it inevitable that he was going to throw up very shortly; nevertheless, he was sufficiently compos mentis to know he was not enjoying this current assignment. He was used to having more time to organise things and he had looked forward to his bender in London as he thought he had plenty of time to arrange things round it. The Bishop was a difficult man to work for, too unpredictable for his liking, but he had no other option, at this stage, than to go along with it since he was owed a lot of money.

When the train pulled into Leeds at 11.50am Petrov gave a sigh of relief. He was feeling a little better now, although when he stood up his head started pounding again. He got off the train and made his way via an overhead walkway from the platform towards the main information area; he was looking for a telephone box which he spotted close to the Arrivals board. He didn't have any change so he had to queue up at the information desk to get a half crown changed into some pennies, threepenny bits and a shilling, much to the annoyance of the clerk behind the desk. He then phoned the Bishop who tersely gave him his final instructions to board the next train to Forster Square station, Bradford, where he was to wait until the American, Rod Trask, met another American off the train from Leeds. He was then to eliminate Trask once the other American had left to go back to London via Leeds. Petrov didn't have any photos to go on but he was well aware of the language differences between American and English. He then realised he'd just missed the connection to Bradford from Platform 3 and would have to wait another thirty minutes for the next train. He was feeling sufficiently better to refresh himself with a coffee from the snack bar in the station before boarding the train from Platform 3 to Bradford.

*****

Rod and I caught the late morning train from Ilkley to Bradford to meet up with Chuck Edwards, who was coming on the 9.00am train from Kings Cross via Leeds. We anticipated he would arrive around 12.30pm if he managed to make the connection in time. If not, he would be around half an hour later.

I was still coming to terms with the fact that John Stonehouse was now the minister in charge of our project and Angela was horrified at the news too. We'd agreed to keep it to ourselves for the moment so I was more in listening mode with Rod this morning. He was excited at finally getting to tell his side of the story to Chuck Edwards and he didn't require me to be in on their conversation, but I needed to direct them to the old offices in Bradford and sign them in, so to speak, with the caretaker there.

'Once you're settled in one of the spare offices I'll head back to Ilkley. There are plenty of trains back to Leeds and Ilkley in the afternoon so you'll both be OK once you've finished your talk.'

'Sure, James, no problems.'

We pulled into Forster Square station and passed through the barrier into the large forecourt, handing in our tickets as we went. I established that the Leeds train was not in yet so our timing was perfect. It arrived five minutes later.

'Rod! Good to see you, buddy! You picked a goddam, right son-of-bitch place to meet, didn't you?' Chuck Edwards announced himself as he swung through the turnstile barrier into the forecourt to meet us.

Introductions were made and I led them both out of the station into bustling Forster Square, across a busy Canal Road and past the imposing statue of William Edward Forster MP, apparently signposting our path with his outstretched right arm. This directed us across Bolton Road and then to the Institute's offices at the bottom of Church Bank. We entered the Institute through the swing door and I signed them in at the reception desk under the watchful eye of a bemused caretaker. He was used to meeting all nationalities but Rod and Chuck were like chalk and cheese to look at — Rod, tall and well-built with a crew cut; Chuck, small, bald and fat! Abbott and Costello came to mind, and I could imagine Chuck doing a more than passable impression of a bald version of Lou Costello. However, both were archetypical Americans and chattered away loudly, as Americans are prone to do!

I checked with the caretaker that they could have all the time they wanted in the office and headed back to the station for the return journey to Ilkley. I picked up a packet of Rowntree's wine gums from the tobacconist in the station to satisfy my hunger until I reached Ilkley. I wouldn't have minded being a fly on the wall in the office with Rod and Chuck but hopefully Rod would fill me in later with the details. I hoped that Rod wouldn't divulge too many details of the Mengele case but I could not influence this at all at this stage. I just hoped he would manage to clear his name and was able to return to his usual work, even though that would be a loss to us as he had become quite useful.

I caught the 1.15pm train back to Ilkley and sat back in my almost deserted compartment to take notice of my journey. We stopped briefly at Shipley station to pick up half a dozen people and then clattered over the old iron bridge as we headed towards Guiseley and the branch line for Ilkley. As I'd often wondered, it was amazing how this branch line had escaped the Beeching Axe in '63, when small rundown stations were immediately closed rather than being updated. I pulled myself together to concentrate on the problems of the moment, in particular, the John Stonehouse complication and how we were going to free Peter Svoboda.

I decided it would be best to involve Hamish totally and that would have to be my highest priority once I got back to the Institute, if he was free to see me. I revised my order of priorities as I soon realised the wine gums were ineffective at quenching my hunger! I stayed on the train until it reached the end of the line at Ilkley rather than getting off earlier at Ben Rhydding.

*****

Bishop Brennan took a phone call which he wasn't expecting and did not appreciate. It was from a rival bishop, who had taken his place in London, wanting to know why he was in the UK. The tone, of course, was all very diplomatic and polite. 'Was there anything he could do to help his Grace during his stay in the UK?'

Brennan managed to fob him off by telling him he was on a private humanitarian mission to give comfort to an old friend who was dying. He realised if any digging was done this could be easily found to be false, yet it was the best he could come up with in the current situation. This bishop was, in his opinion, a do-gooder and to be kept at arms-length; Brennan knew he had strong liberal sympathies and was supported by the new Pope. In fact, he was sure his explanation would be relayed back to Rome within the hour.

His mind was more on what Petrov was achieving at present. It was now 6.30pm and he hoped and prayed that Petrov had located Trask in Bradford. An hour later, an excited Petrov rang with the news he had been waiting for; the American had been eliminated! Hallelujah! Apparently there'd been a minor hiccup in that the American had arrived before Petrov, who had hung around the station for a few hours until, to his relief, the American had returned and been dispatched. Brennan instructed Petrov to get back to Leeds as soon as possible and report to him in the morning to discuss the changed plans for the Institute's opening day.

Brennan thought that, if things went to plan, he could be out of the country by the weekend. He was pleased with Petrov, perhaps he'd misjudged him a little and he should cut him some slack.

*****

Hamish was tied up all afternoon after I got back. His secretary, Mavis, told me he wanted to speak to me but he would not be free until after 5.00pm, so I busied myself in my new office trying to get organised. I called in at Irena's lab to see if she needed any help, but she was just about to leave. I told her I had to wait to see Hamish before I could go, at which she nodded and I went back to my office on the ground floor. I lost track of time and it was 6.30pm when Mavis ran in and said that Hamish was now free.

'Great to see you, James. Had any thoughts about what I should say to Nigel?'

'I think we've got to free Peter before we follow up the Mengele leads.'

'My thoughts precisely, and that's what I've told Angela.'

'There's a major complication, Hamish!' I said, hesitantly.

'I'm all ears,' Hamish said, shifting his sitting position as if to not miss a word.

I then went on to relate what Rod had told me about the real reason for his being in Czechoslovakia and the involvement of John Stonehouse. I also filled him in on the meeting Rod was having with Chuck Edwards in Bradford.

'Holy shit!' said Hamish, uncharacteristically.

The phone rang and Hamish answered it.

'It's Inspector Button for you, James,' he said, handing me the receiver.

'Mr Brittain?'

'Yes?' I said, with an impending feeling of dread.

'We've got a dead American here in Bradford. Can you come and identify him if I send a car over for you now?'

My worst fears were realised and I gave the receiver back to Hamish who had picked up the gist of the conversation.

CHAPTER 14
WHAT SPECIAL RELATIONSHIP?

Angela picked up a note which had just been delivered to her in-tray telling her that Bishop Brennan had entered the country last Friday. Very interesting, Angela thought, wondering why it had taken so long for this information to filter through. She noted that he'd flown into Leeds-Bradford airport which might have something to do with the delay. It could be purely coincidental, but it did cross her mind that people seemed to have started dying since he arrived! It was definitely worth looking into further and James would be highly interested to know that his 'Bête Noir' of yesteryear had returned and was probably in the Leeds area. She looked at the time — 6.30pm. James wouldn't be at the Institute now and she wasn't sure whether he'd be back from taking Rod to Bradford to meet his CIA contact. James had told her about Rod's talks with his brother and the fact that he might now be off the hook. She was glad he'd taken the initiative; it would at least mean she wouldn't be pestered by the Americans. Angela had heard of Chuck Edwards, he was quite high up in the CIA, but she had never met or spoken to him. She needed, somehow, to let Nigel know that Rod was in the country and alive and kicking in Yorkshire. Nigel had learned about the Institute's opening day, and as it was just the sort of thing which appealed to him, he had invited himself to it and got Angela to organise a place on the special train from Kings Cross on Friday. He thought it would be a good opportunity to meet up with Hamish, regardless of the fact that this was going to be one of Hamish's busiest and most important days ever.

Angela was not pleased as to how things were going regarding Peter; Nigel had washed his hands of the whole affair now that the Cabinet had ruled on the way forward. It didn't mean she had to agree with the decision. Wiesenthal hadn't been on the phone again; she didn't know whether that was a good sign or not but she believed that Hamish needed some official backing in his efforts to find Peter. Then there was the news about John Stonehouse being a paid spy for the Czechs! She made a mental note to contact somebody she knew in MI5; it was more their concern than hers but it did make things tricky, and she knew for certain she wasn't going to mention it to Nigel.

She decided to ring the Institute anyway and leave a message with the security man asking James to contact her in the morning. The security man knew who she was and volunteered the unnerving news that James had just been picked up by a police car which had left the car park with its blue light flashing, going hell-for-leather. He couldn't add anything further, but it didn't sound good to her.

*****

Chuck had had a good meeting with Rod and they had managed to buy a decent hamburger across the road from the old Institute. He wasn't certain about Brittain's connection with Rod but he was sure going to follow it up when he got back to the embassy. He had managed to learn the main facts of Rod's mission to Czechoslovakia and was pretty sure he had been told everything, which would determine his course of action when he got back to London. It was interesting for Chuck to hear the juicy titbit that John Stonehouse was on the make for passing technical information to a Czech handler. This would give his section some clout with the Brits — they were always on the lookout for things like this, and the socialist government under Harold Wilson was regarded in a lot of American circles as suspect, to say the least.

Chuck was old enough to remember Attlee's post-war socialist government's incredible decision to gift Rolls-Royce Nene jet engine technology to the Soviet Union, along with twenty-five engines as a good-will gesture! The main condition of the technology transfer was that it was not to be used for military purposes. Not surprisingly, to the Americans anyway, was that the jet engine ended up in several Soviet fighters including the MIG-15, which caused major problems for the UN forces in North Korea in 1950. It was instrumental in shooting down several B29 bombers and directly resulted in the cancellation of daylight bombing missions over North Korea. Stalin was known to have commented, 'What fool will sell us his secrets?' when it was suggested to him that the UK should be approached to assist their struggling jet-engine programme. The rest is history. What Chuck, and most Americans for that matter, overlooked, was the fact that post-war Britain was in dire economic straits, and was seriously contemplating 'selling off the crown jewels' to make ends meet. Sir Stafford Cripps, ex-ambassador to the Soviet Union during the war and President of the Board of Trade in 1946, fully supported the jet engine deal, although no royalties were ever paid. Cripps became associated with the policy of austerity, and as an upper class socialist, he believed that everybody, regardless of class, should share the burden of rationing. Chuck would have appreciated BBC announcer McDonald Hobley's unfortunate Spoonerism as he introduced him to the nation as *'Sir Stifford Crapps'*!

At the end of their meeting Chuck and Rod had shaken hands in Forster Square station, Chuck saying that he would report back positively to the necessary people in Washington DC, enabling Rod to return to the States in the near future.

*****

It was a new experience for me to be chauffeured in a police car at breakneck speed, with a flashing blue light and intermittent siren blaring at important crossroads and traffic lights. We made it back to Bradford in less than half the time it normally took me. I did wonder to myself if it were possible to buy a siren/blue light kit from any motorist accessory shop. The illegalities of it were obvious and I wondered what the penalty was. My somewhat flippant thoughts were brought about by the fact that the two police constables sent to fetch me could not give me any details at all. In fact, I was just left to my own worrying thoughts as we hurtled into the centre of Bradford along Canal Road and then into Forster Square, pulling up in front of the main entrance of the Midland Hotel, which adjoined the station.

I got out of the car quickly and was ushered through swing doors into the hotel's reception area. Inspector Button was standing in front of the double doors which led to the station, deep in conversation with a uniformed police constable.

My heart was in my mouth. I'd had too much time in the car to anticipate what I was going to be shown, and when Inspector Button saw me, the knot in my stomach really began to twist!

'I'm sorry to see you again under these circumstances, Mr Brittain, but you may be the only person who can identify this American.'

'OK, Inspector, let's get on with it,' I said, taking a deep breath.

I followed him through the double doors into a corridor decorated from floor to ceiling in turquoise and cream tiles. It was almost in its original Victorian condition apart from electric light bulbs in glass holders instead of gas lamps. Our steps echoed slightly on the mahogany stained wooden floor as we walked quickly down the corridor, turning right towards the outside door which led to the station. Another uniformed officer was guarding a second pair of doors under the sign 'Victoria Rooms'. We entered a smoky refreshment room with a bar at the far end. It was empty apart from the barman who was busy cleaning up to the faint sound of music which was presumably coming from behind the bar. He'd just finished wiping down a table in front of an open upright piano. Just for a moment, probably because of the American connection, I could easily have imagined Hoagy Carmichael accompanying Lauren Bacall singing *How Little We Know* from the film *To Have and Have Not* — with Humphrey Bogart seated attentively at the bar, holding a Bourbon on the rocks and smoking a cigarette! As I walked further into the room I was quickly brought back to earth realising that the music was Matt Munroe singing *From Russia with Love*. Just then, a photographer holding his camera hurried out of the gents'. Turning to me, Inspector Button said, 'Please don't touch anything when we get inside.' We went into the toilets and he asked, 'Do you know this man?'

'Yes! I do,' I blurted out, looking at the bald head of a man, who was lying face down at a very unusual angle on the floor of the urinal. 'It's Chuck Edwards from the American Embassy!'

The relief I felt, and no doubt showed, was probably obvious.

But where was Rod? Hopefully he wasn't in one of the cubicles. Inspector Button had only mentioned American, not Americans!

'How do you know this man, Mr Brittain?'

'I brought Rod Trask, another American, to meet him here in Bradford this lunchtime at our Institute's old offices, at the bottom of Church Bank,' I volunteered, heaving a sigh of relief now that I knew Rod was probably OK.

121

'And where is this Rod Trask now?'

'I don't know, I haven't seen him since I left them together in the office at about 1.30pm.'

'We need to speak to him urgently. Have you any idea where he might be?'

'He might well be at the Crescent Hotel, which is where we've been staying since you warned us that we were in great danger, Inspector.'

'It's the same modus operandi as the hospital murder,' said the Inspector, as he led me out of the gents' back into the atmospheric Victoria Rooms. This time the rather more pleasant odour of tobacco smoke, a mixture of cigarette and pipe, replaced the acrid urinal smell. We retraced our original path into the tiled corridor. As we headed back towards the hotel's reception area, I glanced up at a St Bruno tobacco advert on the wall and remembered that this was the brand Tony Pickard smoked.

I was desperate to find out that Rod was OK so I walked over to the desk and asked the receptionist to find the Crescent Hotel's telephone number. Behind me, Inspector Button muttered, 'Good thinking!'

'Hello, is Rod Trask in the hotel at the moment?' I ventured to a voice I vaguely recognised at the other end of the line, but couldn't quite put a face to. 'OK, you think he's in his room. This is very important, do you think you could get him to come down and speak to me please? Yes, I'm James Brittain; yes, I'm staying there too but at the moment I'm in Bradford.'

I heard the phone being put down and after what seemed like ages, a familiar voice said,

'James, where the hell are you? I've been waiting for you to show up to give you the good news!'

'When did you last see Chuck?' I demanded, ignoring his question.

'Well, we shook hands in the station just before I jumped on the train back to Ilkley. Why?'

'You left first?' I persisted; I could feel Inspector Button virtually breathing down my neck now.

'Yeah. His train back to Leeds wasn't for another twenty-five minutes so he was going to grab a beer in the hotel next door.'

Inspector Button motioned for me to pass the receiver over. He introduced himself to Rod and broke the news about Chuck Edwards' murder. He told Rod to stay in the hotel where he was as we were coming over to see him directly.

'You've gotta get in touch with the American Embassy!' Rod said, after he'd filled us in with his version of the events of his meeting with Chuck and what he believed he was going to do after he'd left him. Inspector Button nodded and finished taking notes, looking rather worried.

'The shit's going to hit the fan very quickly now, James! Chuck's, sorry... Chuck was a very important US government official; it's going to go down very badly and could cause a major diplomatic incident here in the UK!'

I noted that Rod hadn't mentioned to the Inspector that Chuck was a CIA man. I also wondered what effect the murder would have on Rod — would he now be regarded by the Americans as suspect?

'Just for the record, Mr Trask, could you tell us where you were on Monday 2nd September?'

Rod looked puzzled and thought for a moment.

'I was at the Institute with Irena, and James joined us later on after he'd been to a funeral.'

I nodded in agreement at Rod's explanation.

'I mention this as Mr Edwards was killed in much the same manner as our prisoner at the hospital in Bradford. Not that you fit the description of the man who posed as a porter there, who is suspected of being the assassin, but did you notice anybody watching you while you were in Bradford with Mr Edwards?' queried the Inspector.

Rod shook his head, mentioning that the station was quite busy and there were plenty of people hanging around; nobody stood out.

'He got Chuck instead of me!' Rod suddenly erupted, as if he'd just had a Eureka moment. Fortunately, he didn't take his clothes off and run naked around the Crescent Hotel's snug bar!

'You mean, if Mr Edwards' train had left first, you would have been the one murdered?' the Inspector said, looking puzzled.

'Yes, the target was an American who was staying in the Bradford area. He got us mixed up, don't you see?'

I'm not sure the Inspector did see but he seemed to go along with it for the moment. The time was approaching 9.30pm and the Inspector was obviously keen to go. He suggested that Rod should stay within easy reach as he might want to ask him further questions in the next day or two, and then left.

*****

Angela had received the news of Chuck Edwards' death after her call to James late on Wednesday evening. It was now Thursday morning and she had just received the summons from Nigel, which she had both anticipated and dreaded.

'Did you know Chuck Edwards had travelled up to Yorkshire to meet with Rod Trask and James?' said Nigel icily. 'What else haven't you told me?' he fumed, not giving Angela time to respond.

She thought quickly of a string of information which she had kept to herself, but knew the best strategy for dealing with Nigel in one of his moods was one of silence.

'You may as well know that when this is all cleared up, I will arrange a transfer for both you and Brittain as I don't want either of you on my team in future!' he seethed. 'My minister has just had a very uncomfortable meeting at the American Embassy, and there could be major political repercussions over this!'

'I've just heard about this too. Apparently Rod Trask had been the target for assassins in Prague and Munich and was lying low in Yorkshire after he escaped. He'd arranged for Chuck Edwards to visit him in Bradford and he believes he was the real target, not Chuck — it was a case of mistaken identity!' Angela said, finally managing to get a word in edgeways.

Nigel digested this information and appeared to calm down a bit but was clearly still agitated.

'I suppose Brittain told you this?'

'Yes, he'd been asked by Trask for a place to meet Edwards; the Wool Institute's old offices in Bradford seemed a good place as they are virtually empty now.'

'Brittain shouldn't get involved in American problems; we have enough on our plate at the moment!' Nigel moaned on again.

Angela noticed that he referred to 'James' when things were going his way but it was 'Brittain' when they weren't! If she and James were axed, no doubt in the interests of economy, she would probably be the one out of a job. James at least had a position at the Institute to fall back on.

'Can James get Trask to be at the Institute's bash tomorrow?' asked Nigel.

Angela agreed to find out and to organise things with James.

*****

Bishop Brennan had just had a good meeting with Petrov; he'd decided to overlook his recent shortcomings in London since the final outcome was satisfactory. In fact, he gave him one hundred pounds cash as a down payment on a job partially well done, to focus his attention on the matter in hand tomorrow. Brennan had been able to find out that the special train was due to arrive in Ilkley just after noon. Since time was short he had arranged to drive Petrov over to the station. His driver had even done a dummy run to eliminate any unforeseen problems, such as roadworks, etc. Brennan was going to accompany them, he would be able to give a final briefing to Petrov on the way, and, in fact, he was quite looking forward to it. Coaches were going to be on hand to ferry the VIPs the short distance from the station to the Institute. He'd decided that the best way for Petrov to infiltrate the party was for him to wait at the station, and tag along and board one of the coaches. He did need a smart suit so that he could blend in, so he had just sent him into Leeds to Marks and Spencer to buy one, out of the money he'd given him, of course! He was banking on a certain amount of confusion and it was unlikely that they would be checked against a list before they were allowed to enter the Institute, especially if he arrived with the main group from the train. There would be a list of people present, so Petrov should try to locate one of these and identify his targets from it, namely James Brittain and Irena Svoboda.

*****

Friday morning arrived and Angela hadn't been looking forward to the train journey from Kings Cross to Ilkley with Nigel as he could be heavy going, but she had been pleasantly surprised — not with his sparkling wit, but with the other distractions on the train.

They were in a first class compartment; in fact, everything on the train was first class. They were served with a late breakfast and coffee was available for the whole of the journey, as well as stronger drinks if required. The Institute's London office had laid on a fashion parade with all the latest wool fashions modelled by svelte girls who gave everybody a twirl, and coped incredibly well with the motion of the train. Even Nigel was momentarily distracted when the models showed off the finer points of botany wool sweaters at disarmingly close quarters! Angela made a mental note to check out the prices of some of the outfits, although she did wonder if they were in the shops yet.

After the fashion parade, the bigwigs from Australia and New Zealand who were also on the train moved around chatting to the VIPs. They were all big men, in every sense of the word, with effortless charm and the ability to talk to everybody and make each one feel really important. Nigel lapped this up and commented after they had passed that they were 'pleasant chaps, for Australians!' On boarding the train each passenger had been given a lapel badge showing their name and organisation; Angela's and Nigel's stated that they were from the Ministry of Information.

They had just left Leeds and were now on the short journey towards Ilkley. Nigel had confided in Angela that a mission was to be sent to South America in an attempt to locate Mengele, and that James was needed for this mission. This was going to be quietly carried out under the auspices of negotiations between the Falkland Islands and Argentina, which were regarded as good cover. Angela was also needed to liaise with the British Embassies in Argentina and Uruguay and to keep Nigel informed of developments. She had some misgivings about this news but decided to mull things over with James and Hamish as soon as possible.

The train slowed and pulled into the station. Angela looked out of the window and noticed a well-dressed, middle-aged man standing on the platform. There was something about him that seemed out of place, apart from his short haircut, but she couldn't put her finger on it. She soon forgot about this as they alighted from the train and were led from the platform to a small car park where several coaches were waiting. By this time there was almost a holiday atmosphere, reminiscent of a day trip to Brighton or Blackpool, and an air of expectancy. Angela looked out of the coach window across the road to the Kings Hall and Winter Garden building, where a large banner draped across it announced, 'Ilkley Welcomes the New Institute's Guests'. It was a 'right good Yorkshire welcome', as James would have said.

The coaches set off, made their way through the centre of Ilkley and turned onto a side road which Angela remembered from her visit to Betty's Café with James. No sooner had they set off, it seemed, than they pulled up outside the Institute's gate, from where they were ushered down a flagged walkway towards the Institute's main entrance. In the wide grass verges alongside the walkway were white poles, from which flags of many nations fluttered in the light breeze of a very pleasant, early September day. They were ushered into a large marquee which had been erected alongside the main building. Chairs had been arranged on three sides of a large, rectangular fish pond, facing a table at the far end. It was clear to Angela that there was going to be a formal welcome to the opening ceremony and that speeches would be made from the top table. She followed Nigel into the marquee as he hobbled gingerly along the walkway, where they were shown to seats by the Institute's staff. She saw that Hamish was among the people now taking their seats at the top table so she pointed him out to Nigel. She was looking around casually at the incoming guests, some of whom she'd noticed on the train, when almost directly opposite her across the pond, she spotted the man she'd seen on the platform at Ilkley, who couldn't possibly have been on the train. He was the only person present not wearing a badge, and despite his obviously brand new blue suit, he was sporting heavy duty brown boots! She was close enough to see his right hand which was the size any navvy would be proud of; he was obviously not an office worker. Despite the weather being pleasantly warm, a shiver ran up her spine and she wondered who he was. There was probably a completely rational explanation but his presence worried her.

'Good afternoon, ladies and gentlemen. Welcome to the official opening ceremony of the Wool Institute,' said a large man standing behind a microphone at the top table. Angela immediately switched her attention back to the matter in hand.

CHAPTER 15
RETURN OF THE *HOXTON CREEPER*

I was still coming to terms with the murder of Chuck Edwards. Rod had remained at the Crescent Hotel on Thursday, kicking his heels and wondering what effect it was going to have on him, whereas I had been roped in as one of the guides to escort guests round the Institute's laboratories and pilot plant facilities, and had spent Thursday rehearsing to make sure everything was in place for the tour and that everything could be accomplished within the tight schedule.

We heard that the four hundred or so visitors had now arrived and were in the marquee receiving the official welcome. This was planned to last for approximately thirty minutes before the tour of the building took place, so we guides made our way into the large glass-sided reception area and waited for the guests to emerge. At Nigel's request, Rod was at the Institute for the party and Hamish had suggested that he be part of my tour group so we were both together. Since speaking to Angela a couple of days ago, both Rod and I had digested the news that Bishop Brennan was in the area again and decided that the series of recent events all bore his hallmark. I planned on having a ride over to Leeds as soon as possible to see if I could flush him out. I had a good idea where he might be staying and I could make discreet inquiries at the cathedral. Irena was not involved with the guests but all the Institute's staff were invited, after the tours were finished, for drinks and refreshments with the guests. At present we had to make sure the proceedings went as smoothly as possible. There were approximately twenty guides and we had each been instructed to collect a batch of twenty guests and lead them on different predetermined routes to avoid congestion.

The guests began to emerge from the marquee and I was one of the first guides to collect and greet my group of visitors, who were all keen to see what the Institute had to offer. I guessed that after sitting on a train for two and a half hours, then being ferried by coach to sit down again in a marquee, most people were glad to stretch their legs for a change! I led my group downstairs from the main reception area into the testing section, which was fully air-conditioned to enable each wool sample to be tested under identical conditions. I had to almost to drag the guests away from the fabric tensile strength testing machines, which were vertical, miniature versions of the rack favoured by the Spanish Inquisition. The fabric abrasion machines were not as popular; maybe they rubbed some people up the wrong way! We then made our way through the ground floor laboratories where dyeing demonstrations were taking place in oscillating Dyemaster machines, followed by an inspection of the washing machine area where shrinkage tests on wool fabrics were carried out in a cube-shaped washing machine, unsurprisingly called a Cubex! Rod muttered to me under his breath, 'Have they tried this machine in place of a concrete mixer to increase cocaine yields?' I shook my head but agreed that the mechanical action would be very reproducible!

It was time for us to leave the main building and head for the pilot plant. I caught a glimpse of Angela and Nigel in another group as we entered the spinning hall; Nigel looked completely bored. He should have realised that at this point in the visit Hamish was too busy to see anybody. I conducted the guests through the pilot plant where they showed intense interest in the large scale equipment capable of producing virtually all types of wool fabrics, as well as knitwear and carpets, from the raw wool stage to the finished article. We then made our way back to the marquee where guests could mingle and talk to the Institute's specialists over refreshments. It was a very informal affair — I'd become accustomed to the less stuffy Australasian way of doing things. At the Institute, we had one communal dining room for directors and junior lab staff alike; everybody mixed in together, which went down well.

At last I saw Angela and Nigel returning to the marquee in one of the final groups. They made their way over to us, picking up a couple of glasses of sparkling wine on the way.

I introduced Nigel to Rod and they shook hands formally without saying a word to each other.

'Excuse me for a moment,' said Nigel, turning and motioning to the usher who had shown them to the refreshment table.

As he turned, a voice from the door called, 'Mr Trask! Calling Mr Rod Trask.' Rod looked surprised and then saw two men behind the announcer. Suspecting that they were from the American Embassy, he moved towards them.

*****

Petrov had been dropped off at Ilkley railway station by Bishop Brennan, who had again primed him as to what he wanted him to do. He already had misgivings over this job and now he knew he was going to be completely out of his comfort zone. He knew, but Brennan didn't, that he suffered from word-blindness, he had difficulty in recognising words, and he knew that it was not going to be easy for him to identify Brittain and Svoboda from a list of many names. It turned out that there was no list of names because everybody, apart from himself, was wearing a name badge. Nobody had seemed to notice that he wasn't wearing one and he had successfully boarded a coach and reached the Institute, where he had joined a group of visitors on a tour to look at machinery he wasn't used to and had no interest in whatsoever! He felt slightly better after he had downed a couple of glasses of sparkling wine and fortunately nobody said anything to him. As he wondered how he was ever going to achieve his goal, he heard a voice announcing, 'Mr Trask! Calling Mr Rod Trask.' He looked up and saw a man respond by putting up his hand. It was as if Petrov had been struck by a bolt of lightning! He had eliminated Trask, hadn't he? The awful truth dawned on him that he had killed the wrong man in Bradford. The thing that worried him most was that Bishop Brennan mustn't find out before he had completed his mission. This occurrence was an incredible stroke of luck! He quickly put down his glass and followed the man who had left the marquee and was walking stiffly back through the reception area and into the gents'. It was a case of déjà vu; he knew exactly what to do and followed as swiftly as he dared. Nigel had just relieved himself in the stalls and looked up to see a thickset man entering behind him. To his amazement, he found himself in a headlock and then his lights went out, terminally!

Petrov felt a different sense of relief as he completed his task.

It had been easy really, what had he been worrying about? Bishop Brennan need never know the details. He still had Brittain and the woman to deal with. He propped Nigel up in one of the two cubicles, slid the bolt on the door to lock it from the inside and shimmied over the cubical partition by standing on the toilet and exiting before anybody else could enter.

*****

'Nigel's been a long time,' said Angela.

'He went to the toilet; it doesn't really matter as Rod's tied up with the men from the American Embassy at the moment,' I said.

'Yes, but maybe we should see if he's been waylaid, I would like to be in on any talks he has with Hamish, for instance,' Angela said irritably.

We left the marquee and made our way through reception into the main building. There was no sign of Nigel. I looked in on Hamish's office and the room was empty, the adjoining meeting room contained only Rod and the two men from the American Embassy, so he wasn't there. I checked at the desk and the receptionist remembered him coming through reception but he hadn't returned.

I looked in the gents' — one cubicle had the engaged slot on but nobody else was present.

'Are you in there, Nigel? Are you alright?' I said, somewhat embarrassed. No answer.

I bent down to look under the gap between the floor and the door and saw a leg in an unusual position. I knocked on the door. 'Nigel?' No answer.

I stood on the adjacent washbasin and looked over the cubicle wall. To my horror, I saw Nigel slumped against the wall with his head at an unusual angle. I had an immediate flashback to the Midland Hotel in Bradford and the body of Chuck Edwards!

I dashed outside and into reception.

'Get an ambulance,' I said to the startled receptionist.

'The assassin's here, Angela. Where's Irena?' I said to Angela, who was standing by the desk.

'An odd-looking man was asking about Dr Svoboda a few minutes ago; I noticed he didn't have an identification badge on,' she said.

'What did you tell him?'

'I told him she might be still in her lab on the top floor. Did I do wrong?'

'Shit!' I said, dashing out of the reception area and climbing the stairs two at a time, closely followed by Angela.

'I know who it is, I saw him waiting at the railway station and in the marquee, he has brown boots on!' Angela said, just before she ran out of breath.

I burst through the doors into the top corridor just in time to hear a scream. A man staggered into the corridor, howling in pain and holding his head. He made for the doors at the opposite end of the corridor away from me. As he went through the doors I caught a glimpse of his brown boots. Instead of following him I dashed into Irena's lab to see her cowering in the corner by her desk clutching a reagent bottle in her right hand. The look of relief on her face as I entered the lab, closely followed by Angela, told us everything. She had had a very close shave with death.

'I throw acetone in his face,' she yelled as we approached her.

I looked out of the lab window just in time to see the would-be assailant dash down the side of the pilot plant towards the lower gate of the Institute. I was too far away to try to catch him. We ushered Irena down the stairs to Hamish's office on the ground floor and she told us what had happened. It appears that lust might have got the better of Petrov as he encountered Irena and attempted to rape her, but she had the presence of mind to grab hold of the reagent bottle and dowse him generously in acetone. The intense stinging reaction in his eyes made Petrov abandon his mission to eliminate Irena. Self-preservation kicked in and he'd fled. Irena was shocked when we told her what had happened to Nigel, appreciating now how lucky she was.

Hamish appeared and took in the situation. Maintenance men had forced open the cubicle door in the gents' toilet and had taken Nigel's body into the photocopying room opposite. It was obvious to all who saw him his neck was broken and he was dead. The ambulance arrived and confirmed the worst. The toilets were locked and the police informed. It was Angela who cottoned on to the fact that Nigel had put his hand up just as Rod Trask was being called; she had been in a good position to see it all and her instinct had been right about the man she had felt was out of place. Word reached Rod, who was being questioned by the two American

Embassy men. It was now dawning on everybody that he had been the intended victim again; he was visibly shaken.

The incident put a dampener on an otherwise very successful opening day. The majority of the guests were unaware of what had happened and the loss of toilet facilities was explained as a water leak; a minor inconvenience really! The guests departed the way they had arrived, by coach to board the 'six-five special' back to London, well tanked up. The Institute's staff, not involved in the incident, breathed a sigh of relief at the successful outcome of the opening ceremony and took full advantage of the residual liquor stocks; quite a few individuals happily slept under tables in the marquee until the following morning.

Despite it being the weekend, the incident sparked off a series of diplomatic meetings between the Foreign Office and the American Embassy. Angela was recalled to MI6 and I received a telephone call from her later on Sunday afternoon with the news that she had been given Nigel's job temporarily, until they could find a suitable replacement. The situation needed to be handled by someone with first-hand experience of similar events. In my opinion, Angela was the ideal person. She informed me that she was going to fully reopen the Leeds Mill office and wondered if I could invite Hamish to be there at 10.00am on Monday.

*****

Mikhail Petrov was angry with himself for his lapse in concentration. That bitch Svoboda had surprised him with a liquid which made his eyes sting with excruciating pain; he was still finding it difficult to open his left eye which had been worst affected. The euphoria of finally dealing with Trask had excited him to the extent of being tempted to having his way with the woman who, surprisingly, he found extremely attractive. He regarded it as one of the perks of the job. During the war he had been taught that it was normal to take advantage of female refugees who found themselves in the wrong place at the wrong time. They often expected it anyway and he normally let them go. Now he was going to be in trouble with Brennan for not finishing the job. He had failed to locate Brittain and he wondered what he should do next.

His getaway had been pre-arranged by stashing his motorbike against the steel fence just outside the Institute's bottom gate, which was fairly secluded. He walked the bike down to the main road but dared not get on it immediately because he could not see properly. Instead, he pushed the bike along the main road for about a quarter of a mile until he saw an iron bridge over the river leading onto a back road, which appeared to be little used. He lay the bike down on the grass verge and walked to the riverside to bathe his face and eyes in water, which helped a little. The stinging was eased and he now had improved vision in his right eye, so he decided to chance it, started up the bike and followed a sign to Asquith, which turned out to be a village on the way to Leeds via Otley. On the way back he thought long and hard about how he was going to get out of this mess. He'd seen where Brennan kept his money in the office of the church house where they always met. There appeared to be a good supply of cash, enough for him to live in comfort for a few months until the dust settled. He would keep watch on the house and break in when he knew Brennan had gone out. He thought Sunday may be the best time as Brennan should be busy then. He was what you might call a *very* lapsed Catholic in that he'd become critical of religion, as he'd never had any material gains at all from prayer, despite having been brought up to believe that it would solve all his problems.

*****

Hamish readily accepted Angela's invitation to attend the meeting at the Mill in Leeds. He was pleased that she had achieved some significant recognition within MI6, albeit on a temporary basis. I picked Hamish up in my Hillman Imp at the Institute on Monday morning and drove us both to the Mill as I was well-acquainted with the journey.

'Back agin, lad,' said the usual gateman as we drove into the yard.

It was like a trip down memory lane for me; nothing seemed to have changed. Was it really five years since I'd last been here? The table and chairs were the same and Mavis was on hand with her quiet efficiency. I was surprised and pleased to see Rod seated in one of the chairs alongside Angela.

'OK, gentlemen; let's begin,' Angela said, with rather more authority than usual, as befitted her new position.

'I'm very sorry about what happened to Nigel. We didn't always see eye to eye but he was one of the old school and was dedicated to his job. Since I've been given the responsibility of picking up the pieces, I thought I'd let you know my current thinking and any possible action I'm considering.'

We all understood what she was saying and waited expectantly for her to continue. Mavis suggested we help ourselves to the coffee, which she had freshly prepared, before we started. After a short break, Angela continued: 'I, for one, was disappointed with the specific information we got from Peter's father about the whereabouts of Josef Mengele; I see no advantage in keeping this to ourselves and propose to share it with Simon Wiesenthal.'

'I thought the Cabinet had ruled against this?' I commented quickly.

'Nevertheless, it should ensure that Peter Svoboda is released fairly quickly and we owe him something for bringing it to our attention in the first place. The information was, after all, originally intended for Wiesenthal.'

'The Institute would support this wholeheartedly,' added Hamish.

'What about the Americans?' Rod added.

'I'd assumed that a lot of it is already known to them anyway,' Angela commented, looking at Rod quizzically.

'Yeah. OK, it helped my case, you're right, but it wouldn't do any harm to be seen to be cooperative,' Rod said, rather lamely.

'OK, will do. Nigel wanted James and me to go with him to South America to try to locate Mengele. I'm not in favour of this since we are involving Wiesenthal, but I'm conscious that Hamish is about to set off next week to Uruguay and Brazil, I think, so it may be possible for you to put out some feelers while you're there?' Angela said, looking at a nodding Hamish.

I was not aware that this had been in Nigel's mind but I noticed that Angela had omitted to mention anything about his involvement in the Falkland Islands question and the coming mission to try to mediate between them and Argentina. Presumably she was not going to be involved in this; I would have to question her later on this point.

'This leaves the question of who is trying to kill Rod and anybody else who seems to be associated with him. Brennan is almost certainly involved and the more I think about the assassin we witnessed at the Institute last Friday, the more I am reminded of the *Hoxton Creeper* in one of Sherlock Holmes' tales. He has hands the size of dinner plates and is extremely dangerous; he would have no problem in holding his own with Mick McManus in the wrestling ring!'

Angela was right and I had a sneaking suspicion that I had seen him before, especially after the way he moved when I saw him running from the Institute.

'Oh, by the way, the Americans have loaned Rod to us to try and sort this out since each of us has lost an important official — Chuck Edwards and Nigel. I understand the Americans are to carry out an inquiry within the CIA to see if there is any connection here.'

Rod nodded. 'That's right; I'll be free to return to the US of A as soon as it's completed.'

Angela continued. 'I'll contact Wiesenthal with the information he's expecting about Mengele as soon as possible and James will, carefully, try to locate Bishop Brennan and hence the 'Creeper' as a matter of urgency. Thank you for your time, gentlemen, I'll be staying in the area for the next week or two so if you need me, contact Mavis here at the Mill.'

*****

Bishop Brennan waited in vain on Friday for a call from Petrov. He was desperate to find out whether he had been successful. He had approved of Petrov's smart suit but was appalled that he had not bothered to buy a new pair of shoes; did he have to tell him everything? Apparently so!

Sunday arrived and there was still no word. Brennan had to visit the cathedral in Leeds for some minor function at which Bishop Flannery had requested his attendance; he agreed, mainly to keep the good Bishop at arm's length. He returned to the church house around 1.00pm to find the outside door ajar. On entering the study he was confronted by the body of the housekeeper, slumped over the armchair with his neck broken. The drawer, where he kept a considerable amount of cash, was open and empty. He knew exactly what had happened — Petrov had failed in his mission and bolted! He couldn't allow the body to be found in the house, he needed to get it removed as soon as possible to a location where it would not be found for a long time!

CHAPTER 16

JAMES MAKES A LUCKY STRIKE

Peter Svoboda had drifted in and out of consciousness, aware only that he had a dull, throbbing, incessant headache, which drove any thought he might have had out of his brain. He opened his eyes and realised that the throbbing had stopped; he still had the headache but it was bearable, and the room, when it came into focus, wasn't familiar. Where was he? How long had he been in this state? Slowly it dawned on him that he'd been in an accident; no, it wasn't an accident, he'd heard Rod swear and stumble into him which made him fall onto the railway line. Yes, he'd banged his head, he remembered being told this in the hospital. James had visited him and told him Irena was in England and had got the information from the left luggage locker. He remembered feeling very relieved about this, but was Rod alright? The anxiety returned and he tried to turn but found that his left hand was heavily bandaged and a drip, attached to his arm, was making movement difficult. He felt very weak but his brain was clear and it was time to get some answers. He tried to shout for a nurse but his mouth was very dry and his throat sore; the only sound he was capable of was a deep rattle, which was incomprehensible, even to him. After about thirty minutes he heard the door at his side swish open and a young woman, not in uniform, came into view. She saw at once that he was awake and made soft reassuring noises to him, in German, before leaving the room again.

A few minutes later she came back, closely followed by a man in a white coat, with a stethoscope round his neck. Probably the toilet cleaner! Peter thought, smiling inwardly to himself at the stupid thought which had suddenly come into his head; it was just the sort of humour James Brittain came out with, but it seemed to help in situations like this.

The man, surely a doctor, politely asked him how he felt and continued talking to him whilst he shone a light into his eyes and felt his pulse. Peter got the distinct impression that his cognitive abilities were being assessed and that the doctor was satisfied. Peter asked a whole range of questions including when he was likely to be released from hospital. He was told he was now in a private clinic in the north of Austria and the medical staff had been instructed to send for Simon Wiesenthal as soon as the Herr Doctor Svoboda had regained consciousness. Herr Wiesenthal would answer all questions and the doctor told him that, medically, the worst was now over so he should try to relax and get as much sleep as possible, as this would aid his recovery.

Peter didn't want to relax. He was not a very patient man and he had plenty to say on the matter, but the doctor and the young woman ignored him and politely left the room, presumably to ring Simon Wiesenthal, leaving him to his own troubled thoughts.

*****

How things can change in such a short time. Angela, instead of looking forward to demotion at best, was now virtually in charge of the whole shebang! Temporarily, at least, but she was determined to make the most of it. Having fought to keep the Leeds office open after the section change from MI5 to MI6, her present intention to postpone the closure for a while longer may have raised the odd eyebrow but was not seriously questioned. It appeared that Nigel had kept his cards very close to his chest and it was clear that he had put his own spin on what the minister wanted. This was why she had decided to pass on the information to Wiesenthal, in order to secure Peter's release as soon as possible.

She allowed herself the luxury of analysing why she had been given Nigel's job. Realistically, there was nobody else who had her depth of knowledge and time was of the essence. It was the ingrained mentality of most of the powers that be — men, of course — who condescendingly agreed to give her the responsibility. Maybe she was just being too sensitive but in situations where there was no alternative, common sense prevailed. Why weren't decisions made on the basis of the best man or woman for the job? Women had shown during two world wars that they could get the job done just as well as the men; and at a lower wage too. That reminded her, nothing had been mentioned about salary, she must look into that. Maybe she ought to contact Barbara Castle if nothing was forthcoming. Maybe! It rankled that in both the post war periods it had been assumed that the status quo would be reinstated and women would be happy to go back to menial chores as soon as the men returned.

Now to matters in hand. She had had a conversation with Wiesenthal and found him difficult to read. He was happy enough to receive the information, but his sense of urgency seemed to have gone, and even though she had asked him three times when Peter would be released, he had evaded giving a direct answer. The best she could get out of him was maybe a few days after he had received the information. Rod was right, he was not easy to deal with but she had agreed to post Xeroxed copies of everything to his office so he should have it all shortly. She said she'd ring him in a few days' time to make sure he'd got it and she would then insist on a firm date for Peter's release.

She felt more comfortable in the old Mill, probably because it was free from interference from above, although that was only a telephone call away. She had some private matters to attend to first; she was going to move back into her Leeds flat, which had been rented out as student accommodation over the last two to three years. It hadn't been a success as the students had been particularly severe on the furniture. Trashing was possibly too strong a word but Angela had decided not to continue letting it, and was seriously considering putting it on the market. However, with the latest turn of events, she had decided to move in again, at least for the duration of this project. If truth be told, this, as well as helping the staff to keep their jobs, was a factor in opting to keep the Mill open. She'd some fond memories of the place; she and James had had good times together there.

She had not yet contacted anybody in MI5 to sound out if they considered John Stonehouse to be a serious threat to national security. Her contact there was Robert, they had worked briefly together around five years ago and she had always found him to be dead straight with her, and she knew he would appreciate the feedback from an American source. Now that Nigel was no longer around, going behind his back wasn't an issue, and she made a mental note to speak to Robert as soon as Peter was released. She had been shielded from meeting John Stonehouse so far but it would be prudent to be armed with what MI5 could tell her, in order to be better prepared than she was at present. She knew MI5 was run by right–wing operators who viewed the Wilson government with great suspicion. There had been rumours circulating a few months ago about a foiled plot to oust Wilson and replace him with Lord Mountbatten; nothing materialised but she knew they had files on virtually everybody, including James Brittain, who had had left-wing leanings at university. Her train of thought was broken, firstly by Mavis bringing her a cup of coffee and secondly by a telephone call from Inspector Button, informing her that another body had been found with its neck broken in exactly the same way as Nigel's had been! He was almost sure that the killer wasn't anybody connected to the Wool Institute but it was too much of a coincidence. It looked as if the *Hoxton Creeper* had struck again. Button had rung Angela because he would like James to have a look at the body but he had been unable to contact him. Angela agreed to pass on the Inspector's message to James as soon as possible. She knew he probably hadn't got back to the Institute yet, so she took down the details of where the body was found, in Undercliffe Cemetery, Bradford.

The other thing she had to do, sooner rather than later, was to contact the American Embassy. As Rod had said, it would do no harm to keep them in the loop. She was a little surprised that Rod was willing to help out now he was in the clear, but he did seem to be central to things and could be very useful. Angela thought it would be valuable to inform the embassy that she was Nigel's replacement; they needn't know it was only on a temporary basis.

*****

I drove Hamish back to the Institute, and since it was lunchtime, decided to head for the Crescent to pick up some laundry and get a bite to eat. Rod had been offered a lift but he said he had somewhere else to go in Leeds first. He'd seemed strangely quiet in the meeting as if preoccupied by other things on his mind, in stark contrast to the other night when he was desperate to talk to anybody who'd listen! Maybe it was a delayed reaction to Chuck's death, or something to do with the American officials, or both, but

I would ask him later when the opportunity arose.

Hamish and I discussed the outcome of the meeting. Hamish had considered taking me along on his South American trip but after what Angela had said, he thought she was right and I should concentrate on trying to locate Bishop Brennan; after all, I was uniquely qualified to wring a confession out of him, if anybody was! In some ways I was disappointed at missing out on a trip to South America. I had got a taste for foreign travel, although my track record to date was questionable — less than twenty-four hours after I entered Czechoslovakia it was invaded! Perhaps it was a coincidence but maybe it would be prudent for me to keep out of Argentina; who knows, they might be tempted to invade the Falkland Islands if I showed up?

Hamish was fighting off the press at the Institute. They had got wind of Nigel's murder and were camped at the two main entrances hoping to catch people off-guard. The official line we'd been instructed to say was, 'No Comment.' However, somebody had talked, and Bradford's Telegraph and Argus had run an exclusive story stating that an important government official had been brutally murdered while guests were being lavishly entertained! This was hardly the news coverage the Institute needed; the reporter had obviously got the bit between his teeth by trying to make a link between the two Bradford murders and the Institute. Somebody in the know had probably upset him, as he had laid into us by claiming we were 'trying to pull the wool over his eyes by spinning a good yarn,' and 'somebody had been stitched-up'. He even used the phrase that the police were 'trying to pull all the strands together but ought to get weaving!' Even I thought he had overdone the puns!

Back at the Crescent I was greeted by the receptionist, who handed me a piece of paper and told me that a lady had left a 'phone message for me to ring her on this number.' I recognised the number immediately. What had Angela forgotten to ask me, I wondered?

At the second ring, Angela answered.

'James, Inspector Button wants you at Undercliffe Cemetery ASAP; there's been another murder, looks like it's the same method used on Nigel and Chuck,' she said tersely.

I was fairly sure I hadn't been followed after dropping Hamish off at the Institute, but decided to ring him to make him aware of the latest development, rather than go back to the Institute and run the risk of some reporter following me to the cemetery.

'Strewth, James! This maniac's got to be stopped but for God's sake be careful.'

He was not amused and for once lapsed into stereotypical Aussie speak.

He was right, of course, things were getting out of hand and the police seemed powerless to prevent this series of apparently random murders. After a hasty cheese and pickle sandwich, I decided to take the scenic road out of Ilkley, past the Cow and Calf rocks towards Bradford. The narrow winding road needed most of my concentration, despite which I was mentally planning my next trip to Leeds in order to make discreet inquiries about the whereabouts of Bishop Brennan. I decided I would visit the cathedral in the next day or two depending on what I found at Undercliffe Cemetery.

The final leg of my journey was like a trip down memory lane, virtually every stone in the cemetery wall was etched into my mind after my frantic escape from Brennan's heavies five years ago. I drove through the entrance into the small top car park and was immediately approached by a uniformed police constable, who had just surreptitiously flicked a spent Woodbine stub into the untidy shrubbery which partially masked the inside of the cemetery wall.

'Mr Brittain? Would you please follow me?' I nodded as I got out of my car.

As we walked down the main path into the cemetery, I could see a group of people about a hundred yards away to our right standing in front of a canvas screen, which presumably hid the unfortunate victim.

'Thanks for coming so swiftly, Mr Brittain,' said Inspector Button. If pressure was on the police, Inspector Button seemed not to show it.

'It's almost certainly the same killer, as a superficial examination of the body would indicate it's a carbon copy of the last three murders but we'll have to wait for the post mortem to be sure. I'd just like you to see if you know the man and confirm it's not anybody from the Institute.'

An officer held the canvas flap back so I could enter the screened area. I looked at the body of a man, now lying on a stretcher. Thankfully it was not anybody I recognised from the Institute, but I knew his face. It was Father O'Reilly's old handyman who'd moved on and gone to work for the Bishop of Leeds. It must be eight or nine years ago now since I'd last seen him. His name escaped me but it would be easy to find out.

Inspector Button was delighted. This was a very important connection to Leeds where Bishop Brennan was thought to be holed up. I was interested to know how the body was found; apparently a man out walking his dog had come across it dumped into a newly dug grave. The body was wrapped up in an almost threadbare carpet, which he wouldn't have noticed but for his dog who wouldn't leave it alone, and he soon realised it was very suspicious. Curiously, no new graves had been prepared recently by the cemetery staff; it was a mystery to them. The grave, however, was professionally dug and would have passed the cemetery criteria for burials. I had to admit a cemetery was an ideal place to put a body if you didn't want it to be found. This thought had also crossed the Inspector's mind and we agreed that we'd been fortunate to come across it at all. I wondered out loud why the grave hadn't been filled in. It pointed to the killer having been disturbed and leaving before he could finish his grim job. If he had done, nobody would have found the body at all and it would have definitely been a dead-end! The Inspector decided to carry out house-to-house enquiries to see if anybody had noticed unusual activity in the graveyard. I agreed to visit some of the parishioners I knew who might be able to provide the dead man's name. Inspector Button dashed off to the office in the gatehouse to ring for more uniformed officers to carry out immediate house-to-house enquiries and we agreed to confer again in about an hour's time. The Inspector said he expected to be on site for at least another two hours. I walked off to return to my car with the strange feeling you sometimes get when you know you've missed something. No, it wasn't the man's name, it was something else, and it was important!

*****

Bishop Brennan had planned to keep his visit to the UK low key; he was well-known and had good relations with a wide cross section of people in the Leeds area. The minor function he had attended at Leeds Cathedral had served to raise his profile again and brought him, by chance, into contact with a couple of brothers he'd employed in the past to do jobs he couldn't trust to men of the cloth. To put it bluntly, they were crooks, willing to bend the rules if the money was right. They were both devoted Catholics and he willingly absolved them from their sins for which they were truly penitent! They had had a good chat and expressed their willingness to help his grace in any way possible if he needed it in the future. He hadn't realised at the time that he would have need of them so soon, but when he got back to the church house and found the body of his housekeeper he immediately thought of them and rang them. They were scrap metal merchants with a scrap yard on the outskirts of Leeds. He didn't know where exactly, but they had access to all manner of vehicles and they would have to remove the body that night, for a tidy sum.

He explained the job he had for them and offered them two hundred and fifty pounds. After some discussion, he raised it by a hundred and they said they would be over in about an hour's time! They arrived in a brick-red Ford Transit van, which they backed up to the front door, unloaded a roll of carpet and carried it inside. There were two carpets rolled up together or, to be more precise, one carpet and a large rug. They left the rug, rolled up the unfortunate housekeeper in the carpet and loaded it back into the van. As they laid out the rug to the Bishop's satisfaction, he made sure that they knew the body was not to be found. They assured him they had the ideal spot for it. Brennan didn't want to know any details and he duly paid over the money out of church funds. Reg and Jim Oldroyd were originally from the Bradford area and knew Undercliffe Cemetery, where they used to play as kids, like the back of their hands. There was just enough daylight left for them to dig a grave and lower the body, still wrapped in the carpet. Unfortunately, before they had time to fill in the grave they became aware of a courting couple strolling hand in hand along a nearby path. Reg and Jim, not being in the Brain of Britain league, panicked and made a rapid getaway, but not before they'd rubbed dirt over the van's front and back number plates. They didn't even look sideways as they drove away from the cemetery as quickly as possible. On the way back to Leeds they decided that the scrapping of the Transit van was definitely going to be brought forward as from tomorrow! It wasn't taxed or insured, meaning that it could not be traced back to them — they had bought it recently for scrap knowing it was probably stolen anyway.

*****

I got out of the car on Institute Road, less than three minutes' drive away from the cemetery. This area of stone terraced houses was still known locally as Klondike, because the houses there were built in the 1890s when the gold rush was big news.

I walked along to number fourteen which I knew to be the home of Mrs Overend. She had been the late Father O'Reilly's housekeeper, and although I didn't know if she had been kept on by his successor or not, she would remember the handyman. I knocked on the door and it was opened promptly by Mrs Overend.

'James Brittain! Haven't seen thee for a while,' she said in a tone which could have been friendlier. 'What does tha' want?'

'Nice to see you again, Mrs Overend. Just one question really; what was Father O'Reilly's original handyman called? The one who left and went to work for the Bishop in Leeds,' I said, trying to flannel my way back into her good books.

'Yer mean — Jack 'Argreaves? Why what's he done?' she replied eagerly, her curiosity getting the better of her.

'I'm afraid he's passed away and I'm helping the police with their enquiries,' I explained, probably telling her more than Inspector Button would have approved of.

'Are you the housekeeper for Father O'Reilly's successor?' I enquired.

'Aye, I am. Father 'Ammond is a reight fussy so-and-so, if tha knows what I mean?'

And with that I thanked Mrs Overend for her valuable information and turned to leave. She looked disappointed as I walked away from her door with a cheery wave.

Jack Hargreaves was the man; I hastily made a note of it when I got back to the car. I felt I'd really struck it lucky in the Klondike area!

No sooner had I started the car and put it in gear than I shouted aloud, 'Bingo!', as it suddenly came to me that I'd got a good idea who the killer was, or who he reminded me of! The combination of a brief sighting of Nigel's killer running away from the Institute, grave digging, Klondike and miners; could it be the same man who'd got away from me five years ago? Who was the ex-army sapper who had constructed the clever underground hideaway in the Edensor graveyard for the sniper in the failed Kennedy plot? It was something to work on and Angela would have the details of the man's name.

CHAPTER 17
FROM CZECHOSLOVAKIA WITH LOVE

Peter Svoboda had spent a restless night trying to piece together what had happened to him. A lot of it was hazy and he needed to talk to somebody who could help him with real facts, not just platitudes.

'Peter, I'm so pleased to hear you feeling better, I come as soon as I can,' Simon Wiesenthal said diplomatically, as he rushed to Peter's bedside.

If Peter was pleased to see Wiesenthal, he didn't show it; finally he had somebody in front of him who might be able to give him some useful information!

'Where am I exactly? Why have I been moved from the hospital in Munich? And why are you speaking to me in English, when you speak Czech almost as well as I do?' Peter laid into Wiesenthal with all guns blazing!

Wiesenthal chose his words carefully as he didn't want to upset Peter which might set back his recovery and cause further problems, especially for himself.

'We thought you'd be safer here in this private clinic in Salzburg. There is good security here and the medical staff is excellent. They say you are making good progress now,' Wiesenthal purred, hoping to calm things down a little. It worked; Peter visibly relaxed as if some of the pent-up anger which had caused him so much frustration had left his system.

'Have you got the information about Mengele from James Brittain?'

'No, but it's on its way,' countered Wiesenthal, conscious that this was a sensitive issue between himself and Angela Jones, who, until just recently, had proved obstinate about releasing the information. The delay had played into his hand as he couldn't allow Peter to leave until he had received it. Also, Peter had suffered a setback after his removal from the LMU hospital and was not yet fit to be released. Wiesenthal didn't want to admit that his actions might have contributed to Peter's relapse. Nevertheless, things were looking much brighter now and it appeared as if Peter might possibly be fit enough to travel in about a week's time.

'How long have I been here?' Peter barked, realising Wiesenthal was being cagy and he had lost some time.

'You've been here just over a week; it's Monday 9th September and it will be two weeks on Wednesday since you had your accident,' Wiesenthal offered truthfully, realising that Peter was now in full control of his senses.

It was now clear to Peter that he'd been non compos mentis for longer than he'd realised and he was not going anywhere until he regained his strength.

'Is Rod Trask OK?' asked Peter.

'He's in England with your sister and James Brittain. They're being put up by the Wool Institute where I understand that Irena has been employed.'

Peter smiled for the first time in almost a fortnight; at last something seemed to be going right. He felt tired now and Wiesenthal sensed it was a good time to leave; there was nothing further either of them could do at present. He said he would call in again when he had something to report. Peter nodded and, for almost the first time he could remember, drifted off into a restful sleep.

*****

On Tuesday morning, Angela was on the early train to London from Leeds. She had arranged to meet Robert, her MI5 contact, in one of the bars at Kings Cross station. It was convenient for her and she had no intention of telling Robert that she was presently based, however temporarily, in Leeds. She was first there and ordered a bottle of Newcastle Brown Ale, even though it was still mid-morning. She had only taken a couple of sips when he arrived.

'Angela! Good to see you again, this is a little cloak and dagger isn't it?' he quipped as they shook hands, before he went to get a drink from the bar.

'Well, we're in the business, might as well act like it occasionally!' Angela retorted when he returned with a black coffee.

She now remembered that he was teetotal, a reformed alcoholic if her memory served her correctly, and here she was putting temptation in his way! Not a good start.

'I thought you might be interested in a snippet of information we've picked up from an American who recently got out of Czechoslovakia and who is assisting us at the moment,' Angela began, believing that getting down to brass tacks was always a good opening gambit.

'Sorry to hear about Nigel, mind you, it's an ill wind that...'

Whatever snide remark Robert actually made about her promotion was lost as the tannoy announcer bellowed, 'The train now approaching Platform 5 is the...'

Perhaps he was just getting his own back for having to watch her drink alcohol which must have been like a new form of Chinese torture to him.

'...I'm very interested in anything new, it breaks up the monotony.' He finished the sentence with an attentive look on his face once the announcement had ended.

Presuming that Robert was interested in what she had to say, Angela continued, 'This American had been sent to Prague, prior to the invasion, to debrief an agent who wanted to defect to the US. He volunteered the information that a British Cabinet Minister was on the take from Czech military intelligence for supplying UK government plans and policies, as well as information on technical subjects such as aircraft.'

'What's the minister's name?'

'John Stonehouse.'

Angela expected Robert to show some visible reaction but was disappointed.

'You know how paranoid the CIA is over Commies in foreign governments, don't you?' Angela heard herself saying to cover up the lack of response from Robert.

'Not only the CIA! Is this American called Trask — Rod Trask — by any chance?' he added seriously, taking the wind completely out of her sails.

'Yes, how did you know?'

'I inadvertently overheard part of a 'phone conversation

between one of my colleagues and the American Embassy. It appears he's been in trouble and still might be, but could be useful for getting inside information on Stonehouse while he's in the UK, although I don't exactly know how,' Robert said.

'I do! He's been loaned to us to help out with the mess we're in at present. Don't say we've got an American plant?' Angela said vehemently, draining the last third of her glass of beer, none too elegantly.

'I guess they've got something on him, so he's between a rock and a hard place,' Robert concluded.

Angela then filled him in on the likely cause of Rod's dilemma, namely that Chuck Edwards had been murdered by mistake instead of Rod. Robert knew of Chuck's death and that it had caused some diplomatic problems between the Brits and the Americans but wasn't aware of the detail. He was appreciative of what she had told him and was keen to share some of his thoughts with her. It was clear that he was a troubled man and not happy with his lot at the moment. In fact, there was a lot he was not happy about! Angela had been careful to keep the details about Mengele and the Svobodas under wraps for the present; mainly because there was still some doubt as to when Wiesenthal was going to release Peter. Put bluntly, it was rather embarrassing to have to admit to not being in full control of this matter at the moment.

Robert was keen to return to Angela's earlier remark regarding the CIA's paranoia about Commies in foreign governments. He was aware that MI5 had been tipped off a few years ago by Angleton (head of CIA's Counterintelligence Division), that Harold Wilson was a Soviet agent and that he would provide further information if they guaranteed to keep his involvement away from political circles. MI5 refused to do this and the information was not provided. Robert was not particularly left-wing and believed that MI5 should not meddle in politics, but his bosses, or mandarins as he called them, thought otherwise. Angela knew, from her time there, that the hierarchy was pro-conservative and highly suspicious of the Socialist government. She wasn't aware that they were active in trying to bring down the government but Robert advised her otherwise. There were factions within MI5 who were prepared to do virtually anything to prevent another Labour government being voted in at the next General Election. The rumours that Lord Mountbatten had been approached in May, to lead an interim government in the event of a government collapse due to the economic crisis, were correct; he had apparently refused and walked out of the meeting. MI5 had been active behind the scenes in providing black propaganda that Wilson and his private secretary, Marcia Williams, were Soviet agents and IRA sympathisers. It was only a matter of time, in Robert's opinion, before another attempt was mounted. Angela was not sure that Robert should be talking to her in this way but appreciated that he had enough confidence in her to feel able to do so. Maybe he was a little envious that she now worked for MI6 and was angling for a transfer for himself? She didn't ask him. It was clear to her that MI5 and the CIA were working hand in glove in this matter, something which she would bear in mind when she next had further discussions with the Americans.

They agreed to keep in touch and Angela promised to let him be the first to know if they uncovered anything about Stonehouse. She thought she had probably learnt more from the meeting than Robert had, it had been well worth the rail journey.

*****

I informed Inspector Button that the dead man was Jack Hargreaves who had probably been working for the Leeds Bishop at the time of his death. The Inspector thought that, since it was now an official police enquiry, he ought to contact the Bishop's office. I'd told him of my intention of seeing if Bishop Brennan was in the area and he said he would let me know if that name came up as a result of his enquiries. I was tempted to visit my house as it wasn't far away, but I was still not sure if it was being watched. I was keen to get back to Ilkley and meet up with Rod in order to continue our discussions. The Inspector said he would have to wait for extra police to arrive in order to organise and carry out the house-to-house questioning.

The visit to Undercliffe Cemetery had occupied a large part of my afternoon. It was already 5.30pm and there was no point in going back to the Institute at this point, so I joined the rush hour traffic on the way back to the Crescent. The receptionist caught my eye as I was about to make my way up to my room.

'A reporter from the Telegraph and Argus was asking for you about thirty minutes ago, he said he would call back. Dr Svoboda might know what he wants as I saw him talking to her when she came in,' she said helpfully.

I nodded, my good humour of a couple of hours ago immediately evaporated as I guessed the press had somehow had discovered my whereabouts. I decided to knock on Irena's door and see what she could tell me.

'I understand you have been talking to the press?' I said, as soon as she opened the door and somewhat hesitantly allowed me inside.

'Yes, I talk to man about my escape from Czechoslovakia,' she said rather defensively as she closed the door.

'You know that a lot of what we are doing is secret and highly sensitive and yet you decide to broadcast it to the press; you know it's going to be all over the papers tomorrow, don't you!' I exploded.

It was not how I'd intended to handle things with Irena in light of her recent standoffishness but I couldn't help myself; it was less than three days since she'd had a close shave with Nigel's killer, yet here she was drawing attention to herself, and to me, for that matter. She was turning out to be a loose cannon and I just couldn't imagine how talking to the press was going to help her cause, whatever that was, or Peter's, for that matter. My outburst obviously had some impact from the change in expression on her face.

'I thought it would help Peter, you not tell me truth why Peter not here,' she said quietly, with an air of defiance.

It was evident that I was not going to get any further with her at the moment, and the damage had already been done. She made it clear that the audience was now over.

I stomped back to my room in bewilderment more than in anger; our anonymity was likely to be blown sky high tomorrow when the T&A came out, and where the hell was Rod? I'd just realised that his VW was not in the hotel car park when I came in. Where had he gone?

Angela was not in at the Mill and her Leeds flat did not have a telephone, so I would have to wait until tomorrow until I could discuss things with her.

*****

Angela had caught the first available train back to Leeds after her meeting with Robert and had just gone through the ticket barrier when, as she was about to leave the station, she noticed a news placard:

Czech Woman and Bradford Man in Spy Intrigue! announced the headline, to Angela's dismay. She immediately bought the Telegraph and Argus from the newsstand, and there on the front page was a picture of Irena, together with what the T&A claimed to be an exclusive story!

Angela stood, as if riveted to the spot, barely two yards away from the newsstand, quickly scanning through the article which read like a Penny Dreadful of yesteryear. Irena Svoboda had obviously been interviewed by the T&A reporter at the Crescent Hotel in Ilkley after a tip-off from 'a reliable source', claiming that it was common knowledge at the Institute that she, Irena, and James Brittain, had been chased all across Europe, from Czechoslovakia to Britain, by foreign agents who were hell bent on preventing vital technical expertise falling into the UK's hands! Irena's brother was being held to ransom and two murders were also linked to this story, they claimed. The reporter embellished the story in lurid detail by describing Irena as a vulnerable, beautiful Czech scientist enticed into helping the Institute, but now that she was here they were unconcerned about her brother's release. The story likened the escape to the typical James Bond adventure *From Russia with Love* by renaming it *From Czechoslovakia with Love*!

Angela was livid. She could hardly blame James for this latest development but she was reminded that he had a handy knack of drawing attention to himself, and as for Irena, Angela was now convinced that she could not be trusted. Angela's first thought was that James's, Irena's and Rod's cover was now blown; they had to get out of the Crescent Hotel. It wouldn't take Nigel's killer long to cotton on to where they were after he had read the paper. She decided to head straight for the Mill in order to ring the Institute and speak to James and Hamish. Her thoughts, on a personal level, were that the picture of Irena in the paper did her justice and she would certainly have the sympathy of the readers.

*****

I got to the Institute early on Tuesday morning. There were no reporters at the gate and I quickly made for Hamish's office. He wasn't in. Neither was his secretary. I went further along the corridor to my office and rang the Mill, only to be told that Angela had gone to London — damn! I'd forgotten she'd gone to see

Robert; it would be late in the day before she got back. Just then, I caught a glimpse of Hamish as he walked past my door towards his office. I dashed to the door and called him in.

'G'day, James.'

'Morning, Hamish. I'm afraid the shit's going to hit the fan when the T&A comes out today!' I greeted him with the bad news in the vernacular which I thought best summed up the situation.

'Shit!' said Hamish sympathetically, once I'd given him the gist of my meeting with Irena yesterday evening.

'Have you seen the reporter?'

'No, I kept to my room most of the night and came here early to avoid him. It's clear we can't stop at the Crescent now.'

'What does Rod say?'

'I don't know, I haven't seen him since our meeting at the Mill yesterday, he wasn't at the hotel last night and his van's gone from the car park.'

'I think since Angela's now handling the case it would be best if we told Irena the details of Peter's detainment by Wiesenthal, and that we hope he will be free very shortly. Do you want me to speak to Irena?' Hamish said.

I was in full agreement with this course of action. Hamish might be the only person she would listen to in her present state of mind.

'The other thing that bothers me is who gave the reporter details of where we were staying? Is the 'reliable source' someone at the Institute? Apart from Irena, that is,' I said, to a nodding Hamish.

'Yes, it's too much of a coincidence, isn't it? I'll see what she has to say. It'll have to be this afternoon as I've got a technical managers' meeting at nine and that's going to take up most of the morning,' said Hamish, as he opened my office door and made his way swiftly back to his own office.

I spent the whole of the morning and well into the afternoon trying to catch up on work for the Institute. A lot of it was fairly routine and not difficult, but it did, at least, take my mind off my current problems — until my door flew open as Hamish rushed in and slapped the T&A on my desk with a picture of Irena on the front page!

It was worse than I'd expected; the article gave a totally biased account of the Institute's role in the affair and Hamish's fear was that it was going to overshadow the positive publicity generated by the opening party last week. Hamish was then called away by his

153

secretary as Irena had just arrived in his office for their meeting. He took a deep breath, picked up the paper and left.

The phone rang. It was Angela, just back in the Mill office after her visit to London.

'Yes, Hamish has just shown me a copy of the T&A article. He's just gone into a meeting with Irena, maybe we'll have a better understanding of the situation shortly.' This was the best I could come up with, to Angela's agitation. I promised to ring her back as soon as I learned some more.

I'd no sooner put the phone down than it rang again. It was Inspector Button.

'Hello, James, I've just come back from a meeting at the Bishop's office in Leeds. Thought you might be interested to learn that Bishop Brennen has left to go back to Vienna! The current Bishop of Leeds, Flannery, has returned and could not help me with anything regarding Mr Hargreaves. We could have reached a dead end, if you pardon my language!' said the Inspector, tongue-in-cheek.

Inspector Button didn't know about the T&A article and thanked me for the information. We agreed that it was not going to make any of our lives easier with the press breathing down our necks.

I'd no sooner put the phone down when in walked Hamish, closely followed by Irena.

'Irena totally denies telling the reporter a lot of the details mentioned in the T&A!' said Hamish, with Irena nodding vigorously at his side. 'She only mentioned the escape from Czechoslovakia and the journey in the US convoy led by Shirley Temple Black, and the ferry crossing in the VW campervan. However, Tony Pickard has quizzed her a number of times about various things, including personal questions and where she was staying in Ilkley!' Hamish said. 'I think Tony has a few questions to answer!'

CHAPTER 18
AN AMERICAN IN BLACKPOOL

Bishop Brennan had checked in at Leeds-Bradford airport for his flight to London Heathrow on his way back to Vienna. He had reluctantly called it a day as things were beginning to get a little uncomfortable in Leeds after the incumbent Bishop decided to return. Fortunately he'd managed to avoid meeting him by making a hasty, if somewhat inelegant, exit. Petrov's catastrophic blunder in eliminating the wrong American had made Brennan's position untenable and he had no idea where Petrov was at the moment. With the six hundred and fifty pounds he had stolen, he could even have left the country! Brennan doubted it since he didn't think Petrov was sufficiently imaginative or even clever for that matter. He was likely to stay close to the places he knew and was probably on another bender by now. His flight had just been called when he noticed a headline he couldn't afford to ignore, outside the bookshop on his way to Gate 3. The Telegraph and Argus was not the sort of local paper Brennan would normally read, too parochial for his tastes, but on this occasion he made an exception. The revelations about Brittain and the Czech woman, Irena Svoboda, who had been holed up at the Crescent Hotel in Ilkley, took his mind off the rather bumpy flight down to London. Begrudgingly, he had to admire their plucky escape from Czechoslovakia and their ingenuity. It was a pity, he thought, that it was only the woman Svoboda who had caught the 'flu, otherwise events might have turned out differently. The paper did give a lot of useful information of which he had been unaware and he was now beginning to think he might have been too hasty in fleeing the country. He decided that he should make at least one phone call before he boarded the Vienna flight; he checked his itinerary and confirmed that he had a two hour wait before the flight left.

For the remainder of the short flight to London, Brennan realised he had put too high a priority on trying to locate Trask, Brittain and the woman Svoboda, in the UK. Although he had instructed his 'Fats Domino' operative to try to locate Trask's other companion, who, according to the T&A, was almost certainly Peter Svoboda, he'd not come up with anything interesting. Brennan's gut feeling was that it needed following up more thoroughly; he must talk to Johann Schmidt of the BND in Germany and ask him to use his official connections there.

Schmidt listened to Brennan's information with great interest, he was surprisingly amused that Chuck Edwards had been inadvertently rubbed out by mistake; apparently there had been no love lost between Chuck and the BND! He could see that Brennan's position with the CIA could be difficult if it became known he was responsible and he promised not to pass anything on. Schmidt was adamant that Brennan should stay in Britain where he could perform a damage limitation exercise to remove Trask, Brittain and Irena Svoboda by whatever means he thought fit. Could Brennan not make use of his IRA contacts if his own man had gone missing? Schmidt would commit his full resources in trying to locate Peter Svoboda; it was still possible the information had not got into the wrong hands. Funds were not going to be a problem; he'd get the job done!

Brennan put the phone down and then immediately went about retrieving his main suitcase which he'd checked in at Leeds-Bradford to be routed directly through to Vienna. He used his full status as a bishop to ensure the suitcase was found as a matter of top priority. After about forty minutes, an out of breath baggage handler appeared with his bag. Reunited with his luggage, Brennan entered the gents' toilets and re-emerged a short time later in less conspicuous civvies. He was now plain Patrick Brennan, a distinguished, middle-aged Irishman, with a mid-European accent and a passport to prove it!

*****

I'd apologised to Irena for the remarks I'd made to her the previous night. She took it better than I expected and we all agreed that we should find alternative accommodation as soon as possible. It appeared that the press were no longer hanging round the Institute gates, but, nevertheless, I decided I would walk into Ilkley by a back route to the Crescent, retrieve my belongings and see if there was any sign of Rod. I was getting a little concerned for his safety as it was not beyond the bounds of possibility that the killer had got lucky and seen to him.

I had entered the Crescent and got my key, when the manager approached me and said that Mr Trask had been looking for me. Hopefully, I was about to find out what had been going on.

'Ah, James! Gotta confession to make to you.'

'What, another one? You'll be in need of a proper priest if you go on at this rate!' I quipped, as he opened his door to me.

'OK, I'm sorry, I should have let you in on it sooner but with Angela and Hamish present at the meeting it wasn't easy.'

'What's the mystery?'

We decided to go down to the bar which was almost empty, where we could have a drink and talk things over, thus delaying the explanation for a few more minutes.

'The two US Embassy guys who turned up at the Institute's opening last Friday are playing hardball!'

'What way? Why?' I queried, completely baffled.

'They didn't know anything about Chuck's mission but are still not convinced that I was uninvolved in his homicide. They only have my word now that Chuck was going to arrange for all investigations to be dropped. Since I had to tell them about my mission to Prague and the John Stonehouse connection, I've got to stay in this country until this is sorted out. This is why I'm 'helping' you and Angela, to gain useful information for us from you Brits! Sorry.'

'You mean you're spying on us?'

'That's what it amounts to, yes.'

'Why are you telling me this then?' I asked sharply.

'There's more! I've been in Blackpool for the last twenty-four hours.'

'So you thought you'd have a day at the seaside to think things over, did you? Have a ride on the donkeys, build a few sandcastles and go up the tower! You ought to have waited a few weeks, the illuminations haven't started yet,' I added sarcastically.

'No, I was sent there to have a look round, I'd never heard

of the place before. The Labour Party conference is going to take place there at the Imperial Hotel in a couple of weeks' time and I've got to report back on what I've seen, I don't know why! It looks as if it could be a set up and I'm not going to be part of it. That's why I'm telling you, James.'

'You mean there might be an assassination plot on somebody. Who? John Stonehouse? Harold Wilson?'

'I don't know but as sure as hell I'm not going to play ball!' Rod said, deadly serious.

This was a complication I couldn't have dreamed up in a month of Sundays; Rod was right back to square one, with his own side lining up with the baddies.

'So what did you find out?'

'The Imperial is this massive Victorian hotel right on the seafront, protecting somebody there would be a nightmare!' Rod said, with the voice of one with many years of experience behind him. 'You know, Charles Dickens stayed there!'

'Charles Dickens stayed everywhere important!' I said scathingly, wondering what this had to do with the price of fish!

It was that time of year again, party conferences are always held at the end of September or early October, towards the end of the parliamentary recess. I should have twigged if I'd been a bit more on the ball. The Winter Gardens, Blackpool, was a favourite venue too since it could accommodate a vast number of delegates; the annual jamboree was almost upon us. For the average man in the street it was a big turn-off; it was, however, a big showcase for the politicians to score points off their rivals, both inside and outside their own parties!

It was a case of déjà vu for me; I vividly remembered my last visit to Blackpool five years ago and knew more or less where the Imperial was, just past the North Pier and the Cenotaph. I wondered who was starring at the North Pier this year. Perhaps it was Mike Yarwood, the impressionist. If so, he might be persuaded to stand in as a double for Harold Wilson, since it was so close to the Imperial and, from a distance, nobody would be the wiser. He might get more laughs which would help ease the economic measures we're suffering at the moment. I'm not sure that John Stonehouse was in Mike Yarwood's repertoire; in fact, I did not know a lot about him myself, apart from the fact that he'd been Minister of State for Technology under Wedgewood Benn and was now Postmaster General. It was common knowledge that he was just about to introduce a two-tier first/second class postage charge, it was rumoured that he was highly ambitious and wanted to stamp his authority on more than just bits of paper! I allowed myself this digression under the cover of a couple of large gulps of Tetley's bitter while Rod watched me intently, trying to gauge my reaction.

'Have you finished your scrutiny in Blackpool?'

'Well they think I'm still there, I only returned to see you since I owe it to you to, and I thought you might have some ideas I haven't thought about.'

'It doesn't ring true to me. If they'd asked the right questions when they'd been up in Yorkshire they'd see that you're off the hook.'

'How do you mean?' Rod said.

'Well, Inspector Button, for one, could have told them it was the same man who killed Nigel, Chuck and the gangster in the Bradford hospital. I think the Inspector would have mentioned it to me if he'd been quizzed by American Embassy officials. Anyway, it's easy enough to find out if they did ask him. Angela could put in a good word for you; if I remember correctly, you suggested she should liaise with your embassy?'

'That's right, James, I'd hoped she'd already done it. Maybe you could ask her discreetly?'

'I suggest you return to Blackpool and carry on your digging, mainly for us now. Where are you stopping and what's your cover?'

'I'm booked into the Imperial as a journalist from the Washington Post doing some background work on the UK's party political systems.'

'Sounds plausible enough to me, but I think you should polish up your American accent a bit, you're picking up some decidedly north-country 'isms!' I proffered in a lighter vein.

'OK, James, will do, I'll keep in touch via Angela at the Mill.'

Just then, Irena entered the hotel and came over to where we were sitting, obviously intent on joining us both. Rod got up immediately and, with a wave, went out past Irena without saying a word.

'Where Rod going?'

'He's going to see a man about a dog,' I said, realising as soon as I had said it, it was going to raise more awkward questions for me from Irena.

'What dog? Who is man?'

'Never mind, I'll explain later. Where has Hamish suggested you move to?' I queried, bringing us both back to reality.

'No know, Hamish very busy with visitors.'

I had been toying with the idea of spending a few nights at my home in Bradford as it was not likely to be on the reporter's radar at present, and hopefully the killer might be lying low elsewhere.

'I'm planning to move back to my home in Bradford for a day or two, are you stopping here for a few more nights?' I queried.

'No, I no want to be alone here, it's dangerous, I come with you.'

What could I say? We had all agreed the Crescent was too well-known now, we had to move and I was left holding the baby!

*****

The phone call Angela had been dreading having to make, the one to Simon Wiesenthal, had gone far better than expected. He had almost purred down the line to her! Yes, he'd got the information she'd sent and had been through it, he thought it might be a good starting point for targeting Mengele. He had passed it on to his colleagues; she took this to mean Mossad, the Israeli Intelligence Agency he worked closely with. As to when Peter Svoboda would be freed, he confided to her openly that he was now in a private clinic on the outskirts of Saltzburg in Austria, and was almost ready to be released. He hadn't wanted to worry her earlier — Peter had suffered a minor relapse but he was pleased to report that things were much improved now; perhaps somebody could come and collect him at the weekend?

She'd taken note of the clinic's address and promised to let Wiesenthal know the details of who would collect Peter as soon as she had organised it. Her first thought was that James was the obvious choice, but then, since Peter was going to work for the Institute, Hamish's man in Germany might be another possibility. She would discuss it with Hamish.

Before she could dial the Institute's number, the phone rang. It was a security officer at Heathrow airport reporting that Bishop Brennan had cancelled his travel plans to fly to Vienna. Apparently, but for the fact he'd created such a scene over retrieving his suitcase from the baggage handlers, it would have gone unnoticed. He was observed going into the gents' toilets with all his baggage but was not seen to leave. It would seem he must have disguised himself and disappeared, probably into the London area.

Why had Brennan changed his plans mid-flight? Why had he disguised himself? Angela was reminded of her very recent experience when leaving the train at Leeds and seeing the newspaper placard about James and Irena. Her gut instinct was that something similar had happened to Bishop Brennan! This was the strongest evidence yet that Brennan was up to his scrawny neck in it. James and Irena were still very much at risk, they had to get out of the Crescent as soon as possible.

*****

Johann Schmidt had been pleased to receive the call from Bishop Brennan, the lead that had been given to him was the first bit of positive news he'd had for a while. After a few phone calls, he established that the LMU hospital in Munich was the one Peter Svoboda had been in. Under the official pretext of acting for the railway company's lawyers, he managed to speak to the doctor in charge of the case, Dr Riemenschneider, who was most cooperative. Schmidt learned that a Wool Institute in England had paid for Svoboda's treatment and that, in the doctor's professional opinion, they had removed him from the hospital far too early, but they took full responsibility for that. There was one strange thing that the good doctor did not understand; the German representative of the Institute who'd arranged for the treatment costs to be paid didn't seem to know who had called for Svoboda. In fact, he'd been back a couple of times since, asking questions of the staff — most strange, he thought! His name was Hans Klein; he had his signature on documents in his office, as well as his business card. There was another thing, Svoboda had been visited a few times by an American and later by an Englishman, Brittain he thought he was called, who was obviously something to do with the Institute as he'd later on rung several times from England for updates on Svoboda's condition. He too seemed surprised that Svoboda had been collected from the hospital.

Schmidt knew exactly what had been going on! Wiesenthal had obviously been responsible for arranging Svoboda's transfer, but to where? Schmidt's hunch was that if Wiesenthal already had the information he would have let the Institute collect him, Wiesenthal being a typical wily Jewish customer! The first priority was to locate Klein and keep tabs on him as he would likely lead them to Svoboda. The likelihood was that Svoboda was stashed nearby, probably in a private clinic. He immediately set about instigating a search for all likely places within a hundred kilometre radius of Munich.

Johann Schmidt had been a fully-paid up member of the Nazi party from before the war and recruited into intelligence work due to his multilingual talents, in particular Russian and other Slavic languages. He was attached to a unit under the direction of Reinhard Gehlen, head of counter intelligence operations against the communists. As it turned out, Schmidt couldn't have been better placed when the war, from a Nazi point of view, took a turn for the worse. His boss, Gehlen, was a smart cookie who had seen which way the wind was blowing and had already prepared a Plan B. He had microfilmed vital files with important information on communist activists, and details which he knew would give him a good bargaining hand when he was captured. He'd buried the files in fifty watertight drums in the Austrian Alps, in places known only to himself. He then surrendered to the US Army Counter Intelligence Corps (CIC) in Bavaria and played his trump card! The Americans were so impressed that they took him to America realising that they had a very significant anti-communist asset. To cut a good story short, they eventually got him to set up the BND, which was basically the same job he had been doing for the Nazi regime! Not surprisingly, his ex-comrades crawled out of the woodwork to take up their old jobs again. Schmidt was one of the first to do so and he knew he was on to a good thing. After all, what were the allies going to do with all the ex-Nazis after the war? Put them in a concentration camp and exterminate them? No, they were going to use them against the common enemy, the communists. Obvious really!

Simon Wiesenthal had been a persistent irritant to them over the years. His constant one-man crusade, delving into records and quizzing ex-concentration camp survivors, had kept raising awareness across the world of Holocaust activities. The worst event had been the capture and trial of Adolf Eichmann. Wiesenthal was a menace and a potential threat to some of their most lucrative projects. It was almost twenty-five years since the end of the war, for Christ's sake; Germany was beginning to rise again, mainly through the hard work of the old order.

Schmidt and Brennan had collaborated well previously. They had both made significant personal gains from moving Nazi gold deposits from Swiss bank accounts into the Vatican's safe keeping. Things were more difficult now, but the 'New Frontier' of South America beckoned and there were potentially vast fortunes to be made from the lucrative cocaine market. The Mafia-style network of like-minded, ex-Nazi entrepreneurs had gradually built up channels of communication — some would say global, the more reticent would claim continental, at least — that one could call on for support and action when potential problems arose.

Schmidt had BND agents working in Czechoslovakia prior to the Soviet invasion but communications had gone ominously quiet now which was to be expected. One of his agents had turned a Czech StB security policeman who had been keeping Peter and Irena Svoboda under surveillance. The policeman had an insatiable appetite for long-legged Nordic blondes, especially with the name Ingrid. His agent had become expert at procuring these girls and, by means of a little discreet blackmail, had learnt that Peter Svoboda was receiving mail from South America via an intermediary in Bavaria. They knew that he was communicating with his father and had intercepted some letters which described the latter's dissatisfaction at being forced into doing work on drugs research. Unfortunately, Peter Svoboda realised he was being watched and became very careful, which limited Schmidt's ability to gain further information. An important message from an ex-colleague in South America alerted them to the fact that Svoboda's father had disappeared and had possibly sent very sensitive information to Czechoslovakia. This information had to be retrieved before it got into the wrong hands.

Johann Schmidt was well-satisfied with his day's work, but being something of a perfectionist, he would have liked to get a lead on Svoboda's intermediary in Bavaria, who had so far proved to be stubbornly elusive. Nevertheless, that would keep for another day.

*****

Mikhail Petrov had acquired a taste for London when he had been sent there by Bishop Brennan. He'd realised that he could melt into the background as nobody seemed to take any notice of him. Being flush with money, he could afford to stay in a hotel. The only one he knew was the one he'd been sent to before in Bayswater, where he'd felt at home. In order to try to forget the blunders he'd made in Yorkshire, he'd been on a two-day drinking spree. He occasionally indulged himself in this way but he knew when he'd had enough, and it was now time to sober up and take stock of his situation.

After a good long walk he shook off the last traces of his hangover and made his way back to the hotel, where he asked for his key from the receptionist. Before he was able to pick up the key from the desk, a misshapen, claw-like hand grabbed it and he heard a familiar voice.

'Let's have a little talk about some unfinished business, Mr Petrov!'

He looked round into the menacing face of Bishop Brennan!

CHAPTER 19
CHEEK TO CHEEK — AGAIN?

Angela hadn't been able to speak to Hamish about Peter's discharge from the clinic until Wednesday morning, due to his Institute commitments. She knew he was running out of time as he was due to leave for South America on either Saturday or Sunday, she couldn't remember which. He had suggested that Hans Klein should pick up James from Munich airport, as he'd done previously, then they should travel together to the clinic on the outskirts of Salzburg. This would fit in well with Hans's itinerary as he was already due to carry out some demonstrations in Austria to promote wool. Hamish had agreed to contact Hans and ask him to liaise with James to make the final arrangements. He also told Angela that James was authorised to use his own initiative on this trip and organise things through Hamish's secretary. Angela appreciated that in her cash-strapped world the Institute was willing to be so cooperative, but Hamish reminded her that Peter Svoboda was a significant asset to the Institute and he was doing no more than he would for any other member of staff. He also volunteered the information that Irena had made significant progress in the last couple of weeks and was proving a worthy addition to the Institute. He also suggested that Tony Pickard, who Angela did not know, was probably in the frame for blabbing to the T&A reporter, thus leaving Irena in the clear. He did not know what Tony's motives were but he guessed there was some jealousy involved as a result of James's rapid promotion, which had put Tony's nose severely out of joint! He proposed to deal with Tony when he caught up with him; he was on holiday at the moment.

They'd discussed his forthcoming trip to South America.

Angela had had no instructions from above to initiate anything official and she feared the worst — that she might be in big trouble when it became common knowledge that she had given information to Wiesenthal, who had then involved Mossad. Hamish was setting off on Sunday and flying Air France from Paris to Montevideo in Uruguay, on the Buenos Aires, Argentina flight. He was due to spend two to three days in Montevideo before flying on to Sao Paulo, Brazil. Both Uruguay and Brazil were significant wool producing countries and were interested in being part of the expanding global wool market. There had been significant technical advances made recently in wool science and they wanted to be able to tap into this, as well as make use of the slick marketing tools enjoyed by existing paid-up members of the club. There was a cost implication, as always, and Hamish was making this preliminary trip to explain the advantages of joining the club. He was also keen to visit their headquarters and laboratory facilities which were located in Montevideo and Sao Paulo, as well as to meet up with the key people in each country. Originally, his trip also included Argentina, which was just as significant a wool producing country as Uruguay and Brazil, but political unrest this year over the Falkland Islands had knocked this on the head. Hamish was not aware of the impending mission by Lord Chalfont to try to pacify the Falkland Islanders by assuring them of HM government's best intentions towards them, whilst simultaneously attempting to resurrect talks with Argentina about the Falklands! Hamish didn't know because Angela hadn't told him.

Armed with the knowledge of Josef Mengele's movements, he could put out some feelers, unofficially of course, to see what was commonly known, but he did not have time to make any trips into the country. Hamish was meeting up with a colleague from the Institute's Spanish branch who was fluent in both Spanish and Portuguese. Angela made a point, sore, as it turned out, of wishing Hamish a good journey and commiserating with him on his adverse reaction to the recent booster jabs which had been necessary to ward off a range of nasty-sounding tropical diseases.

Angela then took an unexpected call from John Stonehouse MP, who was extremely unpleasant to her!

*****

No sooner had Irena and I set off from the hotel to walk back to the Institute to pick up my car than it started raining heavily, which made me regret my earlier decision to walk from the Institute to the Crescent. It was September, after all, and the weather had decidedly changed into the Autumnal phase with westerly winds bringing frequent showers and bitingly cold winds.

'It's raining cats and dogs!' I heard myself muttering, as we fought our way, heads down against the wind, in the semi-darkness along the back road from Ilkley to the Institute.

'Is this same dog Rod is having?' inquired Irena.

Again I found myself saying, 'Never mind, I'll explain later.' Once more, I'd fallen into the trap of lapsing into colloquialisms which obviously puzzled Irena; it was like being followed around by a child who questioned everything you said.

We finally reached the car park and deposited our belongings on the Imp's back seat. I took off my jacket to avoid its outer wetness wicking through to my shirt. Irena had been more fortunate; she had on a mackintosh which was more water resistant. The journey to Bradford was uneventful. I formed the distinct impression that Irena was in a good mood and was keen to talk about the work she had been doing. I, on the other hand, was preoccupied with trying to sort out in my own mind what state I had left my house in. It certainly wasn't tidy. We'd have to call in at the off-licence shop to stock up on essentials, bread, milk, cornflakes, etc. Irena was going to be disappointed if she wanted any of her Czechoslovakian delicatessen food in the short term. Fortunately, since being in the UK, she had taken a liking to fish and chips and readily accepted the offer of dining out at Harry Ramsden's emporium at Guiseley, which we were just approaching.

Harry Ramsden's was originally, in early Victorian times, just a wooden hut at the end of the tram terminus from Leeds, which rapidly became a favourite with day-trippers because the fish and chips were very good. Subsequently, a massive red-brick building was built, which was said to be able to seat two hundred and fifty people and was claimed to be the largest fish and chip restaurant in the world. Well, it would be if it was in Yorkshire, wouldn't it? Nowadays it catered for passing motor car trade as well as coaches, the trams being long gone. We parked in the large car park, walked through the main door and approached a wooden floor-mounted barrier stating, *Please wait here to be seated*, which reminded me of Betty's Café in Ilkley.

'Table for two, sir?' asked a pleasant middle-aged lady wearing an ankle length black smock. She led us through the restaurant towards a wooden table for two and, as soon as we were seated, presented us with menus. We decided pretty quickly that we'd have the 'Special Fish and Chips with Mushy Peas'.

A waitress appeared very shortly afterwards also wearing a long black smock, with the addition of black boots, a starched white apron and a black and white bonnet. The effect of this uniform was to transform any good-looking girl you'd be happy to be seen out with into a Rosa Klebb lookalike, who you wouldn't! The boots, I assumed, did not contain a poisoned dagger; this might be reserved for the head girl if you attempted to leave without paying. The pot of tea and mixed brown and white bread duly arrived first to partially quench our hunger, followed shortly afterwards by the 'Special Fish and Chips and Mushy Peas'.

I'd been correct in my assessment of Irena; she was in a very good mood. In between mouthfuls of fish and chip, she filled me in with her good news. She'd managed to reproduce the flame resist effect which Peter had developed at the Brno Institute. Although she knew the basic chemical recipe she had been mainly involved on the testing side; but she had succeeded in reproducing the effect on different equipment by using a different fabric of lighter weight than that which Peter had used. Hamish was delighted and couldn't wait for Peter to arrive to enable this formidable team to fire on all cylinders. I was pleased for Irena, naturally; it was a significant achievement and no doubt helped to take her mind off the troubles we were experiencing at present. We finished eating and asked for the bill, and I made sure that I was seen to pay at the cash desk close to the main door, in order to avoid testing my Rosa Klebb poisoned-dagger-in-the-boot hypothesis! There was a larger queue now for the take-away side of the business which was adjacent to the main restaurant entrance. The weather was winding itself up into another sharp shower so we dashed past the end of the queue, which was under cover, to brave the twenty or so yards we had to cross in the open to reach the car.

On the way back to my house I decided there was no harm in sharing with Irena the news of Angela's decision to give Wiesenthal the information he'd asked for, which should result in Peter being released fairly quickly. I could tell, even in the subdued light in the car, that she was extremely pleased with this news and I began to imagine the hypnotic effect of those mesmerising blue eyes boring into me. 'Come on Brittain! Get a grip,' I said to myself, as I'd decided some time ago to try to forget my indiscretions in Czechoslovakia. Now, here I was, in danger of making the same mistake again! I pulled up sharply just before the traffic lights and jumped out of the car, saying to Irena that I was going to get some milk and bread from Calvert's off-licence shop, which I used when I was in Bradford.

''Bin away have thee, Mr Brittain?' said Betty Calvert, once the doorbell had ceased ringing.

'That's right, need a few essentials now,' I said. Betty and Jack Calvert ran the shop seven days a week. Jack Calvert did the early morning shift sorting out the paper boys; they worked incredibly hard and never seemed to have any time off. Betty was usually on duty after tea when Jack could be found in the Green Man pub, where he played a mean game of dominoes most nights of the week. They were the salt of the earth but were incredibly nosey and knew everything about everybody. There was an element of self-service involved; bread, milk, and cereals were stacked on nearby shelves, and more expensive items such as cigarettes and tobacco were behind the counter. I was just about to pay for the items I'd placed on the counter in front of Betty, when the doorbell rang again and in walked Irena.

'Ere! You're that foreign woman I read about in the paper, aren't you?' I could see Betty quickly putting two and two together and was just about to come up with four!

'I didn't believe everything it said about you in the paper. You're not the sort to take advantage of this poor girl, are you, Mr Brittain?' Betty said, deep sea fishing for further scraps of information.

'It's all nonsense, Mrs Calvert, the reporter's made most of it up,' I said sharply, pocketing my change and swiftly ushering Irena out of the door before Betty Calvert could turn the screw anymore!

I quickly drove the short distance to my house, parked directly outside my side door and entered the house, closely followed by Irena. After putting on the lights and igniting the gas fire in the front room to take the chill off the house, I set about tidying up while Irena decided to make a couple of cups of coffee. Three quarters of an hour later we sat down in the front room which was now pleasantly warm. My jacket, which I'd placed on a chair with its back to the fire, was steaming silently, adding to the atmosphere. For the first time since we'd been in the fish and chip restaurant I looked at Irena. There was that same glint in her eyes which I guessed from experience was the precursor to a full frontal assault! Where was my resistance? The only thought which flashed into my head, as she was suddenly all over me like a cheap suit, was Ginger Rogers' question to Fred Astaire as he was attempting to control a runaway Hansom cab in the film *Top Hat*, 'How are you going to stop it?' His classic reply was, 'In dealing with a girl or horse, one just lets nature take its course!'

Nature took an unexpected course when suddenly, out of the blue, there was a sharp knock at the side door, which took both of us by surprise and the wind definitely out of my sails!

'Good evening. Mr Brittain, Mr James Brittain? Good to find you in at last! I'm Reg Mitchell of the Telegraph and Argus. I wonder if you've any comments to make on the article I did recently on your remarkable escape from Czechoslovakia?'

*****

Hamish had dropped in at James's office after he'd finished talking to Angela, but he wasn't in yet. He needed to speak to James before the start of his next meeting in about ten minutes' time. It was unusual for James to be late and it did cross Hamish's mind to wonder if there'd been any complications at the Crescent the previous evening. He had no sooner reached his office and closed the door when there was a sharp rap and in walked James and Irena.

'Sorry we're late, Hamish, the traffic from Bradford was very slow moving this morning. Have you got a few minutes for a chat?' I gasped, a little over-theatrically.

'Eight minutes to be precise! Shoot!' Hamish said sharply.

'Irena and I left the Crescent yesterday and spent the night at my house in Bradford. I had a visit from Reg Mitchell, the T&A's reporter, who'd obviously been keeping tabs on my house. He's no shrinking violet either, talk about pushy — he would almost make Sergeant Ernie Bilko look like a boy scout! I didn't tell him anything but promised him an exclusive story if he kept off our backs for a week or two. I also told him he'd put our lives in danger by raising our profile. We managed to get a verbal agreement out of him. He did say that he'd got most of the information about us at the Institute's gates from a man with a pipe; he thought his name was Tony something, Tony Pickard! Oh, and by the way, Rod's gone to Blackpool on a mission for his embassy, which he's not too happy about.'

Hamish nodded his head rapidly, taking it all in, and then pushed a piece of paper across the desk to me.

'Here's the address of the clinic in Austria where Wiesenthal put Peter. Angela says we can collect him this weekend, so I've suggested that Hans should pick you up at Munich airport again and drive you to the Salzburg clinic, then ferry you back to the airport. Apparently Peter's still a bit weak and might need assistance,' he said, then indicated that he had to go to his meeting by standing up and rushing out of the room.

At last! Things seemed to be moving now; Angela had come up trumps once again. We'd worry about the ramifications once Peter was safe. Irena looked ecstatic again but I felt relatively safe in Hamish's office as I didn't think even Irena would risk any hanky-panky on Hamish's desk blotter!

*****

After what could only be described as a 'summary dressing down' over the phone by John Stonehouse, Angela had, while she was still seething, rung Robert at his MI5 office in London. His advice to her was not to be phased by it as moves were afoot within MI5 to bring Stonehouse to book. It was time, he thought, that Angela talked to Kirk Edwards, her opposite number in the American Embassy, who was Chuck Edwards' replacement, but no relation. Robert volunteered the information that things were looking less bleak for Rod now, so Angela should contact him as it would do no harm to put in a further good word for him. She agreed.

Before she could ring Kirk, James rang to congratulate her on the good news about Peter and to say that he would get things organised with Hans Klein as soon as possible. He also mentioned that Rod had been sent to Blackpool by US officials to snoop around ahead of the Labour Party conference; Rod was not happy about it as he believed it might be a set-up!

The talk with Kirk Edwards went well, up to a point; they were both trying to fill dead-men's shoes, so to speak. Angela seemed to have the advantage as she'd been running Nigel's show anyway, but Kirk had been unprepared for his new role. He had hastily been trying to get up to speed and Angela was on his list of people to talk to, so he was appreciative of her call. He apologised for the way it looked after Rod was 'encouraged' to assist MI6. He'd since learned from MI5 that they had suspicions about John Stonehouse's dealings in Czechoslovakia anyway, and already had a file on him. Unfortunately, due to the Soviet invasion of Czechoslovakia, Rod's contact had gone to ground and they did not know whether he still wanted to defect. It was early days yet and he still might turn up.

Angela filled Kirk in on the history between herself, James and Rod, starting with their cooperation when JFK visited the UK in '63, and the foiling of the assassination attempt in Derbyshire, which had been hushed up. Kirk was not aware of this and was interested to learn of James's subsequent chance encounter with Rod in Prague while on a routine trip to meet up with a Czech scientist, Peter Svoboda, who was coming to the Institute. Rod's close shave in Prague with the two US hit men, which was fortunately interrupted by the arrival of Soviet troops, had not been reported to Kirk either. Rod was instrumental in organising James's escape from Prague in his VW Campervan whilst assisting other refugees to escape on a train to Vienna.

Kirk was also unaware of the attack on Rod and Peter at Munich railway station, when Peter had been pushed onto the railway track. Angela was therefore not at all surprised that he was equally unaware when she mentioned that the surviving US hitman had followed Rod's VW into Germany and threatened James with a gun. He did, however, concede that Rod and his brother had been under investigation in the States for 'anti-American activities', but this had now been dropped.

The thing that really riveted Kirk's attention was when Angela told him about the incident at the Institute's opening ceremony which had led to Nigel's death in a case of mistaken identity. She explained that she and James had seen the attacker, who was built like a wrestler and was no doubt responsible for the deaths of Nigel and Chuck plus two other murders. The same method had been used in all four cases. It was clear that there was a determined ongoing effort to eliminate Rod and he himself firmly believed that certain CIA factions were involved. Kirk expressed doubt about this but agreed that he was not familiar with everything in which different CIA departments were involved.

Angela decided on the spot to pass on to Kirk the information, which Peter had asked to be given to Wiesenthal, as to the whereabouts of both Mengele and the cocaine factories in South America which were destined to supply drugs to the US market. This apparently unrelated information seemed to have stirred up a hornets' nest in that Rod was not the only one on the hit list now! Kirk swore blind that he knew nothing of this, even though she knew Rod had mentioned a lot of it to the two Americans sent to question him.

'And now you've sent Rod to Blackpool ahead of the Labour Party conference. What's all this about? Are you planning to eliminate Harold Wilson or John Stonehouse, or both?' Angela said sarcastically, almost losing her cool.

'I didn't send Rod to Blackpool, he's supposed to be helping you. I don't know a goddam thing about this, but I'll sure as hell find out!' Kirk said, decidedly angry now.

Angela was not sure whether to believe him or not; if he was lying, he was damn good. She thought it advisable to talk to James as soon as possible after this conversation, which ended shortly afterwards, once they'd each regained some composure and agreed to keep in touch.

*****

'Hello, James, it's Angela. I've just had a strange conversation with Kirk Edwards, Chuck's replacement. He doesn't seem to be up to speed with Rod's situation; he claims he didn't send him to Blackpool to snoop on Wilson and Stonehouse, or that there's any sort of setup!'

'It's not a set up for Harold Wilson or John Stonehouse. It's Rod who's being set up!' I said emphatically.

CHAPTER 20
A FALLER AT BECHER'S BROOK

Patrick Brennan (aka Bishop Brennan) had made a second telephone call once he got off the tube in London. It was to his main CIA contact at the American Embassy in Vienna. He was told that Trask had been sent on a wild goose-chase to Blackpool, where the Labour Party conference was to take place towards the end of September. He was staying at the Imperial Hotel and would be there for the next day or two. Perhaps this time the mission could be carried out without a hitch!

Brennan thanked him for the information and wondered if he might have his opposite number's name in the UK; the answer was a blunt no.

Despite being somewhat on the back foot, he had been handed the exact details of Trask's whereabouts for the next few days. All he needed now was to locate Petrov. He would base himself at the Bayswater Hotel where he'd previously sent Petrov to stay until he had sorted himself out. Just imagine his surprise and delight when, as he pushed open the hotel's swing door, he saw Petrov at the reception desk!

'I thought I'd find you here, Petrov,' Brennan lied effortlessly, seeing the look of dread quickly spread across Petrov's face.

'I... I...' spluttered Petrov, suddenly developing a stammer, unable to find the English words he needed to placate the Bishop.

Brennan, ever the pragmatist, followed Petrov to his room, where he'd suggested they could have a quiet chat!

'OK, Mikhail, you've let me down very badly. You've made some big mistakes but now it's time for you to put things right! Are you willing to do that?'

Petrov was still unable to put a coherent sentence together. He couldn't understand the power this man had over him, especially now when he wasn't even dressed in his bishop's robes. He looked so ordinary and under normal circumstances he could have easily crushed him with one arm tied behind his back. Yet all he could do was nod in agreement.

'You now know what Rod Trask looks like, don't you?'

Petrov nodded again.

'Good. He's now in Blackpool staying at the Imperial Hotel for the next couple of days. I want you to go there this afternoon, if possible, and finish the job!!'

Another nod followed. Petrov was regaining some composure as he realised he was being given another chance; nothing had been said about the money he'd stolen or the man he'd dispatched in the Bishop's quarters in Leeds.

'Did you also see Brittain and the woman Svoboda when you were at the Institute in Ilkley?'

'I see Svoboda woman in laboratory but did not have time to deal with her,' acknowledged Petrov, omitting to mention that he'd attempted to have his way with her, being on a high after thinking he'd just dealt with Trask. 'I'm not sure I saw Brittain; many people at Institute.'

'I don't suppose Brittain and Svoboda will still be in Ilkley,' Brennan thought out loud.

He laid out the Telegraph and Argus on the bed in front of Petrov and pointed to the photograph of Irena Svoboda underneath the headline, *From Czechoslovakia with Love!*, and the accompanying article. Petrov gulped and confirmed that that was the woman he'd seen in the laboratory. It brought back the intense feelings he'd experienced at the time.

'We'll deal with Brittain and Svoboda when you've dispatched Trask. Let's see about train times.'

Brennan folded up the paper and they both retraced their steps to the reception desk. It turned out that there was a train from Euston station leaving in about forty-five minutes; they should be able to make it if they left now. To avoid the chance of Petrov getting lost, Brennan virtually dragged him through the hotel door towards the nearest tube station at Queensway. They took the Central line via Lancaster Gate, Marble Arch and Bond St, changing at Oxford Circus onto the Victoria line to the almost rebuilt Euston Station, which was due to be officially opened in October. There Brennan bought a one-way ticket for Petrov to Blackpool North, changing at Preston. He instructed him to look out for the Imperial Hotel which was quite close to the station. He could do no more now other than hope for the best as he watched Petrov head towards the waiting train; he was still wearing those damn brown boots!

*****

I rang the Imperial and asked for Rod Trask. He couldn't be found so it looked as if he wasn't in the hotel at present. I left a message for him to ring the Mill, then I spoke to Angela again.

'I'm going to go to Blackpool; I know Rod is in immediate danger.'

'Do you know who you're looking for?' Angela said, somewhat confrontationally.

'Well, in the first instance, all that may be necessary is to persuade Rod to leave Blackpool. I've left a message for him to ring you at the Mill so you can tell him to get the hell out of there if he rings before I arrive,' I said abruptly.

'OK, for God's sake be careful, we don't want any more departmental losses, and try not to dispose of any US officials, it could start another run on the pound!' Angela said wittily — uncharacteristically so, I thought!

'Will do.'

With that, I put the phone down, left a message with Hamish's secretary and bounded up the stairs to the top corridor, heading towards Irena's lab.

'I'm off to Blackpool to see Rod. He may be in danger and we can't reach him by phone at the moment. Ask your secretary to get you into another hotel for tonight instead of the Crescent, in case I'm delayed and have to stay overnight.'

With that, I turned round and went out of the lab into the corridor, leaving Irena with a frown on her face.

'I come with you,' she shouted down the corridor after me.

'Not this time, we'll go to the seaside another day when it's better weather,' I shouted back, charging through the double doors at the end of the corridor and going down the stairs two at a time.

It was almost 10.30am. I might be able to get to Blackpool in two hours if the traffic was light. I decided to head for the Imperial

Hotel to start with; at least I could leave my car there while I figured out where Rod might have gone. I didn't look back in case Irena was in hot pursuit; she could be difficult to say nay to if her mind was made up. As I drove out of the car park my thoughts briefly wandered back to last night when I'd had a very lucky escape!

*****

Rod had spent the first couple of hours after breakfast going over much of the same ground he'd previously covered. He'd managed to speak to the hotel manager who seemed to have accepted his cover without question as a Washington Post foreign correspondent. In fact, there'd been plenty of interest in his mission and some searching questions such as, 'What was the general feeling in America about the Labour Party?' and, 'Was LB Johnson going to intervene militarily in Czechoslovakia as well as Vietnam?' Although he'd been out of the States for over nine months he still had a good feel for the mood there, especially as he'd spoken to his brother fairly recently.

He thought he'd got enough information on the hotel now and decided to visit the Empress Ballroom in the Winter Gardens complex, which was the main venue for the Labour Party conference. He nodded as he passed a bell boy who wished him good day and then cheekily asked if he was going for a ride on the big dipper at the Pleasure Beach. This, Rod learned, was Blackpool's equivalent of Coney Island in the USA. He was intrigued as it brought back pleasant childhood memories for him of when his dad took him and his brother, Joe, there after the war. They'd been on the 'Cyclone' Roller Coaster and the Dive Bomber and many more rides; maybe the Pleasure Beach was something similar. He would check it out after he'd been to the Winter Gardens, which, he'd been informed, was further on just past the South Pier.

In spite of the weather being very blustery, Rod decided to walk to the Winter Gardens to get more of a feel for Blackpool; he could have easily jumped on a trolley car, which are apparently called trams, locally. He would leave this experience for later. Once he reached the promenade and approached the North Pier, the skyline was dominated by the Tower, which reminded him of a stubby version of the Eiffel Tower in Paris; something else he might have to have a ride up. Once past the entrance to the

North Pier, which also looked interesting, he crossed back over the trolley car rails and the road to inspect the almost endless array of arcade halls, noisy bingo parlours, slot machine joints and food stalls with their strong smell of French fries intermingling with tobacco and sugared popcorn. He discovered later that he had been walking along Blackpool's 'Golden Mile'. He found the people most interesting; mainly Brits from the North of England, with lots of senior citizens enjoying themselves, letting their hair down, if they had any, and eating their sticks of cotton candy. The Brits apparently call this candyfloss.

He soon came to the Winter Gardens complex and found the entrance to the Empress Ballroom, an enormous 12,500 square feet of floor space. He was shown round by the manager who was impressed that the Washington Post was interested enough to send Rod to see the setting ahead of the conference itself. There was even an adjacent overspill area called the Arena, which could cater for extra people or separate meetings. Security was not going to be easy, with so many doors and the many balconies upstairs proving particularly problematic. The architecture was spectacular and everything was on a grand scale. Rod had seen enough and wanted to go away and think about things a bit more. Now was the ideal time to head towards the Pleasure Beach. He was told just to keep walking down the 'Golden Mile', past the Central and South Piers, and he would come to the Pleasure Beach. He couldn't miss it! This was true, the Roller Coaster and Dive Bomber became visible well before he reached the entrance. He was hooked and decided he'd have to have a number of rides, preferably before he had something to eat!

*****

I made good time driving to Blackpool. I drove up the coast road from the south, passing the three piers on the left, with the Tower just before the third or North Pier. The Imperial Hotel appeared shortly after I'd driven past the last pier and Rod's VW Campervan was clearly visible. He was still here; obviously Angela had not managed to speak to him.

'Can I help you, sir?' asked a smartly dressed girl on the reception desk.

'I'm looking for Mr Trask, of the Washington Post, is he still here?'

'No, sir, he went out about two hours ago, I believe.'

'I gave him directions to the Winter Gardens and the Pleasure Beach,' said a porter, who'd been hovering within earshot.

'Great, very useful, thanks. Which do you think he's gone to first?'

'Probably Winter Gardens as he was on foot.'

I knew he was on foot since his VW was here but it was still useful information.

'As I told the other gentleman who was asking about him, both are easy to find, you just keep walking down the 'Golden Mile'!' added the porter, obviously angling for a tip.

'Who else has been asking about him, and how long ago was this?' I queried. A chill was slowly creeping up my back as I realised that my instinct had been correct.

'Oh, it was another foreign gentleman, about half an hour ago, sir, that's all.'

'American?'

'No, sir, this gentleman might be Polish.'

'Shit!' I said under my breath, but it was still audible enough to be heard by the porter.

'Anything wrong, sir?'

'What did he look like?' I continued, ignoring the porter's question.

'Nothing special I noticed, it was his accent that I remember most,' said the porter rather dejectedly, as he realised he'd probably blown the chance of a good tip!

'He was probably quite tall, maybe six feet. Broad shouldered but he was wearing a loosely fitting blue suit. The odd thing was he was wearing brown boots, which definitely did not go with the colour of his suit. Oh, and he had big hands like a navvy! In fact, he was rather creepy!' said the receptionist, who had come out from behind her desk and was looking very concerned.

'Fantastic. Thank goodness for fashion conscious young ladies! May I use your phone to call the police please?' I replied.

What I was really thinking was *Hoxton Creeper*, but I doubted that either the receptionist or the porter was sufficiently well-versed in Sherlock Holmes literature to appreciate this.

'Hello, police? Could I speak to your Inspector please? My name's James Brittain.'

'Hello, Inspector Todd speaking.' said a lugubrious voice at the other end of the line.

'Ah, Inspector Todd, just the man! It's James Brittain, do you remember me from five years ago when I helped you with your inquiries?' I said optimistically.

'Do I just! What's it this time?'

I explained the situation as succinctly as possible and wondered if he might send some officers to both the Winter Gardens and the Pleasure Beach in search of an American called Rod Trask. I emphasised that his men should be very careful if they spotted a large man wearing a loosely fitting blue suit and brown boots, as he was the prime suspect in four murder cases! If we failed to find him, Rod might well become his fifth victim. Rod might have finished his visit to the Winter Gardens by now and already be in the vast Pleasure Beach area so I would head straight for there. The inspector reluctantly agreed to my request. I left a bewildered porter and receptionist staring after me as I dashed out of the hotel, jumped into the Imp and headed south towards the Pleasure Beach. I drove round the outside until I found the car park and a nearby entrance.

I was still trying to persuade the official on the gate to allow me in ahead of the queue, when Inspector Todd arrived with a couple of uniformed officers and waved his badge airily at the gateman, muttering the magic words, 'He's with us,' at which the gateman shrugged his shoulders and we all walked through.

'Where do you think they might be, Mr Brittain?' Inspector Todd inquired.

'Your guess is as good as mine. Rod might be interested mainly in the 'Thrill Rides', similar to those in the States.' I suggested.

'Not much to go on there. That description would fit at least ten rides. It's a big place, you know.' Inspector Todd said, looking round with an increasingly worried expression.

Just then I caught sight of a man who appeared to fit the hotel receptionist's description; I pointed him out to Inspector Todd as he was disappearing round the side of a building.

'That's the way to the Grand National!' the Inspector said.

We all broke into an instant gallop (sorry!) and dashed towards the building. I was leading by a good two lengths as we turned the corner and saw an imposing 'Art Deco' structure, with what could only be described as a flat, disc-shaped roof, from the centre of which rose a large vertical column with lettering reading 'GRAND NATIONAL'. Some twenty people were queuing to enter the ride via a short flight of radial steps. A quick inspection showed that neither Rod nor his pursuer was amongst them. We paused momentarily to catch our breath and Inspector Todd spluttered that the Grand National was one of the best wooden roller coaster rides in the UK, built in 1935 and still going strong. Just then, there was the sound of a commotion coming from further inside the building. It was evident that the ride had just started and we watched as two separate trains, each made up of four carriages, went round a large curve and then came together side by side before starting to rise slowly up a sharp incline. It dawned on me why the ride was called Grand National; it was a race between the two trains. Both were now rising up on parallel tracks, side by side. We had made our way up the steps and could see the two platforms where the trains had been loaded with passengers. As we dashed onto the platform we could see a man in uniform apparently arguing with another man, presumably a passenger.

'The maniac just manhandled me off the train!' the passenger said as we approached.

I looked up instinctively at the two trains, which were slowly climbing up the steep gradient. Rod was clearly visible in one of the seats towards the back of the left hand train. The two trains were close enough together for passengers to reach out and touch hands with their competitors and there was noisy, friendly rivalry taking place.

'There's Rod Trask in the last seat on the train nearest to us,' I yelled at Inspector Todd, pointing at the trains.

This caught the attention of both the man in uniform and the dissenting passenger, as well as Inspector Todd and the two constables, so that we were all now staring intensely at the two trains which were approaching the brow of the hill.

'He shouldn't be stood up! It's not allowed and it's clearly stated in our information and marked on signs visible from the ride!' stormed the uniformed man, waving his arm frantically at the two trains. This was totally ineffective as we were too far away for anyone to hear.

'That's the imbecile who attacked me,' added the disgruntled passenger next to the uniformed man. Unfortunately, nobody was taking a blind bit of notice of him at the time.

The imbecile being referred to was a man on the other train, who was now standing up with one leg over the side of his compartment on the train's running board. He was leaning across the divide between the two trains, attempting to grab hold of Rod, who had become aware of this and was doing his best to fend off his assailant with a rolled umbrella! Initially he was doing a good job by jabbing him in the chest and head until the umbrella was suddenly wrenched out of his grasp. To our horror, we were forced to watch as Rod was dragged partially over the side of the compartment by his attacker who was strong enough to do this one handed; his other hand was firmly fixed to his own compartment. This occurred just as they reached the summit of the hill and the trains started to go downhill rapidly. Unfortunately, we were unable to see exactly what happened next as the superstructure of the ride obscured our view. The screams of enjoyment suddenly changed to those of terror. It was clear that somebody had fallen from the ride. The uniformed man had dashed to a telephone and I could hear him yelling that somebody had fallen at Becher's Brook!

We all dashed outside and followed the sound of hysterical screams coming from a crowd of people. We pushed our way through and the first thing I saw was a foot with a brown boot on it. It wasn't Rod, thank God! There was only one body. One of the constables confirmed that the man was dead, neck broken.

'He gives me the creeps,' said the other constable.

'Yes, it's the Hoxton Creeper,' I said to a confused Inspector Todd and two constables.

CHAPTER 21
A FISTFUL OF DOLLARS

Angela had had a fitful night's sleep so had no trouble catching the early morning train back to Leeds from Kings Cross. The events of yesterday were still etched vividly in her memory. Just after James had rung to say he was going to Blackpool, she took a call from the secretary of the head of MI6 — she was being summoned back to London for an urgent meeting, what was the earliest she could be there?

The chief, or as some in Angela's circle called him, 'Mmm…', in stuttering deference to the James Bond of fiction, was relatively new to the position and Angela had never spoken to him before. Nigel had only seen him a couple of times because he normally dealt with the man who was now his deputy. It was fair to say that his appointment was an unpopular one within the service; he was the first career Foreign Office official to be appointed head of MI6 in its history, all previous ones had had extensive experience in intelligence work. It was a blatantly political appointment; the Wilson government was highly suspicious of some of the service's activities and sought to bring this more under their control by this move. To say the working relationship between Mmm… and his deputy was difficult was an understatement in the extreme! For at least three months into his appointment in the Spring of '68, his deputy, let's call him Mini-Mmm, syphoned off all important operational documents, keeping Mmm… in the dark. The Wilson government perhaps had good grounds for their suspicions, as Mini-Mmm had cosied up to James Jesus Angleton (CIA's chief of Counter Intelligence) while he was on his secondment to Washington, and was exposed to a great deal of the latter's paranoia, some of which focussed on Prime Minister Wilson being a Soviet KGB agent! It was not known how much of it had stuck when he returned to the UK.

Mmm… had been summoned to the American Embassy for a less than cosy little chat. Mmm… was well-known to the Americans as a result of his secondment as First Secretary to Washington some fifteen or so years earlier, and was regarded as a safe pair of hands by both US and UK governments.

The basis for the meeting was as a result of Angela's recent conversation with Kirk Edwards. Kirk had promised to 'sure as hell find out what was going on!' after Angela had accused him of sending Rod Trask to Blackpool, possibly to 'set-up' Labour politicians such as Harold Wilson and/or John Stonehouse ahead of their party conference. In common parlance, the shit had definitely hit the fan!

There were three of them at the meeting, Mmm.., Angela and Kirk Edwards, Chuck Edwards' CIA replacement.

'What I'm about to tell you is highly classified,' Kirk began. 'Rod Trask's mission to Czechoslovakia was primarily to debrief a potential Czech defector who works for their security services. Rod was chosen because he speaks the language fluently and also he was from a highly trusted CIA section. The anti-American activities were blown up out of all proportion to add to his cover but he didn't know this! Apparently this defector had highly sensitive information to offer, and after his first meeting with him, Rod discreetly requested further back up from the US Embassy in Vienna to avoid using any form of communication which could be monitored. This request was not acted upon before the Soviet invasion took place!'

'So who were the two Americans James saw with Rod when he bumped into them in Prague? Or who, for that matter, tried to kill him later on in the day?' Angela queried.

'Precisely! That's what we want to know, too. Also the Czech defector, in the confusion of the Soviet invasion, managed to escape from Czechoslovakia into Austria and turned up at the American Embassy in Vienna, offering his services. He was asked to come back in the afternoon because there was nobody available to see him. He didn't come back and a body fitting his description was fished out of the Danube five days later! We need to talk to Rod as soon as possible to find out what he knows.'

'Yes, but he talked to two US Embassy men at the Institute on its opening day,' Angela said.

'He talked to two Americans but they weren't from the embassy!' Kirk said, grim faced.

'The only thing we know for sure is that this defector named John Stonehouse is a paid informer. There has to be more to it than that and it looks like we've got security issues in both Vienna and London,' he added, looking uncomfortable. Both Angela and Mmm… knew that 'security issues' meant that moles were at work!

'Something else occurred just before I set off this morning, which you ought to know. James thinks it's Rod who is in immediate danger in Blackpool, so he's gone haring off there to try and find him. As you know, Rod was 'instructed' to suss out the Labour Party's venue for their conference by the two Americans.' It was Angela's turn to feel uncomfortable now as she realised the importance of finding Rod and keeping him alive!

'It's clear that anybody close to Rod Trask is also in immediate danger,' Mmm… added.

'We also think Bishop Brennan is tied up in all this. He's recently been in Leeds and people have started dying since he arrived! He was on his way back to Vienna but he suddenly changed his mind and disappeared. I believe he saw the newspaper article about James and Irena Svoboda which gave him further useful information. The only thing which doesn't seem to tie up here is that he's violently anti-communist and wouldn't do anything to aid their cause,' Angela added.

'Probably he doesn't know why he's doing it; he's just in it for the money,' Kirk said cynically, adding, 'we're worried because there's been a series of instances, possibly coincidental, but which lead us to believe that our signals communications may be being read.'

Kirk then went on to explain his fears.

'The source of the leakages was thought to date back to January this year when the USS Pueblo, a signals communication surveillance ship, was captured in the Sea of Japan by North Korea after controversially violating North Korean territorial waters. Crucially, the crew didn't have time to dispose of all vital code radio machines, in particular the KW-7, or to destroy training manuals and relevant documentation. The KW-7 code radio was an improved, highly sophisticated version of the one developed by the

Brits during WW2. It had been confirmed that this equipment and documentation was amongst 790lb of cargo flown from Pyongyang to Moscow not long after the USS Pueblo had docked in Wonsan harbour, North Korea. This was a major embarrassment not only for the US government but also the US surveillance community. The situation hasn't yet been resolved as the North Koreans still have the Pueblo and eighty-two US seamen in captivity. We had originally thought that even if the Soviets had the equipment they wouldn't be able to use it without the specially programmed keys. However, it cannot be discounted that the Soviets have managed to get hold of the keys. If so, it is possible that somebody has provided them with the highly classified keys, either before the Pueblo was captured, giving an incentive to target a surveillance ship, or afterwards, by an enterprising entrepreneur, who realised there was a fortune to be made when it became common knowledge the equipment had been captured! A major investigation is currently underway to look into the source of the possible leak.

'We now suspect that the Soviets may have already cleverly used this to their advantage when they invaded Czechoslovakia, taking the US and UK monitoring stations completely by surprise. There had been no real clues before the invasion from the signals traffic to indicate the troop movements were anything other than training manoeuvres. If it is true that their communications have been compromised it is vital that the Soviets are not aware that we know they are reading our messages, not yet anyway, until we can change things completely, which will take some time. There might be some mileage in feeding them false information for the time being. GCHQ in London will very shortly be briefed about the situation.'

'Right, can you find out if James has found Rod yet?' Mmm... suggested.

Telephone calls to the Mill and the Imperial Hotel proved negative. Neither James nor Rod had rung in. The meeting was adjourned and it was suggested that Angela should get back to Leeds as soon as possible in the morning to get further information. She had to report directly only to Mmm... from now on, and if John Stonehouse interfered she should refer him directly to Mmm... Kirk decided he would go with Angela to Leeds and they agreed to meet up at Kings Cross station for the morning train.

*****

The relief I felt when I realised Rod was safe was tremendous; he looked 'shaken but not stirred,' when he dismounted from the Grand National ride.

'Want a warm beer, Rod?' I inquired, shaking his clammy hand as we met.

'Something stronger, buddy! Jack Daniels on the rocks would do for starters!' Rod retorted, quickly regaining his normal self.

There were things to sort out with Inspector Todd, which seemed to take ages. We had to go back to the Police station and make formal statements. It's a pity that Angela wasn't here, or Irena for that matter, as they were the ones who'd noticed or had been in contact with the attacker at the Institute's opening day. I had only recognised him by his brown boots. It was almost certain that he was the one who'd killed Nigel, and due to the fact that the other three victims were killed identically, he was almost certainly responsible for these as well. Inspector Todd said the man had no identification on him; he had, however, a stub of a one-way rail ticket from London and a receipt from a hotel in Bayswater. This was definitely something to follow up. Before we left the station, Inspector Todd made me promise to not return to Blackpool until after he'd retired, which would be in about fifteen years' time!

Rod and I decided we desperately needed something to eat. Rod really fancied a Hamburger from a fast-food joint he'd noticed on the Golden Mile as he walked from the hotel. This was followed by a good couple of shots of Jack Daniels; an acquired taste, I thought initially, but the rapid diffusion of alcohol into my bloodstream quickly dispelled any lingering doubts. Despite the alcohol, reality had started to kick in and I was beginning to have worrying thoughts. Are we safe now? Is there anybody else out there trying to kill us? I hadn't brought my Ouija board with me this time! The only spirits we were likely to summon up at present were in the liquid form of Jack Daniels Tennessee whiskey, which Rod said was at least 80% proof! If proof was needed then this was good enough for me!

I was still just sober enough to realise we weren't fit enough to drive back to Yorkshire that night and I went in search of a telephone and a toilet. Time flies by when you're enjoying yourself or celebrating an unsuccessful assassination attempt. The Institute was closed and the gateman ('back agin, lad') at the Mill said everybody had gone home. He thought that Angela had gone to London earlier in the day. There was nothing further we could do tonight. Maybe I should make plans to visit Tennessee someday. I felt a warm inner glow beckoning, but as a good substitute, I quickly decided further research was needed into the therapeutic qualities of Jack D!

*****

Rod and I drove separately into the Institute's car park around 12.00pm. I'd been prepared to stay in Rod's Campervan but he wouldn't hear of it and insisted I take a room at the Imperial, he would pay. I'd made a mental note to postpone my Tennessee trip until I'd got the correct dosage; Rod had obviously done this previously and must have built up his resistance with extensive practice. As we walked in silence across the car park to reception, I had a jingle playing in my head which irritatingly wouldn't go away, *A Double Diamond Works Wonders, Works Wonders — So Have One Today*!

'Oh, Mr Brittain, I've been told to ask you to ring Angela at the Mill as soon as possible, if I see you or you ring in,' said the receptionist.

'Is Rod OK?' Angela barked at me full blast over the phone, drowning out the Double Diamond jingle.

'He's standing right next to me. Want to talk to him?' I said.

'No. Get over to the Mill as soon as you can; just you and Rod,' she ordered.

'Angela wants us both over at the Mill PDQ,' I reported to Rod, who looked a little surprised at the brevity of our conversation.

We drove over together in the Imp and parked in the courtyard after being admitted by the nodding gateman. Having climbed the stone stairs to the main office, we were met by Angela and a man who was unknown to either of us.

'Hello, James, Rod, glad you're safe. I'd like to introduce you to Kirk Edwards, Chuck's replacement,' Angela said, breaking the ice.

'Rod. Am I glad to see you! And you, of course, James,' Kirk said, enthusiastically pumping each of our hands in turn.

We discussed the events of our Blackpool adventure in detail over coffee and sandwiches. Kirk declined the sandwiches in favour of a cigarette or two with his coffee. By contrast, I was now ready for the delayed lunch and appreciated the ham and cheese and tuna and mayonnaise selection. Angela told us that Inspector Todd had contacted her and she had agreed to go over to Blackpool to confirm that the body was that of the man she had seen at the Institute's opening party. I made a mental note to mention to Angela that it would be worth taking Irena along as she'd been in closer contact with him than any of us. Mavis, as usual, was there to cater for our needs, until Angela nodded to her to leave us to it. The preliminary banter being over, Rod couldn't wait any longer and said, 'What did your embassy guys say about me, Kirk?'

'They're not our guys, Rod! We'll get onto what you told them shortly but firstly you're not in any kind of trouble, if that's what's on your mind. On the contrary, you're very important to Uncle Sam at the moment!' Kirk said seriously, and before Rod could answer, he continued, 'The guy you went to debrief in Prague also made it out of Czechoslovakia and went straight to our embassy in Vienna. Unfortunately, he was told to report back in the afternoon but he was rubbed out before then! Also, our embassy didn't get round to sending anybody to liaise with you in Prague after you contacted them. The Americans you saw were there to find out what you knew and eliminate you — which, I guess, you know.' This was confirmed by a nodding Rod.

'We obviously have at least one mole in Vienna and probably one in London as well. This is why it's very important to keep what you know as secret as possible. It's OK to mention details in front of Angela and James since you probably wouldn't be here now if it wasn't for them.'

So Rod hadn't told me the full story of what he'd learned from the Czech security man. I was intrigued at what it might be to make it so important. Good on Rod, as well, for keeping quiet.

'September — the man I'd gone to debrief, that's what he called himself — told me that the Soviets now have the capability of reading certain US naval strategic and tactical communications! He didn't know the full extent of their capabilities but it was enough to make a difference. He told me not to broadcast it via normal communications as he might be uncovered,' Rod announced.

'How long has this been going on for?' I chipped in.

'Since February, he thought.'

'Signals Intelligence (SIGINT) was thought to have been seriously compromised since the USS Pueblo was captured by North Korea in January this year, which fits in with what September said. This is the first direct evidence that supports our worst fears,' Kirk added, drawing heavily on his cigarette as if to emphasise the point, before exhaling silently.

I, of course, had followed the news about the capture of the Pueblo. The US authorities had played down the importance of it at the time but the news coverage was mainly dominated by the worsening situation coming out of Vietnam on a daily basis.

Angela got up, walked over to the window overlooking the courtyard and opened one of the small top ventilation windows to its maximum reach before sitting down again. This action broke my train of thought and I too now realised that the room was thick with smoke; we were in danger of having to put the light on to see one another. Then I took a closer look at Kirk Edwards; he was a small, wiry man in contrast to Chuck, his corpulent predecessor. His brown, tar-stained fingers continually fidgeted with his cigarette packet and lighter which were placed strategically in front of him while he spoke, instantly ready to satisfy his next nicotine craving when the last cigarette had been spent. He was the classic example of a chain smoker. I was amused to see that he was addicted to the Lucky Strike brand; he would no doubt have felt at home in the 'Klondike' region of Bradford. Maybe Kirk would be able to confirm the rumour I'd heard years ago that some packets of Lucky Strike contained a single tobacco/marijuana cigarette as a bonus! Now was not the time but I didn't know anybody else who would be as well-qualified to tell me, since he was probably in the four-packs-a-day league, at least. Maybe I'd broach the subject when I got to know him better and we were in a more suitable joint!

The open window slowly began to make a difference and I made a conscious effort to concentrate on the matter in hand.

Rod continued, 'I only met September once, for about an hour and a half. We had arranged a further meeting but the invasion put paid to that. He had been attached to the Czech Embassy in London as a Labour attaché for a time and that was how he met Stonehouse and recruited him. Stonehouse was paid five hundred pounds per year, approximately a third of his parliamentary salary, to pass on information. Most of it was low grade material but they knew he was very ambitious and hoped he might achieve a position of real significance with time. September had been recalled, but still kept in contact with Stonehouse. It was earlier this year that he stumbled across a file that alerted him to the fact that the Soviets were reading our communications.'

'Why did September want to defect?' Kirk asked.

'After returning to Prague from London he was informed that his career had come to an end as he'd failed an allegiance test. He therefore put out feelers to the CIA. He also mentioned that Sir Barnet Stross and Will Owen, both Labour MPs, were informers as well as Stonehouse. He knew that some TUC officials were involved as well but they were being 'run' by KGB officers, so did not contact them.'

The irony was not lost on me that it was probably as a result of Stonehouse's legitimate dealings in negotiating an agreement between Britain and Czechoslovakia to set up a joint cooperation programme, involving exchange of information and R&D specialists, which made Peter Svoboda eligible to join our Institute. This agreement had only been finalised in March this year.

'What did you tell the two Americans and who were they?' Kirk asked.

'They said they were on a short visit to our embassy in Vienna and had asked to see me before they flew back home. They both had Bronx accents, Scott Olsen was the one who did the most talking, he was the one who got shot. Al Vaughan was the other one. I told them about September and the Brits who were on the make. I didn't mention the communications problem at the first meeting as I wanted to check them out. They didn't buy into why I wanted to see somebody in person from the embassy; they knew there was more, that's why they arranged to see me later, they'd been spooked by James and Peter Svoboda coming into the joint,' Rod continued.

So big Al, aka 'Fats Domino', was the one who'd had his nuts rattled with the baseball bat by Irena, well before season started in May, I thought to myself.

'At this stage I'd already decided to go to Vienna myself since these guys didn't ring true. I should have refused another meeting with them but they asked me to run them to the airport later on,' he added.

'So you never told them about the communications leak at all?' Kirk queried. Rod nodded in confirmation.

'The only person I gave that information to, before today, was Chuck Edwards, at the Bradford meeting which James set up.'

'Good, let's keep it that way,' Kirk said, apparently satisfied enough to ignite what appeared to be the last cigarette in his Lucky Strike packet.

Mavis then entered the room and suggested to Angela that she might want to take a telephone call from Mmm… as he said it was important.

Whilst she was out of the room, I told Kirk that I was due to go and collect Peter Svoboda from the Salzburg clinic as soon as possible. Much to our surprise, Kirk immediately suggested that Rod should go with me.

At this point, Angela returned to the meeting with a worried expression on her face.

'The ten $100 travellers' cheques you brought back from Munich, James, were forgeries. Almost perfect forgeries according to Citibank!' she announced. 'Citibank is under increasing pressure from forged travellers' cheques, they have started appearing in different countries and these are the first that have surfaced from South America. We need to know more as soon as possible. Citibank is worried that if it gets any worse, its financial credibility could be seriously compromised — it could go bust!'

CHAPTER 22
MOLES ARE KNOWN QUANTITIES

It was only four days since Wiesenthal had visited Peter Svoboda in the private clinic in Salzburg, but in that time Peter had improved, both mentally and physically, by leaps and bounds. He still had the occasional headache which soon disappeared after taking a couple of pain killers. He was able to walk round his room and out into a corridor but not any further, since the door, from the corridor, was locked. He had no access to a telephone and, being impatient by nature, he was fast reaching a stage of frustration at being unable to contact anyone. Even though there were five rooms leading off his corridor, all the other doors were locked and he seemed to be the only one in residence. He had only brief, infrequent conversations with the nurse who brought him his meals and the doctor who now only looked in on him every two days. When he asked to speak to Wiesenthal again he was simply told that arrangements were being made for him to leave very shortly since he was improving rapidly; 'Just be patient, Dr Svoboda.' That was something he was not good at; being a patient, patient!

He realised that they were right and he had no reason to doubt Wiesenthal, especially since he was the one who had arranged for him to be moved into the clinic, thus hopefully keeping him out of harm's way. Now was the time to take stock of the situation, things were beginning to look better and even he knew it. It was Friday 13th September — maybe in his case it was a good omen. He allowed himself the luxury of reliving his escape from Czechoslovakia; he was amazed that he and Irena had actually avoided being intercepted by an advance party of invading Soviet troops. He was the one who had decided that they would have a better chance of delivering the information to Wiesenthal if they split up. Irena had been against it but he had insisted that if he didn't make it, she would have a better chance of getting to the Institute if she tagged along with James. He had seen the way James had looked at Irena in the inn and knew she could easily twist him round her little finger if she put her mind to it, and he almost allowed himself a smile as he imagined James's feeble efforts at fending off Irena in full flow — obviously it had worked!

Peter's escape to Austria by car via Brno, much to his amazement, had gone without a hitch; the border guards had fled and he had been able to drive across the Mikulov-Drasenhofen border without any trouble. The only inconvenience on the way had been when it rained; when he and Irena had separated, in the heat of the moment he had handed the windscreen wipers to her, without thinking, and she had gone off with them to the Constans Hotel. In communist Czechoslovakia, windscreen wipers were a prized commodity, and to leave them on the car unattended for any length of time was an open invitation to a thief.

He was able to think clearly now and to prepare himself, at least mentally, to face the outside world again. He was looking forward to going to England to join Irena at the Institute, where she seemed to have been fortunate enough to find employment. He was pleased about this and very grateful to James Brittain, who he now regarded as a valued colleague, even though he thought him a little eccentric, but he had been true to his word, which was an attribute rarely found in the modern world.

Now that he was in the right frame of mind he could channel his thoughts towards the whereabouts of his father. Was he still in Brazil? Peter was also frustrated at not knowing the contents of the package in the left luggage locker in Munich station. One person who might know was his Uncle Berthold; he was the go-between who had set all this up in order to foil snooping secret police. His uncle was a medical doctor in practice in Salzburg, Austria, close to the German border. Peter had already decided that he must visit him before heading for England, which brought him back to his uncertainty about the arrangements that were being made for his release from the clinic. Peter's Uncle Berthold was his father's younger brother, who'd stayed in Czechoslovakia with his family when the rest of the family had fled the country just before the Nazi invasion. He'd survived internment in a concentration camp, but

Peter knew little about this as his father had never talked about it. There was also an older brother, who had got out of Czechoslovakia with his wife and two sons at the same time, but Peter's father had no idea where they were. Perhaps his uncle could shed some light on the present whereabouts of this branch of the family.

*****

Bishop Brennan had hung around the lobby of the Bayswater hotel waiting for Petrov's report from Blackpool for the last couple of days. Surely by now he must have something to report? At the time of ensuring that Petrov caught the Blackpool train from Euston, he'd stressed the importance of ringing the Bayswater hotel only when he had something important to say. He wished he'd organised a hotel for him to stay so he could contact him. He was worried that Trask might not be in Blackpool now and that a good opportunity may have been missed.

After his talk with Johann Schmidt of the BND a couple of days ago, he now had a much better grasp of the situation in which he was involved. Schmidt had been perfectly frank with him this time, as he was seriously worried that the lid on Josef Mengele's whereabouts in South America was going to be lifted, which would result in a scandal on a scale comparable only with that of Adolf Eichmann's show trial, which would do immeasurable harm to the cause. Brennan knew that Schmidt was a person he could do business with, as they sang from the same hymn sheet, metaphorically speaking.

What Schmidt didn't know was that Brennan was one of several priests working under Bishop Hudal who, after the war had ended, had ministered to German speaking POW's in internment camps. Bishop Hudal performed this service himself in Italy, with Brennan acting for him in Austria and Southern Germany. 'Ministering' included organising and supplying false identification papers for ex-SS Nazis, many of whom were classed as war criminals. Brennan was responsible for enabling Josef Mengele to escape via safe houses in Austria and Italy, followed by a sea-passage from Genoa to Argentina. Hudal had set up this route personally by writing to President Perón of Argentina to request a safe haven for these wanted Nazis. This escape route became known as one of the Ratlines. Hudal himself was responsible for the escape to Brazil of Franz Stangl, commandant at Treblinka extermination camp, as well as for Gustav Wagner who ran the Sobibór death camp. He had also arranged the escape of Adolf Eichmann, architect of the Holocaust, to Argentina. Eichmann had been later captured by Israeli intelligence agents, smuggled to Tel Aviv where he stood trial and was eventually executed in 1962.

US authorities initially turned a blind eye, although the Ratlines were later officially recognised by the CIA, who used the same routes to spirit away useful Nazi scientists and men with special skills who might be useful in the fight against communism. This was when the CIA had first recruited Brennan. He had also joined Opus Dei at the time of its rapid expansion around 1950 when it was given official recognition by Pope Pius XII, since when his rise had been meteoric, mainly due to the support of Cardinal Spellman in America, resulting in his appointment as Bishop in Vienna.

Schmidt was prepared to put his full resources at Brennan's disposal in order to counter the potential threat from the bad publicity it would generate if Mengele were caught and put on trial in Israel. There was strong evidence now that a new Germany, which would stand firm against communism, was emerging from the ruins and ashes of the Third Reich. This was being forged by the survivors of the old order, some of whom had made mistakes, yes, but time had moved on and nothing was to be gained in the long run by raking over the old ashes from the past. This was an unfortunate metaphor, but Schmidt and Brennan were too insensitive to appreciate the cost in human suffering caused by people like Eichmann and Mengele.

Brennan was not happy to learn of Schmidt's other headache, probably even more serious than the Mengele question, as it potentially jeopardised the whole East-West balance, giving the Soviets a distinct edge over the Americans. This was the fact that US Signals Intelligence (SIGNIT) had been compromised. Schmidt didn't know all the details but he'd just heard from one of his BND agents in Czechoslovakia, who'd managed to escape to Vienna with the StB security man who'd been watching Peter and Irena Svoboda. This StB man had followed them from Brno to Prague, and while reporting in to his station, had learned that a disgruntled former Czech agent (September) had been observed talking to the American, Rod Trask, in Prague, and was now attempting to defect to the CIA where, if he should be successful, he would be capable of giving away important information about SIGNIT. The Soviet invasion had put paid to September being picked up and he had escaped into Austria where he had headed for the US Embassy in Vienna. Unfortunately for him, on arrival at the embassy, he had initially spoken to the one man who had been pre-warned about his possible defection and had arranged for an unwelcome and rather inadequate swimming lesson in the Danube. The StB security man had been rattled and fearful that his indiscretions should be discovered, so confessed all he knew to Schmidt's BND agent. Both had then fled Czechoslovakia, after the promise of an almost endless source of leggy blondes in Vienna answering to the name of Ingrid being sufficient to convince the StB man to throw his lot in with the BND.

The more Brennan and Schmidt discussed this topic, the clearer it became to both of them that Brennan's CIA contact at the US Embassy in Vienna was a Soviet mole. Brennan had been used to try to eliminate Trask, firstly by the two American Mafia types he'd employed in Prague and then by Petrov in the UK. This annoyed Brennan intensely, what on earth was the CIA playing at employing agents who were easily turned! It was not the first time that he'd bemoaned the fact that 'you just can't get the right staff nowadays.' He'd thought it strange that he was not allowed to know the name of his CIA contact in London, which would have made it easier to arrange practical details. Perhaps they would only have said that if his contact was already dead! Yes, Chuck Edwards must have been the other Soviet mole in London. There was some consolation in the fact that, through Petrov's incompetence, Chuck Edwards had been killed in Bradford instead of Rod Trask. Maybe, Brennan concluded, it was divine intervention after all!

Schmidt had said he would deal with the Soviet mole in Vienna and intensify his efforts to locate Peter Svoboda. Meanwhile, Brennan was to carry out a damage limitation exercise in the UK and arrange for the elimination of Irena Svoboda and James Brittain. Hopefully Petrov had already dealt with Trask in Blackpool.

Brennan's attention was suddenly drawn to a news item on the television in the hotel's lounge. The Blackpool police were asking for the public's help in identifying the body of a man who'd been killed in a fall from the Grand National ride at Blackpool Pleasure Beach. A photograph of the man was flashed up on screen — the unmistakable face of Mikhail Petrov!

*****

I knew Rod was not pleased with Kirk Edwards' suggestion that he should accompany me to pick up Peter from Salzburg as soon as it was mentioned. Knowing Rod, I could sense by his body language that he was against this, but he didn't say anything at the time.

However, as soon as we had left the meeting and were in the car on the way back to the Institute, he burst out with, 'For Christ's sake, James! What's more important, a few counterfeit $100 travellers' cheques or the Soviets being able to decode our communications traffic?'

Before I could answer, he continued, 'You're damn right it is!'

'You mean you're not going to go with me?'

'I've gotta go, he's the boss but I might be more useful here in the UK,' said Rod, still seething, but obviously relieved to be able to get it off his chest.

'Kirk might want you out of the way for the time being until he's sorted out the moles in the UK and Vienna. You might be better off out of it for a few days,' I speculated.

'I hadn't thought of that. You could be right.'

With that, we drove more or less in silence, each preoccupied with his own thoughts, until we reached the Institute. I told Rod I would ring Hans Klein immediately to see when he was expecting me, or rather, us now, since Rod was tagging along to collect Peter from the clinic. I suggested it might be useful if Rod was around when I spoke to Hans, in case we all needed to agree on something in particular. Rod nodded and we made our way into the Institute. I'd hoped to catch a final word with Hamish before he left for South America, but his secretary said he'd left for home just before lunch in order to placate his wife, since he was going to be away for some time.

I didn't need to ring Hans since Hamish's secretary handed me my flight tickets and a typewritten itinerary. I was leaving on the 9.30am flight from Manchester to Munich tomorrow, Saturday. Wow! It was 3.30pm now and we needed an extra ticket for Rod. Hamish's secretary hastily rang the travel agent in Ilkley and they agreed to do it, but we would have to pick up Rod's tickets up from their offices once they'd arranged things. For convenience, I decided to stay overnight at the Crescent, where Rod still had a room. Then we could both leave together in the morning to drive over to Manchester airport. I decided to call in at Irena's lab to tell her the latest news about picking up Peter up this weekend; I anticipated she would be relieved.

'I come with you,' Irena announced when I told her.

'It's too short notice, Irena, and I'm not sure Hans Klein has enough room in his car for all of us,' I ventured hopefully, also conscious of not wanting to explain extra costs later on and the possible accusation of 'taking the Institute's football team out on a jaunt!'

'Where Peter is?' Irena demanded. I showed her the typewritten itinerary which had the name, address and telephone number of the Salzburg clinic. She made quick notes in a form of shorthand in her notebook, looking satisfied.

'I give clinic ring and speak to Peter,' she said dismissively, indicating she had all the information she needed and I could leave now. I didn't seem to be able to read Irena sometimes, not that we had a love-hate relationship, but she was unpredictable which made it difficult to have a stable working relationship with her at the best of times. Women! Maybe it was a hormone thing?

Our flight from Manchester touched down in Munich around 12.30pm local time and so far everything was going to plan. I felt I knew the ropes at this airport having travelled through it before when I had come to visit Peter in the LMU hospital. As we queued up to go through passport control, I noticed that, as luck would have it, the same officer was on duty as on my previous visit when he'd noticed a missing exit stamp on my passport. This time he didn't bat an eyelid and we sailed through. Maybe Saturday was a good day for him and his mind was on Bayern Munich's game this afternoon.

The massive frame of Hans Klein was clearly visible as soon as we entered the Arrivals hall. He shook me warmly by the hand as I introduced him to Rod. As he led us quickly out of the busy hall towards the car park, I had a strange feeling that we were being watched, but with no concrete evidence I couldn't share this with Hans or Rod for fear of being thought foolish. Hans's car was a big BMW, it had to be because he was carrying a lot of equipment in the boot and the overspill was on part of the back seat, meaning that both Rod and I had to place our small suitcases on our knees. Hans explained that he was due to give some technical demonstrations at a trade fair in Austria on Monday and

Tuesday next week, which necessitated his carrying all this. It was fortunate that Irena wasn't with us, as we'd have been hard-pushed to squeeze another two into the car. I purposely sat in the back seat so I could surreptitiously look over my shoulder occasionally to see if we were being followed. It was difficult to tell, but again I had the same strange feeling as in the airport.

Munich airport is to the north of the city, and once we had joined the ring road and were heading towards Austria on Autobahn E52, I began to relax a little as the miles slipped by. Hans had said it was about a two hour journey but, with it being Saturday, the traffic was light and he thought he could do it a little quicker. Most of the journey was in Germany, the border between there and Austria formed by the Salzach River, with Salzburg virtually just over the border. With a bit of luck and a following wind we might make the early evening flight back to Manchester. It crossed my mind that the river must be salty since 'salz' is the word for salt in German. I wondered if they did fish and chip dinners at any of the motorway rest areas, as I was feeling decidedly peckish by now. Rod didn't seem to be bothered and, to my surprise, I must have nodded off, for I was suddenly conscious of the car breaking to a stop. I looked out of the window and we were at the border crossing close to the Salzach River. Good, we were almost there.

'Guten Tag; Papiere bitte,' said the border guard as soon as Hans had wound down his window. I hastily fished my passport out of my inside jacket pocket and handed it to Hans. The guard briefly thumbed through our passports and then looked through the back window at me and the residual pile of equipment on the back seat. He motioned for Hans to get out of the car, indicating that he wanted to look in the boot. I couldn't hear exactly what was being said but Hans was getting very agitated and his voice was getting louder.

'Scheisse!' said Hans loudly as he got back into the car and slammed the door shut.

'No got papers for equipment,' Hans explained as he started the car and turned off the road, as directed by the guard, towards the rest area where he'd been told to arrange for the right papers.

'Can't we leave the equipment here to be picked up after we have collected Peter?' I volunteered helpfully.

'Maybe. We see,' said Hans, still livid. I could see as we approached the rest area that it was fairly small with a bijou café, toilet facilities and telephones. Hans immediately went inside and started talking animatedly with a woman. I wondered if it might be a good chance to have a sandwich but Rod thought we ought to get into Austria first.

'No safe room for equipment. Bloody Austrians! They like make things difficult for us Germans.' Hans then looked over towards the border control post on the motorway and noticed that it was obviously change-over time for the guards.

'Have idea, get in.' Hans took off his jacket, telling us to do the same. He then used all three jackets to cover the equipment on the back seat leaving just my suitcase sticking out. He jumped into the car and proceeded to reverse the wrong way up the one-way slip road, back towards the motorway. The rest area was positioned in no-man's land between the two borders. Hans was carrying out a highly illegal manoeuvre, and it was fortunate that we met no car legitimately approaching the rest area. Once back on the motorway, Hans drove straight up to the border post where he stopped as before, we showed our passports to a fresh guard, Hans presumably indicated we had nothing to declare and bold as brass, we drove into Austria! Hooray. Believe it or not, we had wasted the best part of an hour in crossing the border.

A quarter of an hour later we drove through some large gates up to the entrance of the clinic, which looked like the country house it might have been at one time. We were shown into a waiting room with two people seated at a table; one was a rather frail looking Peter Svoboda, with a big grin on his face. Opposite him sat Irena Svoboda!

CHAPTER 23
KITH AND KIN

Bishop Brennan was reluctantly coming to terms with Petrov's demise; he had been jolted back to reality by a call from Johann Schmidt who'd excitedly reported that his lookout at Munich airport had just seen Brittain and another man being picked up by Hans Klein. He'd had Klein under surveillance and it looked very much as if they were going to meet up with Peter Svoboda. They had been seen heading towards Munich, or possibly Austria, in a grey BMW, and unfortunately Schmidt's man didn't have transport to follow them. Just in case the destination was Austria, he'd had a word with customs at the Austro-German border to delay their transit if they arrived there. It now made sense to him that Wiesenthal had probably stashed Svoboda in an Austrian clinic, perhaps in Salzburg, a possibility which he'd originally overlooked when he'd organised the search for a clinic within 100km — he should have extended it to include Austria.

Schmidt was wondering if Brennan might now be more fruitfully employed in Austria. Brennan readily agreed and arranged to meet Schmidt at Munich airport. It was now early Saturday afternoon so once he had found out the flight times, he would ring back with details of his travel itinerary. He spoke to the man on reception asking him to find out flight times to Munich and also to prepare his hotel bill and have it ready when he returned after packing his belongings. He would be glad to leave the UK and to wash his hands of the sorry mess Petrov had landed him in.

*****

Angela had originally arranged that she and Irena would visit Inspector Todd in Blackpool on Saturday morning in order to confirm that the body in the mortuary was the same man they'd seen at the Institute. The Inspector agreed, but Angela's efforts to arrange this were unsuccessful as Irena had left the Institute early and was not expected to return before Monday. The visit would have to be postponed, which gave Angela the opportunity to tie up one or two loose ends of her own. She needed to bring a few personal items from her London flat up to Leeds so that she could base herself closer to the Mill. Her Mini was still down in London anyway, so this weekend was a good opportunity to finalise things there. She also had the receipt from the Bayswater Hotel which James had given her after he'd found it on the *Hoxton Creeper's* body; it would be easy for her to check this out for herself and it would also be quicker and probably helpful for the Blackpool police as well.

'Hello, I'm looking into the movements of a man who, I believe, stayed here a few days ago. Can you help me?' said Angela to the man on the desk at the hotel, giving him the receipt.

'Yes, a foreign man, Mr Petrov I think,' replied the receptionist, checking his register. 'He left us on Wednesday, is there anything wrong?'

'Yes, I'm afraid he died in an accident,' Angela answered truthfully, without further elaboration.

'I wonder if the gentleman he met here before he left is aware of this? I've looked up the flight times for Munich for him and he's just about to leave, shall I give his room a ring for you?' said the receptionist helpfully.

Angela was somewhat taken aback by this but managed to look suitably interested and before she could answer, the access door from the stairs opened to reveal Bishop Brennan, dressed in his civvy clothes and clutching a suitcase. Angela's attention was immediately drawn to his misshapen, claw-like right hand as he deposited his room key on the receptionist's counter. She remembered James's vivid description of the Bishop. He was smaller than she expected, with grey hair, mean, thin lips and piercing eyes. This was the first time she had seen him.

'This lady was just enquiring about Mr Petrov, Mr Brennan.'

Angela now merited the full attention of those piercing, cold, blue eyes, and although she was not conscious of any perceptible change in his expression, his face took on a menacing look, which sent a shudder down her spine.

'What do you want?' was all he said, after what seemed like ages.

'I'm seconded to the Met and we've been asked by the Blackpool Police to follow up on Mr Petrov's whereabouts immediately prior to his visit to Blackpool. Were you aware that he'd been killed in an accident, Mr Brennan?' Angela queried, looking him directly in the eye.

'No I wasn't and I only met him once immediately before he left; in fact, I showed him the way to Euston Station,' lied Brennan, without any trace of emotion.

Angela could see he was trying to figure out how she knew he'd stayed at this hotel. She wasn't going to help him so she continued by asking him for details of exactly when this had been.

'You say you're from the Met Police?' Brennan queried, avoiding a direct answer to her question, his eyes narrowing even more which Angela found very uncomfortable.

'The young lady had Mr Petrov's hotel receipt,' volunteered the very helpful receptionist, waving the document in front of Brennan. Angela was grateful for this as she was acutely aware of the fact she did not have a warrant card to back up her claim to be from the police.

'I see. As I said, I met Mr Petrov here at the hotel, three days ago, on Wednesday that was, and he asked me for directions; I cannot add anything further to that. I have to go now as I have an appointment to keep,' Brennan said, somewhat on the defensive as he realised Angela was probably who she said she was and he hadn't the time to waste by being obstructive, which would have been his preferred option.

'Where can we find you if we need to contact you again?'

'I'm going to Germany on business; I'll be back here, at this hotel, in three to four days' time,' lied Brennan again, effortlessly.

Angela hadn't the authority to detain him so just nodded as Brennan picked up his suitcase and left the hotel.

'Here, Miss, you'd better have this back,' said the receptionist, handing Angela Petrov's hotel bill.

'Were you on duty when Mr Petrov and Mr Brennan met last Wednesday?'

'Yes I was, and it didn't appear to me that they hadn't met before!'

'Go on.'

David, the receptionist, was very chatty and filled Angela in on what he knew. Brennan had basically accosted Petrov at the desk when he picked his room key up, under David's nose, and Petrov appeared to be flustered almost to the extent of being unable to speak. David thought Brennan had said, 'I thought I'd find you here.' They had moved away, presumably to Petrov's room, before leaving the hotel together after Petrov had paid his bill. This was about an hour before Brennan signed into the hotel. This was crucial information and went a long way towards substantiating Angela's previous suspicions that Brennan was the man who pulled Petrov's strings.

On the one hand, it had been an incredible stroke of luck running into Brennan, but on the other hand, Angela had been totally unprepared. Was there any way in which she could have handled it better? David had remembered the flight details he'd given to Brennan. There were two flights to Munich from London, both early evening. Somebody was going to have to shadow Brennan. A telephone call from the hotel to her London office confirmed her fears that it was too short notice to organise anybody from there, given that it was Saturday afternoon. All details of the Salzburg clinic were at the Mill in Leeds where, at the moment, there was nobody who could easily find them, meaning it was impossible to get a message to James. Shit! She found herself running through the list of deficiencies she would be accused of if things went wrong and it got out. There was nothing for it but to follow Brennan to the airport herself and see if she could organise things from there once she knew which flight Brennan was on. Angela did not normally get involved in fieldwork but she was more than capable of handling it in an emergency.

She thanked David profusely and gave him a number to ring if and when Brennan turned up again at the hotel. She then dashed out of the hotel towards Bayswater Road where her Mini was parked and set off; first of all to her flat where she picked up a few essential items, after which she headed towards the airport.

*****

Johann Schmidt was in a really good mood. Things were beginning to fall into place now as a result of meticulous planning, hard work and dedication, he told himself. He'd been thoroughly trained in the art of Teutonic efficiency, although he would have quibbled with the use of 'art', science was the word he would have chosen. Semantics aside, his systematic search for the whereabouts of Peter Svoboda's clinic and his go-between, thought to be in Bavaria, had revealed a rich vein of very promising information; it might even be the mother-lode!

His decision to widen the search for a private clinic beyond the 100km radius had revealed one in particular, in Salzburg, which looked very promising. Although information on patients was highly confidential, a call by one of his operators posing as a government official looking to place a number of important fictitious clients with them, revealed that they had the spare beds, but for security reasons one floor of the clinic had been sealed off. Even better, a routine search of the Salzburg population register had revealed a Dr Berthold Svoboda who had a medical practice in the city and was of Czech origin. He was believed by some of his patients to be a survivor of Auschwitz concentration camp. Schmidt had access to old records, which listed an inmate of the same name who had been forced to work for Josef Mengele on some of his special projects. Although Svoboda was a common Czech name, this was too much of a coincidence. The opportunity of being able to cash in two bad-Czechs in one place was too good to miss!

He'd subsequently received a call from Bishop Brennan from the airport in London informing him of his flight details, and telling him that he'd been questioned by a plain-clothes policewoman at the hotel of whom he had been highly suspicious. He'd decided to travel as the Bishop using his special Vatican passport in case of customs problems. Schmidt wished he'd not arranged for Brennan to return, as he now would have to pick him up from the airport. This was a distraction he could do without, as he was hell bent on targeting both the Salzburg clinic and the good Dr Svoboda at his surgery. Nevertheless, Brennan's man who'd come close to dealing with Peter Svoboda in Munich and knew what both he and the man Trask looked like, would prove useful. Schmidt had asked Brennan to contact him before he left London. Brennan was a good man to know as he said he was on good terms with the current Archbishop of Salzburg and could arrange comfortable accommodation for both of them near the cathedral; this meant sumptuous luxury to Schmidt which he looked forward to.

Yes, it had been a good day for Johann Schmidt as he prepared himself for travelling from his offices in Pullach to Munich airport. He estimated the journey would take about an hour, which included parking his car and making sure he was present at the Arrivals hall to meet Bishop Brennan. It meant they were unlikely to be able to progress with their investigations until Sunday, as it would be at least 10.00pm–10.30pm before they arrived in Salzburg.

*****

I don't know about you but I don't function at my best without a regular intake of food. It was a good eight to nine hours since I'd had breakfast and it must have been the same for Rod, but he seemed better equipped to live off his reserves — maybe he was distantly related to the camel family, though I was the one who'd got the hump! Of course I was pleased to see Peter Svoboda, he looked a bit pale and frail but that was to be expected, the sparkle in his eyes was enough to tell me he was raring to go. After we'd got the pleasantries out of the way it was clear that the clinic was keen to see us off the premises as soon as possible. I was told firmly that there was no tea and biscuits available for visitors picking up patients. It was clear Teutonic rules encroached into Austria as far as Salzburg anyway, a rule is a rule and 'must be obeyed.'

Hans Klein came to the rescue by suggesting that he knew of an eating place close to his hotel which was only about ten minutes away. He would take us there and then drop off his equipment before ferrying us back to the airport. A frown appeared to pass over Peter's face but he said nothing. Irena said she was hungry too and would very much like one of my omelettes. She then went on to tell everybody as we piled into Hans's overladen BMW that I was shit-hot cook. I agreed but confessed it was limited simply to omelettes. I was not yet in the mood to tackle Irena as to why she had come over to Salzburg independently to pick up Peter, without mentioning it first.

Hans was true to his word. He drove us swiftly into Salzburg's Altstadt and parked outside the Kasererbraeu Hotel, which Hans said had been here since 1342. On another occasion I might have been more interested but the imminent promise of food overrode other emotions. I was soon appeased by a swift glass of lager and the traditional white sausage and mustard appetiser. Peter waited until we were well into our main course before announcing, 'I need to contact and talk to my Uncle Berthold before I leave for England.'

'But we'd planned to go this evening,' I said rather sharply.

'It is very important; he is the one who left the information in Munich station for me!'

Conscious that Hans was listening to the conversation and would not understand the implications, I enquired as to whether it would be possible for us to book into the same hotel as Hans. He'd only had a lager and the appetiser, so took my hint to go and find out if there would be sufficient rooms for us all tonight. Then I made another attempt to persuade Peter to either change his mind or to contact his uncle sooner by telephoning him for instance. I was also somewhat nervous about prolonging our stay in Austria or Germany and was keen for us all to get back to England and relative safety as soon as possible.

'My uncle may have further information, and news of my father, and this might be the only chance I get to meet him. I look for his telephone number now!'

With that, Peter stood up quickly and went to the bar where he demanded a telephone directory from the busy bartender. I felt I'd achieved a partial success; obviously Peter was as much aware of the dangers as l was. I sensed that Rod was uneasy by the way he was shuffling uncomfortably in his seat.

'Goddammit, James, it looks as if Peter knows even less than we do about the Mengele information; this trip could be a complete waste of time for me! We gotta have a talk with this uncle of his. We might just as well since we're here.'

I glanced across to the bar again and saw that Peter had been on the phone and was making his way back over to us with a smug expression on his face.

'I find him! Uncle Berthold come here in twenty minutes.'

Just then, the large frame of Hans Klein squeezed through the narrow doorway and confirmed that we could all have rooms if we wanted. It was pretty obvious we were going to be tied up now for some time so I diplomatically told Hans that we would stay the night, but could he please leave us now as we had some private, non-Institute business to discuss. I could see he was disappointed as he'd been given a whiff of the intrigue but said he could usefully spend the time unloading his equipment from the car into the hotel for safe-keeping and then make preparations for the exhibition next week. With that, he drank the remains of his lager and waved goodbye.

Rod and I had the same idea almost simultaneously. 'Great minds think alike, fools…,' flashed through my mind as we both got up to use the telephone. Angela was expecting us to pick up Peter and return to the UK as soon as we could, and according to Rod, Kirk Edwards would be under the same impression. My calls failed to locate Angela both at the Mill in Leeds or in London; I did leave a message with the duty officer at the latter, who said that he would pass it on if she rang in. Rod was more successful, he'd managed to speak to his Lucky Strike boss, who'd reported that Angela was on the trail of Bishop Brennan after unexpectedly running in to him in London! He didn't know where she was at the moment, although it looked like Brennan was now on his way to Munich. I didn't like the sound of that! How I wished we could just drive back to the airport and get back home.

I was the last to use the phone and my attention was drawn to the commotion coming from our table near the window. I could see that another man had joined my companions and judging by his age, it was almost certainly Uncle Berthold — a fairly tall, late middle-aged, thick-set man with a good head of greying hair and a studious appearance. The commotion got even louder as I neared them and then to my surprise hugs were exchanged, which was to be expected between the uncle and his nephew and niece, but with Rod as well? I was no wiser as I sat down next to them as they were speaking in Czech. To my amazement, Rod was actually in tears. In fact, they all were!

It was Irena who put me out of my misery by explaining that her Uncle Berthold had nearly had a heart attack when he came in because Rod was the spitting image of his elder brother Tomas who he thought had been killed with his family in the war.

'So what? Many people have lookalikes.'

'No, you no understand, Rod's father is Tomas Svoboda, Josef and Berthold's elder brother! And Rod is our cousin!' shouted Peter ecstatically.

CHAPTER 24

THE HILLS ARE ALIVE WITH THE SOUND...

It was a new experience for me to witness at first hand a red-letter day in the history of the Svoboda family. I realised there was little chance now of my persuading them to break up the party as it was pretty obvious it was going to last most of the evening and probably well into the night as well. I was wishing I'd not sent Hans Klein away as he would have made a useful drinking companion and we could have had a meaningful discussion about his forthcoming exhibition and presentation next week. The animated conversation, taking place in front of me, was totally incomprehensible and I might as well not have been there. Berthold Svoboda's initial appearance had been transformed from one of a studious, shy man to a carefree father-figure, which of course was exactly what he was.

I was naturally delighted for them all. As the tally of lagers on my beer mat began to mount, it looked like I was destined to pick up the tab, but I wasn't worried as I shouldn't have any trouble claiming it on expenses. It became fascinating for me as I was an only child and never had the distraction of any siblings to worry about; it was also a powerful reminder to me of how strong emotional ties are within families. To a degree, since losing my mother, my last relative, I had become somewhat of a loner, not by choice but out of circumstance; it was only on occasions like this that I realised what I might have been missing. Fortunately, I was able to channel my energies and emotions into my job, which at the moment gave me little time for anything else. For Berthold it was as if he'd been released from his chains and the years began to roll off him; even though I couldn't understand what they were saying, I was able to understand their body language and they were having a whale of a time. Fortunately, Irena was seated next to me so I did not have the unnerving distraction of her mesmerising blue eyes to worry about — dammit! I mentally chastised myself for thinking about the consequences of allowing Irena to get into one of her 'good moods'.

The spell was momentarily broken when Berthold took time out to visit the gents'. I took the opportunity to give Rod a look which implied, 'Come on, Rod, fill me in on what's been said?'

'Gee, James, I never realised I was going to find my long-lost relatives! My dad never said much about before the war and I vaguely remember some relatives coming to stay with us. My dad changed his name to Trask; I guess he felt guilty about leaving Berthold and his family behind in Czechoslovakia just before the Nazis walked in. He thought they had all been killed.'

'Yes, but has he told you anything more about the information he placed in the left luggage locker at Munich station?' I pressed, hoping we might still be able to conclude things more speedily.

'Not yet, it's all been about family matters, the good times when we were all together before the war. I think he's winding himself up to that shortly, James.'

Rod was right, when Berthold returned he became more serious and mentioned briefly his correspondence with Josef in Brazil and the important information he'd left in Munich station. Being a very methodical man, he wanted to describe things in a strictly chronological order and I could see there was no point in trying to steer him off the course he had set himself.

I was included in the conversation now. Rod took on the task of giving me a running commentary of what Berthold was saying and we all chipped in for clarification when something was unclear. I was totally unprepared for what I was about to hear.

Soon after the Nazis invaded Czechoslovakia in June 1940, all Jews were rounded up, their possessions were seized and then they were told they were being sent away to a place in the north west region of Bohemia called Terezin (Theresienstadt in German), an old fortress city which had been converted into a ghetto. They survived there under terrible conditions until early 1943 when they were transported in cattle trucks to Auschwitz concentration camp. Unbeknown to them at the time, Hitler's Final Solution policy had condemned the Jews of Europe to be exterminated. From then on, Theresienstadt became a transit camp for Jews on route to extermination camps such as Auschwitz, Treblinka and others. Berthold, his wife and four-year-old twin girls endured an almost unbearable journey before they arrived. It was clear to me that this was probably the first time Berthold had told his story to anybody since then; he said he had been waiting twenty-eight years to unburden himself to somebody who would really understand his misery and guilt!

I couldn't understand why he felt guilty, was it because he had survived?

Like most people at the time, I'd been captivated and appalled by the witness accounts in the daily TV coverage of the Adolf Eichmann show trial in Israel. I could truly testify that it was not the same as sitting opposite a living, breathing survivor of the said atrocities.

There had been a crude sort of selection process as the wagon loads of Jews arrived daily at Auschwitz. Camp doctors, among them Josef Mengele, segregated those capable of work who were admitted into the camp. Those who were deemed unfit were sent immediately to the gas chamber. At the time, Berthold had not fully understood the implications of this and was only conscious of the fact that he had been separated from his wife and two girls. He had attracted attention, as it was stated on the accompanying forms he was a medical doctor and pathologist with extensive experience. As a result, he was led away separately by a guard at this stage, and that was the last time he saw his wife. Berthold almost broke down at this point but recovered sufficiently to cover his grief by finishing his glass of lager in one draught, prompting Peter to attract the waiter's attention for a refill all-around. The tally was again recorded in bold pencil marks on my beer mat, with a flourish!

On the day after his arrival he was interviewed by Josef Mengele who was the doctor in charge of carrying out research involving human experimentation. Berthold noted that, unlike many of his colleagues, Mengele relished the segregation process so he could select suitable twins, dwarfs and people with deformities for his experiments. In the case of twins, one twin was infected or treated with a substance and after a period of time, both twins were killed. Berthold's job was to take comparative post mortem samples for the reports. His girls were subjected to this and he was forced to carry out the pathology on their bodies. He didn't elaborate as to what experiments had been carried out on his two girls, but at this point he broke down uncontrollably.

This was about as much as I could take and my bladder was sending me urgent signals which I could not ignore any longer. I excused myself and made a rapid exit to the gents'. On my return the barman caught my eye. He was holding the telephone in his hand and indicating that he wanted me to take a call. It was Kirk Edwards on the line ringing for Rod; the barman had not totally understood who he wanted to speak to.

'Hi, James, it's Kirk. You still there? When do you expect to be back at Munich airport?'

'Tomorrow morning now.'

'Jesus, James, what's the delay?'

I explained that Peter Svoboda wanted to debrief his Uncle Berthold thoroughly before we finally left, as we may be able to extract further useful information from him about Mengele.

'Shit, James! Angela's expecting to meet up with you all at the airport this evening; she should be landing about now.'

'What the hell's she doing over here?'

'She's followed Brennan, who's obviously left the UK unexpectedly for Munich, and she is worried that you're in immediate danger. For Christ's sake, hurry up.'

I didn't need any reminder to get a move on, but we were close to getting to the nub of the information we needed and maybe I could force the issue when I sat down again. Kirk did not need to speak to Rod but said he would relay the information to Angela when she phoned him, and he would pass on our contact details. I was half tempted to ask Kirk if he'd come across a Marijuana Lucky Strike cigarette yet as I was desperately in need of a lift of some sort at the moment!

As I re-joined our table, Berthold was describing his Zombie-like existence under Dr Mengele who seemed completely oblivious to the misery he was inflicting on defenceless and innocent people of all ages. Towards the end of the war, Auschwitz had been abandoned in order to avoid the advancing Red Army. Of the inmates, those who couldn't walk were shot, and those who could endured a forced march to a new labour camp where, mercifully, they were eventually liberated by US troops. Berthold had been very

213

active with the US army section, working with Simon Wiesenthal to gather evidence of Nazi war crimes. He had been sure that he had seen a priest talking to Mengele in one of the camps and had reported it to the authorities. In the meantime, Mengele had escaped, and the priest, by the name of Brennan, when questioned, had denied any contact with the prisoner; he had been believed because he was a priest!

It became immediately obvious to me that Berthold was desperate for justice for his family and for the thousands of 'patients' on whom Mengele had performed his hideous experiments. It was a legitimate crusade, and the chance to bring Mengele to book as Eichmann had been was a major incentive. I now saw a chance to move things to a final conclusion and asked a direct question of Berthold.

'Do you have any more information about Josef Mengele, further to what we recovered from the left luggage locker at Munich?'

'Yes, I've had a recent letter from my brother Josef identifying the town where he's presently earning a living as a vet,' Rod interpreted Berthold's words verbatim.

'Where is it?' I exclaimed excitedly.

'It's at my surgery for safe keeping at the moment.'

'No, where's the town Mengele's holed up in?'

'It's somewhere in Brazil, I can't remember exactly, but it's in the letter.'

The effects of the lager were beginning to get to me and I could see that Berthold in particular was showing similar signs, oscillating from laughing bouts of high emotion to sobs of despair. I muttered under my breath to Rod, without thinking, that he was getting a bit 'Brahms and Liszt!'

Rod, it appeared, didn't understand and neither did Irena, who'd overheard and waded in with, 'No, it's Mozart, Wolfgang Amadeus Mozart, everybody knows that. Didn't you see the Mozartplatz as we came in?'

Why don't I think before I speak?

'I just wondered if now would be a good time to have a break? Perhaps Berthold could go back to his surgery and retrieve this letter for us so we can take it with us first thing in the morning, to save some time,' I said as diplomatically as possible.

Peter had been relatively quiet throughout the meeting, simply keeping us all topped up with drinks. The increasing frequency of my hints to bring the Svoboda reunion party to a close were obviously not to his liking, and he finally cracked, launching into a series of invectives at me, with a face as black as thunder! All very well but he'd forgotten to switch his speech mode from Czech to English so the impact on me was substantially wasted. I got the gist though from his posturing. Rod diplomatically kept quiet.

Berthold, clearly not as drunk as he appeared, placed a calming hand on Peter's shoulder and sat him down again uttering some reassuring noises. It worked. He then announced, via Rod, that I was right and we should do as I said, meeting back here in a short while for a final farewell! Peter, still not totally happy, acquiesced reluctantly but insisted that he should accompany his uncle to make the most of this reunion. Peter, I could see, had certain character traits in common with Irena — headstrong was one that immediately sprung to mind. I could foresee that together they might be a handful at the Institute in the future, but Hamish was perfectly capable of getting the best out of each of them, despite their idiosyncrasies.

Just then, Hans re-entered the inn. He glanced in my direction and caught my eye with a look which implied that he was unsure as to whether he should he join us. I waved him over, sensing an opportunity to take advantage of Berthold's suggestion.

'Perhaps Hans would be kind enough to drive Berthold and Peter over to the surgery to pick up the document?' I enquired, promising Hans there would be a drink or two in it for him.

This was agreeable to all concerned, and after Peter and Berthold had made another essential trip to the gents', they left. I breathed a sigh of relief, at last things were moving again and we were a step closer to learning Mengele's latest whereabouts. Rod confirmed that Peter could not shed any light onto the forged travellers' cheques, so he was right in the respect that it had been a wasted journey on his part. However, if he had not come he would have missed out on the reunion of the Svoboda clan. Next, I tackled Irena, educating her on the rhyming slang definition of Brahms and Liszt! This was greeted with a look of indifference. Rod added that in the US it could mean that you were angry. I could not see any rhyming connection in that and preferred our interpretation.

The barman, phone in hand, waved in our direction, indicating that there was yet another call for us. Rod said he would go as it was probably Kirk again. It wasn't; it was Angela for me, from Munich airport.

'James, it's Angela, listen up, there's been a serious development. Brennan's been dealing with an ex-Nazi who's now an influential figure in the German security services. I'll explain the details later but it looks like they know where Peter Svoboda was holed up in Salzburg. The clinic's been raided and some of the staff roughed up. It looks like you got Peter out just in time. They are almost certainly heading your way, so get back to Munich airport as soon as possible tonight then we can get back home. I've got some back-up here.'

'Shit! Peter and Berthold Svoboda have just left to go to Berthold's surgery to pick up the latest letter from Peter's father telling us where Mengele is living at the moment. Hans Klein has just taken them there in his car. I don't know the address!'

'You'll have to find out; they could be in grave danger.'

I hurried back to our table and quickly updated Irena and Rod with Angela's unwelcome news. Our exit was irritatingly delayed by having to pay for our meals and drinks. None of us had any Austrian schillings, and I was the only one with travellers' cheques, so, with a bit of persuasion, I convinced the barman to accept one by including a good tip! We quickly headed for the hotel via the Mozartplatz; Irena made sure I was aware of the imposing statue of Mozart which dominates the square. Somewhat out of breath, I countered by informing her that Salzburg was also famous for *The Sound of Music* film which had been a sensation in the UK. Our current predicament was somewhat similar to the Von Trapp family as we were also attempting to escape from Salzburg out of the clutches of perceived Nazi thugs. Apparently this was not in Irena's repertoire and she was unimpressed by my knowledge. I could even have given a passable rendition of The Hills are Alive — admittedly in a lower key to Julie Andrews' version — but judged it would not have made any difference at all!

This was a minor interlude for me, which acted as a distraction from the terrible images playing through my mind, reawakened by Berthold's harrowing experiences. We soon arrived at the Kasererbraeu Hotel. Hans had checked us in and our luggage, such as it was, had been taken to our rooms. Irena set about interrogating the man on the desk as to the whereabouts of Dr Svoboda's surgery; she seemed to be able to understand the Austrian-German dialect better than I could so I left her to it. I excused myself, got my key to Room 15 and headed there, where I was physically sick. The combination of the meal, too many lagers and Berthold's story had got to me and I was completely drained. After a wash I sat down on the bed and almost immediately fell asleep. I was jolted awake by a sharp rapping on my door; I jumped up immediately and opened it to see Irena standing there.

'Peter dead!' she said.

Momentarily confused into thinking I was still at the Constans Hotel in Prague, I blurted out, 'What? Again? Are you sure?'

'Yes, it's correct, nobody could have survived,' Hans added as he came into view, closely followed by Rod.

Hans explained he'd taken Peter and Berthold to the surgery and parked across the street. The two of them had entered through the front door and the lights went on, and about thirty seconds later a loud explosion had rocked the building, followed by a second minor one which sent flames shooting out of bursting windows. Within seconds, the whole building was a raging inferno! Hans, even though he was in his car and behind closed windows, had to move the car away as the heat was unbearable. The paint on his car was blistered. He knew it was hopeless for anyone inside to have survived so he had come back to the hotel as soon as possible.

'Perhaps you can tell me what this is all about? I was nearly killed tonight!'

'Sorry, Hans, you're right. We think it's ex-Nazis who want to keep Berthold and Peter quiet because they have certain information about wanted criminals. I think Angela was right, we need to get out of Salzburg now!' I said, picking up my luggage and indicating the rest should do the same.

I waited for them at the top of the stairs before leading them down towards the foyer, when I heard, 'Jesus, dumkopf, TRASK, for fuck's sake. Don't you understand plain English? Has he been here?' It was the unmistakable voice of Fats Domino, in full cry. Irena looked at me with terror on her face, she knew exactly who it was and this time she didn't have the advantage of a baseball bat handy to rearrange his wedding tackle. Rod didn't look too happy either. We hastily retreated up the stairs and headed for the emergency fire exit. Soon we were all out and making for Hans's car which was conveniently parked in the next street. I ran my hand across the blistered wing of the BMW while Hans opened up the doors. It must have been an intense fire.

'Freilassing! We take road,' muttered Hans, as the BMW's engine fired first time and we made our way through the deserted streets. I realised Hans was going to keep off the motorway and take an alternative route back to Munich airport.

I'm pleased to report that the return journey went without incident; we were all very quiet and preoccupied with our own thoughts. I began to realise I had been woefully unprepared for any complications, and I wasn't looking forward to seeing Angela or the inevitable inquest on my return to the UK.

*****

One week later, Angela and I came out of an MI6 meeting which was in effect a 'Court Marshall' of our work on the Mengele case. Angela hadn't been sure whether she would keep her temporary job promotion, or for that matter her job at all, since she was highly critical of her own performance and judgment. I knew I could still have a job at the Institute but that was not the point. In the end we were both exonerated and not blamed for Peter and Berthold's deaths. I was bitterly disappointed not to at least have found out where Mengele was last seen but it was not to be. It was noted that the firebomb planted in Berthold's surgery was a highly professional job and that ex-Nazis were still very much active in the background, although nothing could be traced back to Schmidt of the BND, or Bishop Brennan for that matter.

Rod was repatriated back to the States after making sure that he and Irena would meet up again in the not too distant future. He wanted her to meet his brother and his dad, Tomas, her other uncle. In the meantime, Irena resigned herself to working hard at the Institute to forge a new future.

I was gutted that Bishop Brennan had once more escaped justice; I really wondered how he could look himself in the mirror every morning. I could easily make it a private mission of my own to personally hear his confession before I dispatched him!

One small consolation for me was that the head of MI6, Mmm..., commented, 'Look, Brittain, you could be very useful to us in the future as an agent, you have impeccable scientific cover which will stand up to the tightest scrutiny. Just keep your nose clean and a low profile and give Germany and Austria a wide berth in the near future. This is not like the movies; you're in the real world now!'

Angela looked me squarely in the eye and said, 'Want a lift back to Leeds? They've agreed to me keeping the Mill open and I'm going to be based there for the foreseeable future. Perhaps we could meet up again when the dust settles?'

AUTHOR PROFILE

Keith was born and bred in Bradford, West Yorkshire, and still lives there willingly! He was trained as a chemist and became a wool research scientist at the IWS Technical Centre in Ilkley. Following the collapse of the wool market in the 80s, he was 'encouraged' to find pastures new and started working as a private consultant, trading as Envirocare, assisting companies with the new health and safety regulations. The endeavour was successful and Envirocare Technical Consultancy Ltd was formed in 1994, based in Bradford.

A few years ago he stepped down from the day-to-day running of the business ventured into producing collage artworks, made entirely from stamps, with brightly reactive phosphor bands under UV light. Three large collage impressions of famous Bradford people — David Hockney, J.B. Priestley and Sir Ken Morrison — were created. A fourth collage ('Bradley Baht 'at') celebrated the Tour de France coming to Yorkshire. The pictures were exhibited in Bradford's Pop Up & Fabric galleries in 2011, 2012 and 2014.

Keith is also delighted to be to be participating with a colleague as EDPAL in the new Longitude Prize.

'From Czechoslovakia with Love is Keith's second book. His first novel, The 63 Steppes, was inspired by his re-reading John Buchan's The Thirty-Nine Steps. For more information visit www.stuckonstamps.co.uk

Publisher Information

Rowanvale Books provides publishing services to independent authors, writers and poets all over the globe. We deliver a personal, honest and efficient service that allows authors to see their work published, while remaining in control of the process and retaining their creativity. By making publishing services available to authors in a cost-effective and ethical way, we at Rowanvale Books hope to ensure that the local, national and international community benefits from a steady stream of good quality literature.

For more information about us, our authors or our publications, please get in touch.

www.rowanvalebooks.com
info@rowanvalebooks.com